UNIVERSAL LINKS

UNIVERSAL
LINKS
a book of sci-fi stories

Sean M. Clor

Clor, Sean (1971–2009)
   Universal Links
   ISBN 978-0-692-09416-7

Cover and interior text design and layout
by Stephen Tiano, Book Designer

www.tianobookdesign.com

All proceeds from the sale of the book will go to the Muscular Dystrophy Assoc. in Sean's name.

Dedication

*T*his book is dedicated to everyone who has a dis-**ability**
and who through determination, support, strong will
and faith show that their **ability** far exceeds
any impediment that life can place
in the way of their drive
to succeed.

*M*ost of all to our son Sean who embodied all these traits
and succeeded in making his legacy
come to life in spite of over 30 years
of his wasting disease.

Contents

Introduction

On March 9, 1971, our first child was born. We named him Sean Michael partly because of my (his father's) Irish background and because Sean is Gaelic for John, my legal first name. Born in Buffalo, New York, where my job had moved the family a year earlier, Sean was soon joined by his brother, Jason, sixteen months later.

Because they were both boys and only sixteen months apart, they grew up like twins. In addition, moving several times caused them to be best friends and playmates. Together they would play, and as boys do, get in trouble, but overall they adapted and grew up together.

As Sean grew, we began to notice he had some problems with balance, walking, and getting himself up from the floor. Initially we took it to be just his awkwardness growing up. However, after some concern about worsening issues, we took him to a children's hospital, where he was diagnosed with Duchenne muscular dystrophy. The doctors who spoke to us when testing was over gave us the prognosis that he would not live past his teens. Our lives began to change dramatically.

A few years later, Sean had had several surgeries on his legs to keep him walking and wore full leg braces to keep him mobile. As even those began to fail, he found himself in a wheelchair full time, and several years later, he began to need a ventilator to help him breathe. This is how he spent the

rest of his life as his muscles began to fail him
slowly each year.

During this time, thanks to Apple, computers came on the scene, and, though limited in his
arm and hand movements, Sean was able to use
his mind and artistic talents to build his dream
of writing a book.

He began his task to build his legacy, as he
called it. While his hands still worked, he drew, and when they began to
fail, he was able to utilize what was called a head-master that moved the
cursor on the screen, and with what little strength he had remaining, he
clicked the mouse.

In his teens and early twenties, he drove his powered chair with his chin
and eventually with his tongue and began to spend more and more of his
time in front of his computer.

By this time his hands were unable to move and his neck muscles were
failing, and through help from MDA, we were able to acquire a computer
with a retinal scan. Throughout this time, his writings and artwork were
done without any physical or mechanical assistance. His drive got him out
of bed every morning, regardless of how he felt, through his routines, and
in front of his computer with the mantra that he had to finish his book.

Sean led as full a life as could be expected for someone with his disease. He attended movies, went to museums and summer festivals here in
Milwaukee, and, with the help of his wonderful crew of nurses, actually
lived in his own apartment for three years. But, as said before, his overall
passionate drive was to finish his book.

Sean passed away in 2009 at thirty-eight years old, twice the age we
were told to expect, after telling us that he was almost finished with his
book. As his father, I have spent many hours sifting through the hundreds
of files he left and marveling at his imagination, artwork despite his hand-
icap, and, most of all, drive to achieve his dream. It's what kept him going.
This book is a small offering of some of his talent that overcame his MD
and gave his family and friends such joy.

John Clor
March, 2018

Strike Team Zero

1   On Shaky Ground

Early morning, 0600 hours, May third, a Saturday. The year was 2091. The sun's gentle glow had graced the barren hilltops of the Anti-Lebanon Mountains, retreating from Syrian Rebel fighting in Damascus well inside Syria. They were diverted in mid-flight to European Russia. The chopper was headed for the Gobi Desert in Mongolia near the North Korean border at the time. The small commando unit was told by intelligence that trouble was brewing there. They were told that they would be briefed further on the way.

Commander Jennings was speaking to the helicopter pilot on the radio.

"Keep low over the highland rises… uh, H and I fire making the LZ very hot… Refuel at relay station Romeo November eight four … This is Victor Yankee, over," Stryker communicated to Alpha Base.

"I read back Romeo November eight four … Red Charlie, over," the pilot responded.

"Radio check, Red Charlie, authenticate by XO—read over six on one hundred and twenty-four megs," Jennings said back to Stryker.

The radio squabbled in the background while Preston unbuckled himself and made his way to the front of the chopper like a stewardess trying to keep her balance. He leaned over and grabbed the receiver out of the pilot's hand.

"I authenticate Preston, Wayne, Colonel, one, oh, niner, four, eight, one, over," the colonel spoke into the receiver.

Radio squabbles again.

"Roger, Preston, six on Red Charlie," the commander said back to Preston.

They'd been en route for seven hours. They were hauled out of a camel hole in the desert and shipped off to who knows where on some priority orders from ARLAC command. The Syrian lines were nearing the breaking point. Although they got good support from DEFCON artillery bombardment and sweep squadrons to maintain the perimeter, their supply lines had worn thin. Sixteen hundred men couldn't fight without food or clean water or Zyrathine to ward off viral infestations. So ARLAC pulled the plug. It took some doing, but with the help of a handful of crazy GL jockeys and the citadel Washington, in sixteen hours, they called it a day and were on their way home. Not home like their ancestors might have known. It was a temporary command base and a dusty bunk still warm from its previous occupant, simple but welcome comforts.

"Victor Yankee, this is Red Charlie. Request—"

The pilot was interrupted by a sudden, jarring mechanical rattling.

"It's the left nacelle," the copilot shouted as he cracked a window open.

"Turbine manifold's smoking," the copilot reported. "Real, Red Charlie—all after request," the receiving end of the radio said.

"Having mechanical difficulties, Victor Yankee. Stand by," the pilot said to the receiving end of the radio.

"What's the problem? Is something overheated?" the pilot said to the copilot.

"Magnetic failure. I'll engage a backup," the copilot said to the pilot.

"No! Delay that! Check the recirculation pumps," Stryker recommended.

"Lieutenant, if that's an Arling ML-19, you could be redlining the trivalve and she'll pop her seams from a magneto overload. Reroute the primary pumps through the balance fan and gyro by stick. She'll buck a little on turns, but it'll ease the pressure," Stryker suggested.

Switches clacked and the rattling died off.

"That was fast thinking, sir," the copilot complimented.

"Thanks, Lieutenant." The pilot did the same.

"Victor Yankee, this is Red Charlie. We request ATC freak for VOR guidance, over," the pilot said to the other end of the receiver.

"Roger, Charlie, you are on 98.2 VOR acquisitions. Flash—Charlie, standby … Uh, immediate stand-down at Romeo November has been canceled … Strip alert in effect. Watch for Snakes in the air, over," the radio voice said.

"Roger, Victor Yankee. We will advise you on procedure, over," the pilot said to the receiving end.

"It's going to be a hot one, Colonel. They're launching the Snakes," Stryker alerted.

"Hold on tight, Stryker, and don't stick your head out too far. You know those Snake pilots are trigger happy," Preston cautioned.

"That's an affirmative, sir," Stryker agreed.

The airwaves had been abuzz with chatter all morning, massive movement of air cavalry and mechanized units. Snakes in the air were a definite sign of something major; the "Snakes" were the heaviest engagement helicopters they had—antiquated twenty-first-century choppers loaded down with heavy weaponry used in destructive, last-ditch strikes against well-defended enemy positions. Something big was going on to the north, and their unit, Strike Team Zulu Oscar, would no doubt be in the thick of things. The helicopter door slid open, giving them the very loud sound of engines. Air rushed by, and the door gunner loaded his mini-gun.

"Looks like a damn Boy Scout camp down there, Colonel. Everyone's pulling up and packing away," Forward Lt. Jake McKinley commented.

"It's a big operation, McKinley. Everything's kept hush-hush, no details," Preston answered.

"Every big operation is hush-hush, Colonel. With all this radio silence, I wouldn't be surprised if the enemy already knew about this big dance number before we hit the briefing room," Jake said with concern.

"Welcome to the war, Jake," Preston simply spoke. "Colonel, ETA four minutes. Let's buckle down back there," the pilot said.

"Hey, gunner boy, why are you showing the heavy barrel? It's our base, you know," Armstrong said.

"Better keep back from the door, Sergeant. This LZ is going to be h-o-t. There were reports of Syrian resistance in the hills laying heavy fire on the base," the gunner replied.

"Stryker, what's the story on the rebel units from Syria?" Preston asked.

"There have been forward observer reports of strong small arms fires from the surrounding hillsides. The flats were green a few minutes ago, and then wham! Someone popped a whole load of DH-12s near the northeast observation tower, and all hell's broken loose. Scuttlebutt has it that the Iranians pissed in the Syrians' pot. That's all I can make from the chatter, sir," Stryker answered.

"Has there been any confirmation of BARE (Battle, Armored, Robotic, Exoskeleton) units?" Preston inquired.

"I've heard a few reports from recon, maybe a couple of tin can jockeys, nothing bigger, I hope. The big problem will be touching down in a free strike zone. With this wind, we could sweep out into the crossfire," Stryker informed.

The door gunner from the helicopter buzzed a few rounds at the rebels with the mini-gun; bullets glanced off the helicopter's hull.

"Lock and load, gentlemen, it's getting thick out there." Bullets rattled against the metal alloy of the chopper, the men readied their weapons, the radio chatter increased, and explosions went off in the distance.

They were dropping into a world of fire. If it was only rebels, they would be lucky. But if the mighty Korean Army was waiting on the landing pad with Armored Battle Suit units, they could be flying into a world of hurt. Their orders were priority, briefing with high command in twelve hours. The rebels must have sensed that something was going down and were mad as hell no one invited them. If they were lucky, the rebels weren't receiving support from the enemy. But they'd long since run out of luck. They were running on grit, anger, frustration, and fear.

"In one minute, thirty seconds, girls," Stryker alerted.

Bullets riddled the chopper, the control panel sparked, engines whined in another turn, the mini-gun continued to fire short bursts, and distant fire and explosions became more intense.

"My HUD's blown. I can't read the ILM gauge," the copilot said.

"Lovely, Lieutenant, take the stick," the pilot said.

"Red Charlie to Victor Yankee, we have lost instrumentation, visibility poor. Please advise us on landing procedure, over," the pilot said to the receiving end of the radio.

"Smoke's too thick. I can't—"

The bullets pierced the windshield of the cockpit and hit the copilot.

"Windscreen's too starred, Colonel! I can't see ..." Stryker struggled.

"Armstrong, help me kick out this glass. Dexter, help that man," Preston asked for assistance.

Armstrong helped the colonel kick out the windshield as it shattered some more.

"He's taken it through the windpipe. We've got to get a compress on the wound," the pilot recommended.

"Apply pressure with your hand. I'll get the med-kit. Mr. Krychovski, could I have your assistance?" Dexter asked.

Dexter opened the med-kit and removed forceps, gauze, and syringes. An explosion rocked the helicopter and the gunner growled.

"Krychovski, stabilize that man. I want him ready to haul in a hurry," Preston commanded.

"She's holding steady, but I'll need someone to get on the horn and spot me an empty pad," Stryker said.

Dexter ripped open a bandage pack to patch the copilot's wound. There was more mini-gun fire from the door, shell casings tumbling on the floor, and an alerted KLAXON in the distance.

"Crap! Watch those hot casings! Lieutenant, approach is Romeo November, channel B!" The pilot cursed.

"This man is choking. I must administer an air line," Krychovski alerted.

"Romeo November, this is Red Charlie Seven on final approach, come in," Stryker said into the radio receiver.

There was more machine-gun fire. Bullets struck the hull of the chopper and riddled the cabin. The gunner cursed and cocked his weapon.

"Watch yourself, compadre, thumper coming through," Armstrong said mockingly.

Armstrong unslung a single-shot grenade launcher, loaded a shell, and fired at the Korean Alliance BARE unit. The crew could hear a distant explosion.

"Romeo November, encountering heavy enemy fire, approaching low visibility. Please advise us on where to land, over," Stryker said.

"Hard to see, Colonel, but I think the transmitter may be down," Armstrong said with concern as he coughed.

"Keep trying, Armstrong. Thompson, Krychovski, you boys get ready to pop some smokes to mask our entry. Then lay down a suppressing fire and haul ass. Dexter, how is that man?" Preston ordered.

"Can't vouch for the comfort factor, but he'll make it in one piece if we do," Dexter said with assurance.

"Colonel, this vehicle is not going to have much chance in this crossfire." Krychovski spoke with uneasiness in his voice.

"Romeo November, come in," the pilot shouted into the radio.

"We'll all have to bail, gentlemen, crew and all. Stryker, get on the line and get me the air cav—" Preston said briefly before he was interrupted by enemy gunfire. Bullets ripped through the cockpit, whizzing past Stryker's head, and the crew heard an explosion close by.

"Stryker," Preston said with concern.

"I'm all right, Colonel, but that left nacelle is going to redline if I don't lock it down right now."

"Do it! Armstrong, ditch the heavy gear and strap down for a hard landing!" Preston ordered.

A few rounds pierced the cabin and hit Armstrong, the gunner. "Man down!" Thompson shouted.

"Colonel, I hate to bother you," Stryker said.

"Stryker," Preston answered.

Another explosion rocked the helicopter.

"I'm losing torque in the left rear quarter and the flaps are locked. If we don't find someplace flat in sixty seconds, we'll lose autorotation and she'll flip on her back and slide in," Stryker pointed out.

"Hold her as long as you can, Lieutenant, and try to raise Romeo for advisement. Thompson, what is Armstrong's condition?" Preston asked.

"He got a tracer through the leg, Colonel. He has minutes, tops," Dexter said.

"Romeo, Romeo. Wherefore art thou, Romeo?" Stryker spoke into the headset as he smacked and shook the radio a bit.

The engine whined as it lost power. Explosions, gunfire, and flames were very intense now. They had been through some close scrapes in a gyro-lift transport before, when engines had failed and over-torqued the controls. Luckily, in those crashes they were over the pad, with fire crews standing by. Today, they couldn't even see the tarmac, and they were under heavy fire. This one was going to hurt. There were military personnel scattered about the field, shouting at each other. Also, there were fires burning everywhere, gunfire in the distance, and vehicles driving around.

"Sir, recon reports hostiles advancing on third sector right flank," the ground tech said.

"Any update on the sightings?" the base sergeant asked.

At that moment, a group of fuel drums exploded. Some rocketed into the air and others just completely burst.

"Roger. Tac-Comm reports and BARE units, full brigade, eight strong. They're just north of here, pounding the hell out of our howitzer emplacements," the ground tech said.

"How long, Corporal?" the base sergeant replied.

"They're four minutes, tops. We'll need more support from Air Cavalry to hold them until Red Charlie gets in. Should I call Commander Jennings and tell—" The ground tech was interrupted. The sergeant grabbed the radio headset and slammed the receiver down on the tech.

"Under no circumstances are you to contact Air Cav, is that understood? The CAP choppers are en route. ARLAC says none to spare," the base sergeant commanded.

There was another explosion in the background.

"Fuel dot's hit! Run!" an infantryman said in the distance. At that moment, the dot blew, causing a fiery explosion. "Get me Preston on the horn!" the base sergeant commanded.

As the helicopter descended, they could hear machinegun fire and radio squawks in the distance.

"She's sliding over, sir," Stryker said.

"Easy does it. Armstrong, toss the gunner's web gear. Get over here and balance the ship," Preston cautioned.

"Sir, Romeo's transmitter just came back online. The base sergeant would like to speak with you," Stryker said as he fumbled with the headset.

"Preston here," the colonel said as he grabbed the mike. "Colonel, all choppers have been compromised. You're coming in solo. Landing pad seven is clear of debris, but make it quick. We've got a full brigade of BARE units' metal marching down our throats, over," the base sergeant said.

"Understood, out," Preston explained to his men.

"I can give you another thirty seconds, Colonel, so think fast!" Stryker said with discretion.

"Men, we've got some difficulties. We're coming in without Air Cav to cover our asses," Preston said with disappointment as the troops protested.

"Clearing the trees. Everyone brace!" Stryker said with vigilance.

"They've all been sent on ahead, and with their low fuel margins, they can't be spared. We've got to put this bucket on the ground and dump before the enemy can drill us. Look sharp, people," Preston said with encouragement.

"What's the opposition's strength?" McKinley questioned.

"In addition to infantry units, they've got one brigade of Armored Battle Suits. Armstrong, unpack that rocket launcher and keep it close. Lieutenant, give me status on the situation," Preston informed his comrades.

Explosions rocked the chopper. Heavy gunfire riddled the helicopter, turning it into the same metal it came from.

"Lieutenant, give me some good news!" Preston yelled.

"We only have one hundred feet to go and dropping, Colonel! This is all she'll give. We're starting to shake apart!" Stryker said.

"Keep it steady! Pad seven's clear! Watch the radio tower!" Preston encouraged.

"Sir, I can't see the tarmac," Dexter said.

"Warnings on oil and RPMs. She's slipping," Stryker cautioned. Heavy gunfire rocked the helicopter. There was a loud, metallic stomping, explosions in the distance, and lots of fires.

"Gunner's down!" Thompson shouted.

"Sir, I have a visual on the landing pad!" Stryker pointed out.

"Colonel, we've got a problem. There's an enemy Battle Suit on the landing pad!" Armstrong alerted.

The suit's armor was dark blue. There were gray areas, which were Servodraulic support systems, and red areas were for the power output. Weapon systems included an over-the-shoulder rail launcher, and in its robotic gauntlets, a heavy assault rifle. The North Koreans' design was rather crude and antiquated. It looked like straight out of the box, some assembly required, and batteries not included. The BARE units were basically a powerful extension of the human soldier, allowing them to lift and carry heavy loads.

"Give us evasive action, Lieutenant. Give him a low profile. Men, get ready to ditch," Preston ordered.

"Everyone down, Lieutenant," Preston said.

More machine-gun fire rattled the cabin.

"We are returning fire!" Thompson said.

First a volley of shells was fired from its rail launcher, and then the engine struggled and died.

"Cyclic control jammed! Hang on, this is going to hurt!" Stryker cautioned.

The helicopter spun out of control as the engines caught fire. The Battle Suit walked with an elephant's grace, one metallic step after another, firing on the craft as it plunged its body into it, shrapnel scattering everywhere. The chopper was a piece of junk; it was basically put together using scrap parts from a Huey and Apache helicopters.

"They're on fire!" the ground tech shouted.

"Get a fire team over there, right now!" the base sergeant commanded.

There was burning wreckage, gunfire, and men running and shouting in the distance.

2 Picking Up the Pieces

"Head count! Where's the colonel!?" McKinley asked.

"Sound off, give me report, Lieutenant. How are we?" Preston said, coughing.

"Bruised but breathing, sir. Armstrong took a slug and Stryker's got a concussion. Everyone else was thrown clear," McKinley reported.

"Let's assess the damage before this heap goes up, Thompson." Preston ordered.

There were flames and wreckage. Under a large pile of it, the men heard someone groaning. The enemy soldier cursed, something garbled in

Korean, as he removed his ski mask; it happened to be in McKinley's training to learn some of the language.

"What did you just say?" McKinley put a gloved fist around the soldier's throat.

"Stand down, Lieutenant. That's an order," Preston ordered, sounding out of breath to his subordinate.

"We have orders to interrogate any North Korean prisoners," Preston said with a gasp as he ran, while two MPs dragged the prisoner away.

"McKinley, that psychotic pilot of yours nearly got us killed!" Thompson criticized.

"Hey, I brought that baby down as soft as I could! It didn't help the situation when you were crying like a baby back there. On top of that, it didn't help when that suit walked where the chopper was crash-landing," Stryker said angrily.

"Yeah, smoothest collision with a steel tower I've ever seen!" Thompson complained.

"Let's see you fly it, you little pissant," Stryker said as he grabbed Thompson by the lapels. Stryker knocked Thompson down and they struggled on the ground.

"Ease off, Thompson!" Armstrong calmed.

"All right, that's enough. One more word out of either of you and I'll boot your asses so hard you'll wish you'd bought it on that BARE unit back there," Preston lectured.

"I suggest we haul ass before the fuel catches," Stryker recommended.

"Torque that turkey, eh, Tommy?" Dexter said as he elbowed Thompson in the ribs.

"I think he's still alive in there," Thompson warned.

"No stalling for souvenirs, people. Advance to the bunker by twos, weapons on single fire, move!"

There were fires, people running, the crackle of gunfire, and explosions in the distance. There went another intimate encounter with death. The base forces managed to pacify the Korean infantry. Turned out they had followed a supply convoy to the base in search of food. In less desperate times, those hungry farmers might have simply come to them and asked for food. No thanks to ambitious North Korean generals, these people had been outfitted with fresh weapons and a new hatred for ARLAC.

BARE units or Armored Battle Suits were tough, until they strolled through a drainage ditch cordoned and laced with anti-armor mines. Now things were quiet. The skies were blackened by the flames that continued to rage, but the crackle of gunfire had receded into the hills, fading away with the setting sun. Geostat Command, their atmospheric monitoring center, gave them a clear four-day forecast. That meant being able to march the fields in light detox gear and flash goggles rather than the heavier, CBRN polyacrylic dusters and air-filter hoods. It was a deadly world out there. Even without the enemy.

The men rested, asleep in warm bunks, deep beneath concrete bunkers. It was a much needed relief, short though Preston feared it might be. Command kept rest periods short and infrequent, juggling forward patrols with rear-guard duties to maintain variety and keep spirits up. For the grunts, this short time in dark, warm silence was what they fought so hard for. Preston, however, was troubled as always by emptiness. This was to shelter them from radioactive fallout and enemy raids. The times were hard, food was scarce, women and children wept because of the fact that disease and pestilence had plagued their lives. Preston would sometimes cry out in his sleep and wake up in a cold sweat. He tried to forget those horrible memories but was unable to leave them alone and probably never would. Memory could be a terrible thing, a deafening thunder echoing in the void of silence.

To understand the present, one must consider the past, some of which Preston remembered, but most of which he had been told. It had been a world of plenty, of riches and happiness. A world inhabited by men limited only by the narrowness of their vision and the coldness of their hearts. They had the world, and squandered it away to nothing. Now they fought, killing endlessly for the crumbling ruins of a world that had grown to hate them, leaving them with a war over dust and blood.

3 Remnants of the Past

Once there were grand cities, vast colonies of concrete and steel sprawling toward the horizons and rising to the heavens. In this world of forgotten monuments, the great powers claimed the richest lands for themselves, leaving the hardest soils to the impoverished masses. Countries rose and few names invented and forgotten. Names erased from the map, such as the lost United States, and California, Hawaii, Oregon, as well as Washington State. Lost American cities blown away with the nuclear ashes— Los Angeles, San Francisco, Seattle, Honolulu, and Portland. Though now just names on a map, they were names of power and high ideology. Puppet states of a Western philosophy in whose ashes they now crawled. New frontiers dwindled. The seabeds could be mined, but only at high cost and low yield. Interest in space exploration had waned to next to nothing, and manned flights ceased altogether soon after the start of the twenty-first century. Mankind was running out of resources, running out of riches. The world economy began to deteriorate. Oil prices kept rising, making food rationed because of a shortage of uncontaminated food, as a result of oil prices being too high, raising prices tenfold, and hungry mobs rioted in protest. Economic unrest inevitably led to political strife. The United Nations became a fulltime forum for settling treaty and armistice disputes. The world was poised, waiting for that nudge to push it over. Whether by arrogance or ignorance, the superpowers had hastily overlooked a country that had isolated itself from the rest of the world only to be a sleeper waiting to strike. After their settlement over a century ago, this isolated nation was plagued by political influence, poverty, disease, and poor quality of life. Their economic climb was a difficult and unprofitable venture, and so this small nation lagged behind while the rest of the world languished in prosperity. These people were hard-willed and clever, and vowed to seek their own destiny apart from the world order of Europe, Asia, and the mighty United States.

The progress of North Korea went entirely unnoticed amongst the reports of unrest and economic turmoil in the early twenty-first century. In fact, the stark realization of their approaching dominance came late in 2057, with the built-up stockpiles of nuclear missiles using the uranium purchased from Iran in Syria. Their stockpiles soon were loaded into four launchers mounted on eight-wheeled trucks.

Unable to combat the wholesale takeover of the economic world, riots raged, conflicts exploded, and blood ran red in the streets of the cities. Security forces commanded by former superpowers were maddened, starving masses. The world of structure began to crumble into chaos.

A final, desperate move by the former superpower nations was to announce the World Council for the Benefit of Humanity in 2064. The summit was intended to unite the world against the common foes of hunger, poverty, and disease. The council failed miserably in its original goal, as most of the nations invited found themselves racked with dissent and unable to send delegates. Those who showed found little agreement amongst their leaders as to how best to deal with these problems. The nations of the world knew some country was isolated from the world for way too long, but behind this show of erstwhile charity, a secret agenda took precedence.

The armies of the free world had envisioned the bleak possibility of global conflict, with the massive Middle-Eastern military machine, the Korean/Iranian Alliance, rattling the sabre. Iran built up a stockpile of nuclear weapons and warheads, since the early part of the twenty-first century during the War on Terror, using the United States as a scapegoat. The scenario of Middle-Eastern global dominance must be prevented at all costs. Towards these aims, the military nations of the United States, the Russian Commonwealth, Germany, Japan, and China forged the secret alliance of the American-Russian Liberation Army Command, known later as ARLAC. Effectively a bilateral unification of military commands, the ARLAC would wait in the political wings for some fateful event to throw a crumbling world into conflict. The event in question occurred five minutes after three p.m. on March 15, 2065, during afternoon rush-hour traffic.

Terrorism had then taken the form of mad, random killings and futile hostage crises. But on that day, the world saw firsthand what one isolated and brainwashed country could do with a high-yield uranium-tipped nuclear warhead. The details of an infiltration of one unknown nation were unclear, but in the end, two hundred million people and the entire city of Los Angeles were removed from existence in a blinding flash. Within minutes, the dominoes fell. The nuclear arsenal went active at 3:19 p.m., followed by an alert to the ARLAC forces at 3:21 p.m. An ominous rumble filled the sky during rush-hour traffic, as fiery halos rose slowly into the heavens. The entire western coastline of the United States was hit by at least ten to twelve ICBMs, completely obliterating it from the map.

War had been the inevitable conclusion of the escalating conflicts. The detonation of the first missile in the heart of the city of Los Angeles sealed the inevitable fate of all mankind. Drawn into the conflict, the superpowers were prepared to unleash their nuclear arsenals, but their plans came to a screeching halt when the allies discovered a flaw in them. The allied countries didn't quite think this scenario through—the North Koreans could launch volleys of ICBMs at the United States, but North Korea was such a tiny country the US might risk hitting one of their allies. Then the winners and losers would disappear in a flash of atomic fire. Cities would lay waste to billions of people incinerated or irradiated beyond all medical help. The world machine would grind to a halt, but that was not the end of the US effort. A detachment of hand-picked Special Forces soldiers was selected to go in and do some surveillance or act as forward observers to see where the missiles were fired from. They were going to be secretly inserted into the Gobi Desert on the border of Mongolia and North Korea. In order to figure out this whole fiasco later in 2091, ARLAC devised a plan using a small unit of hand-picked men and a stealth attack transport helicopter, first of its kind. The AH-118 was equipped with a mini-gun and a place for a door gunner to sit, as well as the troops. They would undergo a forward-observing tactical commando recon mission.

The evacuation of what was left of the western coastline of North America remained the prime objective of ARLAC. For now, their forces were weakened by the well-supplied onslaught. They must satisfy themselves with little victories. The current focus of military efforts had been to locate and neutralize the enemy. According to ARLAC, they must stabilize their positions on all fronts, executing swift and well-timed thrusts into enemy lines, searching for a weak point. Their main operations had been the restructuring and refortification of Europe. They gave a large scale of aid to the battered, brainwashed, and flat-out isolated North Korean people. The invasion continued into South Korea while people evacuated into the Gobi Desert in Mongolia and the jungles of India. Europe continued a role on the conflict in the Middle East after what Iran did.

Despite grand strategies and noble causes, Preston could not help but wonder what they could possibly achieve. He was born before the war, his parents now dead and long forgotten when they were living in San Diego. It was difficult to remember details of his late childhood, running hungry through the streets of Las Vegas, Nevada. He joined ARLAC through necessity, a need for a warm place to sleep and a regular meal.

He worked hard, his tormented mind glad for the distraction his duties gave him. He began as a supplies clerk at age twelve, advancing to cook's assistant to laundry worker to munitions handler to messenger. When he was old enough to enlist in active duty, he jumped at the chance. Instilled with a youthful fire, he accepted duty as private first class under Major Wesley Sandburg of the Washington Puget Sound Second Light Infantry. With determination in his heart, young and foolish, he fought for what he believed was a just cause. He didn't question then. He didn't know any better.

4 Lock and Load

"**A**bilene foxtrot zero niner, this is comm. Control, this is Romeo November requesting status and casualty report, over," the tech said into the radio.

"Ox trot to Comt … rol, we've got fires under control, but have … ven men to small arms fire, over," the woman said on the other end.

"Please repeat, Foxtrot, your signal is weak. I say again, please repeat," the tech said.

The transmission was too garbled to make out. Commander Jennings approached the tech.

"I need a perimeter assessment by 0830, Corporal, along with full casualty and damage report from all outstanding units," the commander ordered.

"Aye, sir, most units have reported in, with the exception of Fourth Platoon and Khasvikov's squad," the tech said.

"Who's the CO of Fourth Platoon?" the commander asked.

"O'Neill is the CO, sir," the tech answered.

"Yes, sir, understood. If those men are in and secured within five minutes of departure, I want them and their gear on that vehicle. Any update on the drop-off point?" the commander said.

"Last full sheet reads no change in flight plan. They snagged an embankment on the last takeoff, so they're running six minutes late for in-flight repairs. Landing coordinates are fixed until further notice," the tech explained.

"Right, relay all information to the X-3 Cyclone stealth copter as soon as it comes in, and then come get me," the commander said.

The doors burst open, talking in the background silenced, and Preston approached the commander.

"Colonel, I'm quite glad to see that—"The commander was interrupted.

"Markey, I nearly got smeared across that landing pad," Preston complained.

"There was a little trouble, Preston, but you did make it," the commander said.

"Make it without the benefit of any cover from CAP or the boys at Air Cav! I've got priority orders from Petering himself, and I'm having enough trouble keeping these boys from walking into crossfire out there in the real war without having to worry about being torn apart on my own jump bases!" Preston said, outraged.

"Now, just listen here a minute, Wayne! I don't need you stomping in here spouting like this, throwing priority orders and General Petering's stars in my face! I get enough flak from those rebs in the hills, I don't need this! The orders come in and … " the commander said with anger. "One can be spared, but only under the cover of darkness, and it will be coming from an air force base in the States. Now, look, it's going to take at least two days. I'm sorry, Wayne. That's the best I can do. It's in its prototype stage," the base commander said.

"Five minutes before you come breezing in here, I get all of my air cover yanked, on order from ARLAC Central, signed and dated. I don't like it any more now than then, and believe me, I was pissin' in a hole then. So cool it and take your chatter out on Command, because I've got no say in this. Is that clear?" the commander said fumingly as he began to walk away.

Preston paused for a moment to light a cigarette and calm him down.

"Affirmative," Preston said in a cool voice.

"We took a beating here too, Preston; don't think we're not hurting, either. They're out there with ABS NK support, armor maybe, and they're hungry and mad. Pacified now, but still gosh darn getting pissed on. And now I've got to yank another half of my own personnel to arrange a personal escort for your boys in order to get you to the drop-off point in time for crumpets and tea with the high command … Either way, you're important. Why do we have to go way out there?"

"I don't know, can't say!" Preston said questioningly. "What's this Strike Team Zero thing I keep hearing about?"

"That is classified intel and on a need-to-know basis and you don't need to know yet," the commander whispered to Preston, which intrigued him when the commander said the word yet as he walked away. Preston, with a touch of gray on his brown sideburns, flicked his cigarette butt.

"If there was any little reason to boot your leathery butt for this little insurrection here, I wouldn't hesitate to do it. But as circumstances lie, I haven't got much choice either way. You're important, and God knows why," the commander said in a calm voice.

"Sorry, we all know our parts," Preston said.

"We know it all too well, Colonel. What's your condition?" Jennings said.

"None the worse for wear, we were just out of the Middle-East Afghan mountains with our tails between our legs," Preston said.

"Glad to see you made it all right, though. I'm sure you deserve one heck of a rest," the commander said.

"Certainly do, at least for the men, strung pretty thin," Preston assured.

"Well, get some rest in the sheltered barracks," Jennings suggested.

"The AH-118 X-3 Cyclone, we're headed for a location, code-named drop-off point, huh?" Preston confirmed.

"I hear she got rattled bad by ground fire and enemy aircraft," Jennings said. "You'll need to mount up quick to catch your ride when it arrives."

"Yeah, I'll round up the boys," Preston said as he headed for the enclosed corridor. "Thanks, Commander, and keep the faith," said Preston.

"Good luck, Colonel. Don't take any chances," Jennings said. Preston opened a door and he walked down another hallway that was busy with activity. He thought this as he walked down the hallway:

I'm still on fire about that brush with the BARE unit regular, but I know these base commanders too well. You can spit and hack and holler, but don't get on their bad sides—save the venom for the enemy. It's hard enough fighting blind in a world out of control with friends you can rely on. In these times, if you turn someone off, you may later find your life in their hands. We're all connected, they like to remind us, a network and a team. It's not that I'm not a team player. You've got to cooperate to win, but first you've got to survive.

Preston walked down the hallway until he opened the door to the outside and continued on. There were vehicles driving around and gunfire in the distance amongst bare dead trees under a cloudy overcast sky.

"Hey, Colonel, what's the word? We got warm bunks and two days R and R when the mission is over?" Stryker said as he approached the colonel.

"Yeah and combat pay," Dexter remarked.

"Try injury leave," Armstrong grunted as he dropped his duffel next to his bunk.

"You boys know you deserve all of it and I'd give it if I could, but we've got export orders from command," Preston commented. The men groaned and someone threw a canteen, almost hitting him.

"You know I don't write 'em," Preston said.

"Yes, we know, you just read 'em," Dexter sighed.

"Correct, I got the wire just before the extraction from Glory Point this morning. We're catching a stealth chopper to the drop-off point east of here when it arrives in two days. Get some rest and I'll see you guys in a couple of days. We're catching a chopper in its prototype phase. We are going to be secretly inserted into the Gobi Desert on the border of Mongolia and 18 North Korea, using a stealth attack transport helicopter, first of its kind. It will be here in two days, so be ready; its code name is the X-3 Cyclone. The AH-118 is equipped with a mini-gun and a place for a door gunner to sit. That would be for you, Armstrong, as well as you guys. It will be sent out from New Castle, Delaware Air Force Base. It looks sort of like a Black Hawk hybrid," the base tech confirmed.

"It's funny how ARLAC keeps cutting us diggers short on our sit-down between tours. Must be to keep us from noticing we aren't getting anywhere," Armstrong remarked.

"Ground pounders beware," Thompson said.

"All speculation aside, Sergeant, I think this one may be wrapped in with something big. The gunny who gave the release was dropping names like Petering and Randall," said Preston.

"Witch Bitch Randall of Air Cav?" Stryker commented.

"The same, Lieutenant," Preston said.

"The way her snake-jockeys were running a few minutes ago, I'd have thought she was fighting for the other side," Stryker said.

Meanwhile, two days later, during their gearing-up …

"I'm quite certain, Lieutenant, there is some reasonable explanation for their departure," Krychovski said assuredly with his Siberian accent.

"Krychovski is right, Stryker, I've been told they've got high-priority reassignment. I've got a feeling, with all the base-stripping and troop transfers, that they're gearing up for a major operation," Preston confirmed.

"I assume this may have something to do with the Timan Geostat satellite relays," McKinley said.

"Beg pardon?" Stryker asked.

"ARLAC Central's been on Code Red hush-hush ever since the— What is it called, Corporal?" Preston said.

"The Upper Timan Declination Spectrograph," McKinley clarified.

"Exactly, ever since the Geostat relayed this picture from the eastern border of Mongolia in the Gobi Desert, everyone's been walking on eggshells. It takes me forty-five minutes now just to get authorization for a case of foot powder. I've had to red ball half our replacement gear. So don't step on any toes, gentlemen. We've got enough problems without anyone pissing on the hand that feeds us. Understood?" Preston explained.

"What about this Proteus thing I've been hearing about? What's the scoop on that?" Dexter inquired.

"There's been no confirmation of the Proteus Orbiter," McKinley said.

"There's none that we've been told, McKinley. Durgood in supplies has been hearing stories from the armor boys about finding tanks lying in the middle of nowhere, melted to slag, with their crews still inside … " Dexter said.

"Yeah, total meltdown," Thompson interjected.

"Just rumors, gentlemen. Probably propagandist horseshit spread by Korean/Iranian Alliance weasels to keep us scared. Let's keep focused on the task at hand, shall we?" the colonel mentioned.

Meanwhile, a couple of days later ...

"Gather up the gear and hoof it to the rail launcher emplacement. The chopper has arrived and is gassed up on the helipad. I've got to file some routine interim half sheets and AARs, and I'll be with you in five," Preston informed as the troops gathered up their gear and headed out.

"Oh, Stryker," Preston said.

"Yes, sir?" Stryker answered.

"I didn't get a chance to commend you for the top job you did with that gyro. Finest piece of flying I've seen in quite a while," Preston complimented.

"Wal, garsh, Colonel, twarn't nuthin'," Stryker replied.

"It may seem I'm always on your case, but I don't forget the job you put in around here. Just tone down the offside antics, and you'll be up for promotion fairly soon. Then you'll be rid of me for good," Preston said.

"Colonel, I must admit, it hasn't all been bad," Stryker admitted.

"No, Terry, we've got our points of friction, but I think under it all, we're on the same wavelength," Preston conceded.

"Aye, aye, Colonel. See you in five and thanks," Stryker said.

Stryker picked up his gear and hurried to join up with the troops.

"That leg still looks a little raw. Did you get it checked, Armstrong?" Thompson asked.

"Yeah, the medic told me I got lucky. It was one of those steel-jacketed slugs, so there was no torn tissue. Clean puncture. Hurt like a mother, though," Armstrong answered.

"How's it to walk on?" Thompson probed.

"Well, it jabs a little, but Doc gave me some morphine for the pain. Lucky it didn't hit the bone. Those twelve millimeters can shatter six-inch cinderblock," Armstrong said.

"Good thing it didn't hit your head, then," Stryker said with concern.

"Man, Stryker! Don't you quit? I'd thrash your ass like I always do, but as you see I've only got one good leg," Armstrong threatened as a Humvee drove by.

"Soldiers coming through, so haul ass, get out of the way!" said the ground tech as another Humvee went by.

"The way you talk, Armstrong, you'd only need one," Stryker remarked.

"He's got a point. You're not exactly the most modest man among us," Dexter said to Stryker as they all laughed.

"Then let me humble myself and say, I'm feeling a bit weak from my medication …" Armstrong said as he dropped his duffel bag again.

"And will you please carry my gear for me?" Armstrong continued as everybody laughed.

"C'mon, Armstrong, I've got the field radio!" Dexter said to hurry the men along.

"Let's keep up, Lieutenant," Thompson encouraged as Stryker picked up his duffel bag.

"Aw, man!" Dexter complained as a group of troops rushed by.

"Oh, Stryker, thanks for bringing that tub down safe back there, man. You really tucked our asses in real nice," McKinley said.

"I did my best not to mess up my lovely hair, at least," Stryker said jokingly.

"There is much to be said about your abilities, Lieutenant. I commend you, fellow comrade," Krychovski complimented.

"Well, I must admit I'm a little rusty on the GLT, but we got down all right. That BARE goon in the tin suit wasn't helping any …" Stryker commented.

"Crap, when I saw that OV standing there like Dirty Harry with a rail launcher, I thought we were going to buy it," Dexter said in the distance.

"Dexter, who is Dirty Harry?" McKinley inquired.

"I'll show you later in the bunk shelter video relay," Dexter said.

"What I'd really like to know is where the Snake flyers were when we were getting chewed apart?" McKinley asked.

"They had priority orders, Corporal," Thompson explained.

A vehicle approached the men.

"What's the matter, Dex, got no faith in my abilities?" Stryker said as he stroked his blond hair.

The vehicle stopped with a load of wounded and lots of shouting in the background as men approached.

"Don't get me wrong, Stryker, but we nearly … got … killed … " Dexter said.

Men were screaming in pain. Medics rushed about; some were using their equipment.

"Give me a hand with this man, Lieutenant!" the nurse said.

"Sure!" Stryker said as he rushed over.

"My eyes … My eyes … My eyes …" said the wounded soldier as the man was lowered onto the gravel.

"Hold on there, man. We'll get you fixed up," Stryker said calmly.

"I can't feel … my eyes! What … happened?" the wounded soldier said a little louder.

"I need to get a compress on. Get his helmet off," the nurse said.

Stryker removed the soldier's helmet and the nurse tore open a bandage.

"Oh, man, what the heck!" Stryker cursed as he looked away for a moment.

"Aaaugh, why … can't … I … see?" the soldier complained.

"Nurse, what … " Stryker began to ask.

"The sergeant says an enemy BARE unit used a flamer on him and started a brush fire," the nurse whispered to Stryker.

"Oh, my goodness! My goodness! My goodness!" Stryker said weakly.

"Oh, my goodness, oh, my, oh, oh … " the soldier said as his voice died off suddenly.

"Lieutenant?" the nurse said as she nudged Stryker.

"Huh? Oh, I'm sorry! I just never got used to it." Stryker said nervously.

"Yes, well he's sedated now, Thank you!" the nurse said calmly.

"Sure!" Stryker said.

"Coming through!" the medic alerted.

There were people strolling fast through the corridor in the medical wing of the base. There were gurgling noises coming from patients being on life support.

"Burn victim! Coming through!" the medic said again.

"Lieutenant Stryker, we must go quickly," Krychovski said.

"Eh? Yeah, let's go," Stryker said sickly.

Stryker picked up his duffel bag. There were a lot of people rushing through the hallway. The groans and activity slowed down.

"Are you all right, Lieutenant?" Krychovski said with concern.

"Yeah, I'm all right. I care too much, I guess," Stryker said with sympathy.

"One can never care too much, my friend," Krychovski interjected.

A whine of a helicopter rotor started up and a chirping noise could be heard as the blades picked up speed. There were voices in the background and gunfire in the distance.

"Move it, Terry, the colonel's here already!" Dexter hustled.

"This is the last bus leaving for the Wasteland, immediately, all aboard," Armstrong said aloud.

People went up steps into the chopper. The colonel slid the door shut as the rotor blades began to gain momentum. The wounded were stacking up as they left. Young bodies, maimed and torn, like so much meat for the grinder. The grizzly face of death was all they'd known, and yet its glare was all the more real with each new glance. One could not hear the cries and not wonder, *How close have I come to becoming that?*

While the others amused themselves with war stories, Dexter reminisced about his past … He remembered his most recent mission, where they were in a small town in Afghanistan. They had to take care of some Syrian rebels hiding out in abandoned buildings. When Dexter was finally in place to flush out an insurgent, he saw the second flare go off; he knew the perimeter had been breached. Dexter didn't hear any alert go out over the shortwave, so the rear observers hadn't seen enemy forces yet. He slipped in around this shot-out building, setting his scope to passive night vision, and took a look into an undeclared fire zone without rear cover or flanking fire.

"Whatcha staring at, Dex? You've had that look since we left," Thompson asked.

"Huh! Oh! Who me? Oh, that! I was just reminiscing about our past," Dexter said as he checked his HK MP-20 submachine gun.

"He must've been out of his flippin' skull."

"That's Dex, gentlemen. He's one slip short of a section eight," Armstrong commented.

"We like to think it's that Cherokee blood in him. Don't mix well with the rest, and makes him a little out of it," Stryker said.

"What is the Cherokee?" Krychovski asked.

"Native American, Krychovski," Stryker replied as he opened his canteen.

"For some reason, the lieutenant always thinks he's on point," McKinley said.

Anyway, he thought about the scenario again. He slipped across the western barricades so he got a clean view, and he popped the IR. Dexter took a long guzzle from his canteen. There were two columns of sappers tiptoeing through a break in the concertina wire. Dexter saw at least thirty-six in all, backed by a carriage team and mortars. Spotters didn't see them. Three dozen clanking bomb boys could stroll into camp without anyone seeing them. He couldn't call in to confirm, because from twenty yards, that carriage gun would've heard him and drilled him in. Without ranging fire, he couldn't pop a thumper into the bunch and book. Climbing back over the barricade was a good way to catch one in the back. He did the only other thing he could do, set his piece on auto and opened fire. He figured the only way to warn his guys was to give 'em some hostiles to shoot at, rather than these slinky sappers. He opened fire at the spotters. He was on the hog that night, and Dex thought they had one of those crazies on the wire. The damn lights and motion sensors were down while they switched generators. Just motherfricken luck they slipped in when they did. He buzzed around quick and they flashed the backups and dropped a Willy-Pete on the field. Base commander looked like he needed a change of shorts, which was understandable. Armstrong was there with the eighty machine gun and he just had to let it fly. That was one funky mad minute. He must've dropped twenty of 'em before they vented the tower with the carriage. Lucky Thompson pulled him off the hog, or he'd have caught a mortar round in his lap. There should have been cover from armor, at least just a Bradley, or a Scout drone in case. Fourth Light was executing an RIF of the city to root out dug-in resistance. They had him pegged down pretty good. Dexter could squeeze his way out of a guarded footlocker.

Dexter opened a food pack.

"Be sure, Sergeant, that when Dexter wants to miss somebody, he misses 'em," Thompson said.

Armstrong was on the hog that night, and just his luck, Dex saw the flares pop off. Well, Dex never missed anything. He could read in his sleep, so they said. Understandable, McKinley responded not even a Bradley or a scout drone. Dexter thought again, because the Syrians breached their defenses for the command hut. Lucky he hit them from behind, though. He could warn the CP, but he couldn't use the radio, because the enemy could hear him. Everyone was clear by then. His message came and it was hard to make out.

While the troops were busy talking all of a sudden, Dexter just burst out laughing.

Thompson said, "Let me guess. It's the latrine incident, isn't it?"

Dexter nodded with bright red rosy cheeks, trying to contain his laughter.

"That's life on the jump CP," McKinley interjected.

The team couldn't spot for artillery, either, because the enemy had breached their perimeter and were onto the base. Armstrong laid it down thick for them, but the point man and his friends broke out and made for the command hut. Luckily he didn't try to hit them from behind, though.

Dex couldn't kill them, but he could warn the CP. Then he thought he could have used the radio. Then he thought, as he chuckled, if the message wouldn't have been dramatic enough. He remembered he rolled a smoke grenade into the bunker. It worked—immediate evac. The Furies busted in and wham! Everyone was clear by then. Then he thought to himself, too bad the major was in the latrine at the time, as he let out a big laugh that he couldn't contain.

Red Furies came next. They were basically suicide bombers. They rushed in with nothing but forty pounds of thyrite on their backs and a dead-man switch. This was one last glorious service for the motherland. Usually guys with diseases or terminal cancer were chosen for the job.

"The major had taken the wrong tablets that week. You know what bad water can do to you," Armstrong said, trying to contain his laughter as well.

"Luckily no one saw the major dive from the building with his pants around his ankles," Dexter remarked as he chuckled.

The colonel unbuckled his harness and leaned over his seat to check on his men. At the drop-off point, Stryker eased the chopper down smoothly at a base.

5   Shuffling Through the Scuttlebutt

"Well, Colonel, what's the scuttlebutt?" Stryker inquired after setting the chopper down at a midway refueling station.

"Gentlemen, rest yourselves for a couple of hours. We're scheduled to rendezvous with the drop-off point at 1400 for a quick dust-off," Preston reported in.

"I hope you've booked the suites for us, sir. I'd like something with bay windows and a shower," Thompson said jokingly.

"And room service," Armstrong added.

"I can't give you the Holiday Inn, but you can rest your hides for a bit before we get briefed. I've been informed that there will be shower passes for everyone, and a special surprise—ice cream," Preston said as the men gave each other high fives and shouts of approval.

"Suit up in light field plate by 1330. I've got some reading to do, so I'll be in the officers' cabin," Preston said.

The door opened and closed in the officers' cabin. A door opened up and there was a sound of boots walking on the metal catwalk in the hallway and another door closed.

"Situation is green, Colonel. We've got to go through the Kazakh to the Ishim Valley, but the latest from Geostat indicates heavy invasive contaminates have settled south of the Urals. It'll be touch and go from there," the base commander informed.

"Keep me posted, Captain. I'll be in my quarters," Preston said.

"Roger," the base commander said.

A door opened up and closed quietly. Preston sat down and poured himself some coffee. He pulled his chair up to the desk and positioned himself. He stirred and sipped his coffee with one hand and paged through a folder that he had in a briefcase with the other. He set the cup on the desk while he looked through the folder some more.

This is priority one data for authorized eyes only. Do not accept from courier if seal is broken. The coding is F-Branch, indicating that intelligence put the file together. Lord knows what the half-wits at Intelligence would want to tell me, Preston thought to himself as he ripped open the seal, looked at some of the contents in the folder, and took another sip of his coffee.

Field reports, standard. The estimates of the enemy's strength on Ural and East European fronts. There were no casualty reports. The ARLAC had held the territories of Kazakhstan and Scandinavia for quite a few months now; that wasn't news. What were new were the reports of heavy fighting. ARLAC had panicked ever since the North Koreans invaded South Korea and then had the newly formed North Korean/Iranian Alliance, which came marching across the Gobi Desert into Mongolia and took them by surprise with their new walking machines. They even brought over their four nuclear missile launcher trucks, and now it seemed they wanted the land back. It was strange—there weren't any important resources to be found there. Just some empty fishing waters and sterile farmland. But now their new offensive was to nuke or invade China and Russia.

It appeared that the North Korean forces were bracing for heavy assault, bunching their units closer along key positions. They'd been at this too long not to know when something was brewing. The Russians knew that an invasion was imminent; it was only a matter of time. Then it happened; they rushed the South Korean border and people fled in panic using aircraft and seafaring vessels to evacuate into China and Japan. Some refugees who didn't make it out of South Korea were either shot or trapped.

Invoices and requests for spare chopper parts were ordered to build a stealth helicopter gunship transport, first of its kind and classified. From the army's scrap yard of spare parts, Apache cockpit and nose turret, fuel injector from a Huey UH-1D, twin Packard jet turbines, a rotor assembly and swash plate from a UH-60 Black Hawk, CH-47 Chinook fuel tanks and landing struts, and finally a fuselage from a Russian Hind gunship. There was definitely something going on at R and D.

The design was horrendous. He'd be surprised if this thing would run without blowing up, much less fly. They'd included a few design specs, but not a whole lot else. No explanation for this jury-rigged monstrosity. Needless to say, he didn't like the looks of it.

Then the authorization for special equipment came through.

The list was long and detailed.

"I can tell just by looking that we'll be isolated, probably behind enemy lines. No mention of a radio pack or signaling gear. No contact with ARLAC after insertion," Thompson complained as he sifted through paperwork. It would be another bad sign.

6   Your Move

Colonel Preston briefed the troops on the current situation. He began, "During the Great Defensive near the Canadian border, many refugees were killed by a cloud of nuclear fallout. There were twenty-two people killed. Even the attacks didn't seem that intense. Less than sixty percent of our forces in that field have engaged enemy positions." If ARLAC wanted to break the ring of fortifications around Eastern Europe, they would have to concentrate, find a weak point, and exploit it. This list of artillery strikes and ground advances seemed irregular, almost random. There was no strategy here, except perhaps to keep the enemy off-guard. Maybe something was brewing.

"Current estimates of contaminant concentrations from Geostat. It was a reliable system of aging weather satellites that kept us informed of toxins in the atmosphere. However, our reliable Intelligence department had informed us that our global spectrographic imaging system was in danger of being destroyed by GSKs or satellite destroyers. The presence of these high-altitude, missile-carrying aircraft has not yet been confirmed, but it was suspected. Several orbital relays have mysteriously malfunctioned. More salt in our wounds.

"Confirmation of a grade-seven SSTO launched twelve days ago, where South Korea was the only nation left with the resources to launch manned or unmanned space vehicles. Our own Geostat consists of pre-war weather and Earth resource platforms that have been reprogrammed. The Koreans have continued the traditions of NASA, the ESA, and the Russian space programs. Their Single-Stage-to-Orbit vehicles allow transfer of payloads twice the capacity of the twentieth-century shuttles. Security Services has refused to speculate whether or not this may be the Proteus satellite on its maiden voyage.

"Our inside sources have known for quite some time of the development of the Proteus weapon system. Apparently, the scientists had discovered a means of altering the molecular structure of matter, resulting in an odd 'fusing' effect. If such a procedure were used against human beings, the effect would be gruesome, at best. Although tales of tanks and crews melting into heaps of metal and flesh have circulated following this launch, there is no evidence to confirm such happenings. At least, as far as we've been told. Security Services and Intelligence will do anything to keep up morale."

Colonel Preston ran this thought through his mind: *Some fuzzy video-tech relays of high-altitude reconnaissance pictures. The desk jockeys have made sure to circle the enemy units just in case we forgot what they look like. We color-coded shock troops in green, support vehicles blue, light armor yellow, and tripods red. It's almost funny how the experts on the enemy have never actually seen them in action. Theirs is a world of photos. Ours is a world of fire.*

It appeared to be standard triple-cluster formation, with two forward sentries and a rear-scout command tripod surrounding each unit of infantry. The Korean Alliance method of war derived from the tradition of deforestation. The mammoth tripods marched forward, pummeling the earth with concussion and carriage guns. The cannons, firing either anti-armor squash-head or high-explosive concussion rounds, scattered tanks and hard point emplacements; gunners behind the rapid-firing carriage-style machine guns swept the field, suppressing smaller units. As the devastating machines marched past, ground units moved in to eliminate stragglers. The advance came in long lines, sweeping clean the battlefield like some enormous deadly tide.

It appeared that the Korean forces were bracing for heavy assault, bunching their units closer along key positions. They'd been at this too long not to know when something was brewing.

7   Plan of Action

Colonel Preston flipped past a satellite photo he'd just looked at. Color Geostat spectrographs. The inset dated them at March 12, 2091, and May 20, 2091, the Omega-Divine declination. The comparison between the pictures was striking. The first was an unremarkable scan of the northern tundra, a blend of grays and browns, scarred by the bloody gash of the Ural Mountains. What was revealed in the later scan, however, undoubtedly lay at the center of this operation. That was, if this was not a computer error. Nowhere on the Earth's surface was there such a large patch of green.

The intercom crackled.

"Attention personnel, prepare for CBRN system initiation. Don filter hoods and await further instructions. This is not a drill," the base commander said.

An alarm echoed off throughout the base. A cabinet opened up and Preston pulled a respirator over his head. A door opened up and a tech stepped in, also wearing a respirator.

"Air purge in two minutes!" the tech said.

The door closed loudly and there was faint scrambling and talking outside Preston's door.

"The base's atmosphere has been compromised … Prepare for air purge in ninety seconds! All non-essential personnel brace for decompression!" the base commander said.

Preston breathed into his respirator as he waited the situation out.

When Preston had his first toxic-invasive drill, he was understandably tense. The outside air had become so polluted with chemical toxins, radioactive dust, mutated viruses and bacteria that a deep breath at the wrong instant could lead to a long, excruciating death. The CBRNs, chemical, biological, radioactive, or nuclear systems, were efficient to a point, but during waves of highly toxic contaminants, complete isolation was required. As a result of the volatile winds that had plagued the Russian plains for thousands of years, they were especially at risk. Geostat helped to locate larger pockets of toxins, but early-warning sensors were essential in order to prepare for the next "toxic wave." In a hard point bunker, the atmosphere could be purged and sealed, creating a stable and safe internal environment. In the field, bulky and often unreliable rad-tox gear and respirators were all they had between our vulnerable lungs and some of the deadliest substances known to man.

"Decompress in fifteen seconds, all external vents to locked position. Initiate pressure seals. The ventilation system will purge in five, four, three, two, one!" the commander alerted. There was a loud sound of air escaping and being filtered out. Then the sound of grinding pumps, the thud of closing valves, and the hiss of air returning could be heard throughout the base.

"Standby … " the base commander said over the intercom. It had become a ritual for Preston, as ordinary as cleaning a rifle or brushing his teeth. That was something that simply needed to be done to ensure their survival. In a moment, they'd declare the air safe and return to their tasks.

"Stand down CBRN alert. Cabin integrity is maintained. Resume standard operations," the commander said over the intercom as he clicked on the button. At that moment, Preston removed his respirator and returned it to the cabinet. He then took in a deep breath of fresh air, then sipped and stirred his coffee some more.

In the years following the atomic war, an odd, peaceful quiet fell over the land. The radiation from the blasts settled quietly into the soil, and for a short time, man thought the threat was over. Not in the least. Almost immediately, deadly, incurable diseases began to appear, taking thousands of weakened refugees by surprise. The effects were devastating. His own father was killed in a matter of hours as a mutated virus caused his lungs to deteriorate rapidly. As he watched him gasp and writhe, lying in the ruins of their home, he cried for the last time. He stared into his eyes, put his gun to his head, and ended his pain. That was his only remaining memory of his father, but one he would never be able to forget.

Winds kept most of the disease and poison out of the cities, so they were safe if they stayed among the ruins and found shelter when it rained. Regular doses of Zyrathine given by the militias kept the blood from becoming too anemic due to the radiation. However, other symptoms, such as the nausea and hair loss, could not be avoided.

The threat of radiation had died considerably, and remained significant only in a few heavily nuked areas. However, they were told that their life expectancies had been severely cut short by the irradiation; cancer and leukemia were rampant killers. He personally had sixteen tumors removed during his forty-two years.

The viruses had grown steadily worse, and the Korean/Iranian Alliance had presented a new threat: chemical warfare. The taboo weapons of the twentieth century had become the staple of twenty-first-century warfare. All manner of toxins, from primitive mustard gases to nerve toxins and emulsified sterilizers, had been introduced into the air and water. As a result, every member of ARLAC carried a polyacrylic poncho and air filter, on the battlefield and off. Due to the destructive effects of many chemicals on the human reproductive system, isolated "baby camps" had been established. In these hidden underground bunkers, the one-half of one percent of the population still able to procreate were breeding the next generation of soldiers. Instead, their governments discontinued that project and had something else in mind.

He never gave children much thought, really, but donated sperm and DNA when he was a young officer. He was declared sterile at age twenty-four, anyway. It wasn't because his wife, Laura, didn't want them, it was that she wanted to help the refugees in the Midwest. She would have been a perfect mother. She had that adaptive quality. Sometimes he thought nothing fazed her; she would glare into the face of adversity and continue to toil. Forever the optimist, his beloved Laura, may she rest in peace.

They met during the Great Defense. She was fleeing Montana, her family killed by the radiation after the missiles hit the coast. But somehow she managed to persevere, and gave her time as a medical volunteer, inoculating children, feeding the aged and the dying. He was twenty-two, still young and bright-eyed when he saw her. Until then, he had never looked at a woman in that way; as fate might have it, he undoubtedly never would again. She had a simple elegance that rose above the dirt and the ruin of the world around her. Something in her fought it all back, and when they were alone, he could forget the sorrow the world had made for itself. They were married the night before the evacuation, when she would leave for the Russian heartland, while he remained to aid in the defense of the last strongholds of the North American continent.

He'd lost so much of himself those two days, and he could not bear to recall the nature of his actions. One never thinks oneself capable of sheer, hateful brutality. It took a man pushed to the brink of madness.

In the showers of fallout and blood, he became lost in the back alleys of the city of Las Vegas. Dazed by inhumanity and numb with fatigue, he stumbled mistakenly across a familiar boulevard. He did not realize until it was too late that they had mine-swept the street hours before.

The Grasshopper mine was designed to propel the explosive upward before detonation. He had only time to realize his mistake when he heard the pop. He awoke sometime later, his chest torn ragged, his face burning from within. When he could see through the wall of agony, he realized he had been pulled clear, into the rubble of the buildings. The man who had rescued him took his hand and smiled. He mumbled something in his good ear and left, and only then did he realize that he bore the uniform of the Korean/Iranian Alliance. Preston lay there for quite some time, lacking the strength even to pick the shrapnel from his blackened face. He felt fluid entering his lungs; his heart strained against a cold, steady pull. He lay quiet and waited to die.

In his feverous state, his mind wandered. He thought of the soldier who pulled him from the street. He had unconsciously conditioned himself to believe that each of the enemy wished him dead, and yet along came this man, whose compassion had driven him to pull him from the path of his blood-thirsty brethren and let him pass away in peace.

Preston thought then of his father. In a way, this man had given him that same final wish: a peaceful exit from this terrible world. How many fathers had begged mercy from as many sons from a world of hatred and pain that they themselves had created? Had they made this world, men like his father? Was this war some conspiracy by humanity, for humanity, and against humanity? Did he make the same mistake then, betraying himself to that final nothing?

He felt oddly at peace in the face of such impending uncertainty. Death was not his enemy. He had lost his fear of Him long ago. And yet he was at war, as of yet. Who was his enemy? Certainly not the people of Korea. He had just seen how they, like his people, were given to pity, compassion, and generosity. Why then did the fighting continue?

The outline of Laura's face formed in his mind's eye. To her he would give everything. For her he would do anything. As he lost his fear for his own life, he replaced it with fear for hers; he fought on solely for her. Fought whom? Fought to protect her from the enemy? Fought the violence of war?

Perhaps all this mess was for the war itself. Somehow that answer felt right. The war was his enemy; in it was embodied all that he despised and loathed. If he could rid himself of it, he could let happiness again into his heart. Satisfied with himself, he strained to move. Somewhere, out there in the land of the living, Laura needed him. He would not disappoint her by dying.

He dragged himself from the ruin into the darkness beyond. All about him, among the fires of the city, roamed the triumphant North Korean soldiers. He heard no rejoicing; they had paid the price in blood and tears. But the city was theirs, and he had little hope of salvation.

8   The Horrors of Reality

Alas, he did not realize! Suddenly the sky was alive with planes. They had held long enough, and careful ARLAC pilots strafed the streets with hot vengeance. He managed to fire a signal flare, and was spotted by a gyrolift medvac. They pulled him from the plains of death and swept him to safety.

The surgeons made no guarantees, but he had been exceedingly lucky. They reattached his ear, though he could no longer feel it, and his cheek had lost much of its scarry texture. The recovery was long, and not without hardship. He was alone in a room of the dying, but the duty of love spurred him on. Within a month, he was walking. In two, he could speak and see clearly, and he took his leave to search for Laura.

"Would Colonel Preston please report to the main hangar?" said the captain over the intercom.

He shouldn't have let himself wander like that—only got halfway through the file. He didn't doubt this last section was important. "Archangel Project." There would be a full briefing, but the brass loved a well-read soldier. He did try his best.

Preston safely tucked the folder in his briefcase and zipped it closed. He then opened the door and then closed it again. He walked across the metal catwalk to the control room where the radar and satellite monitoring was.

"The captain's in the forward section, sir. He'd like your advisement on some visual contacts," said the tech.

"Affirmative. Inform the troops in back they've got fifteen to be in impermeable greens and slick-hats," said Preston.

"Aye, aye, sir," the tech replied.

Donning a respirator, Preston walked through compartments, climbed up and down ladders, and opened and closed pressure doors and hatches.

He pressed buttons and flicked switches. There were tone sounds as doors opened and closed and Preston removed his respirator.

"Captain, I've been informed of some visuals?" Preston inquired.

"A group of unaffiliated partisan units, bearing 309.7 degrees, two miles northeast. They followed us, parallel course, and don't seem to be trying to mask their movement. If I thought they might know about the rendezvous with the drop-off point, I'd think," said the captain.

"How many?" Preston asked.

"Private, rerun that last section of video," the captain commanded as the private rewound the tape and played it.

"They're bunched tight, with a couple of horses and what looks like a motorcycle riding point. Forty-two at our best count," the captain said.

"Have they made any aggressive advances?" Preston questioned.

"None yet. But we're certain they've seen us," the captain replied.

"What is the current ETA to the LZ?" Preston asked.

"Nine minutes ... Mark," said the captain.

"Keep an eye on them and contact me if there's any change in their relative position. Whether they make a move or not, I want a volley of smoke packs and some warning fire to keep them off while we transfer. I'm sure the drop-off point can lend some support if things get too heavy," Preston suggested.

"Will do, Colonel, and good luck," said the captain.

"Thanks for the rest stop," Preston said with gratitude.

Everyone laughed and gathered up their gear.

"Don't fall too far behind now, Armstrong. We'd hate to have to leave you behind," said Stryker.

"You do, and I'm sure I'll peg your ass with this thumper so you can stay behind and keep me company," Armstrong said.

"Oh, tough guy, *hermano*?" Dexter said.

"Bad to the bone!" Thompson replied.

"Bad to the core!" Armstrong remarked.

"Y'all come back," Thompson interjected.

"And we'll give you some more!" said Armstrong.

They gave each other high fives and cheers of approval. The door opened and closed.

Outside, the X-3 Cyclone had the rotor blades spinning and ready for takeoff.

"Welcome back, Colonel. I hope your cabin was comfortable. Wouldn't want you to be too jealous of us grunts back here in the meat wagon," Stryker said.

"Oh, I'm quite jealous. None of you had to read the ream of paper Intel and SS handed me before I got on," said Preston.

"Is this any indication of our next assignment?" Armstrong inquired.

"Count on it, soldier. Now in five minutes, we'll be ready to lift off to the drop-off point. She'll only be on the ground for a ninety-second slow taxi, so haul it. Keep clear of the prop wash and landing gear and you'll be okay. Any questions?" Preston said.

"Do we get aisle or window seats?" Dexter said jokingly.

"Dexter, you've got point. Everyone else, follow Quinn, ten-yard spread. Jog it until she touches down, then double time. Oh, and one more thing. There may be some partisans out there trying to crash our little party. The base gun turrets will lend some cover fire, but don't stop to say hello. All right, hoods on, three minutes," said Preston.

"Though I walk through the valley of the shadow of death ..." said Thompson.

"Man, you are screwed up," Armstrong commented.

"Couldn't hurt, you know," Thompson remarked.

"You always say that. You're supposed to get fired up when you're prepping, not prayed down!" Armstrong said.

"He's just a little twitchy knowin' you'll be covering his ass, Armstrong," Stryker said.

"Lieutenant Stryker, those silver bars have protected you from more harm than your field plate ever will," said Armstrong.

"You got that right, Sergeant," Stryker remarked. "Weapons on single fire, gentlemen. Let's conserve our ammo—don't make any unnecessary moves," McKinley suggested. "You are set for lift-off when the light reads green. Standby ..." said the captain.

"Lock and load, safeties off. Look sharp!" said McKinley.

"Major, I need you to arrange for the troops' accommodations, full decon and bunks, once we board. I've got a priority meeting with brass, so I'll send word later," said Preston.

"Don't worry, sir. I'll have it all taken care of," McKinley assured.

"I can count on you, Jake," Preston agreed.

"All right, Dex! Let's make sure we don't step in anything this time!" Stryker said.

"Don't worry, my friend. The spirits are with us," Dexter assured.

"What's this, a Native American charm necklace?" Thompson asked.

"You might say. Grandpa gave it to me, says it goes back to the old tribes. Good medicine," Dexter explained.

"There is much wind and dust. The landing will be … touchy," Krychovski said.

"There!" Thompson said.

Of all the machines of war, the citadels were by far the most impressive. They lacked the menacing quality of the robotic drones and tanks, or the awkward quaint of the towering tripods. There was some odd, elusive grace about them. He supposed the tradition of the super carrier went back to the Second World War, with the Boeing Liberators and Superfortresses. Big, powerful, flexible machines. They needed something to match the supremacy of the ARLAC F-63 Skyblazer sky jet squadrons, but with less demanding fuel constraints. It had to be big, to carry effective payloads, but turbine power ate too much precious fuel. The answer was to return to the prop. Speed wasn't a requirement, so the designers went back to the older bombers. What they came up with was remarkable.

It was difficult to describe the scale of the citadel: imagine a Superfortress expanded to ten times its normal size. What resulted was a massive twenty-engine aerial bunker. Measuring nearly two hundred and fifty yards in length and three hundred wingspans, the drop-off point and others like it were capable of carrying vast amounts of cargo over long distances. The normal crew complement was one hundred and twenty, but she could carry four hundred more in her belly. A few had been modified to service makeshift hangars capable of repairing, refueling, and launching chopper and gyro lifts in midair. Despite the furious power of the Korean/Iranian Alliance tripods, the citadel remained the most powerfully armed vehicle ever built and there were five of them.

She'd circle at least twice and find the best approach, then set down on her massive twenty-foot tires and drop a crew ramp to pick them up. She was vulnerable on the ground, and spent a minimum amount of time during pickups. Somewhere inside her broad belly, a brooding assembly of high command officers awaited their arrival. Somehow, Preston was not looking forward to this meeting.

A ramp thudded to the ground.

"Easy, boys. Don't stick your heads out too soon . . ." McKinley cautioned.

The outside aircraft noise was louder now.

"She's a marvelous beast, this drop-off point," Krychovski commented.

"Yes, Leonid. She is," Preston agreed.

There was gunfire in the distance.

"Looks like our party crashers are right on time," McKinley said.

"Rock and roll!" Dexter remarked.

The troops scurried down the ramp, the citadel engines cycled down, and there was more gunfire in the distance.

"She's more damaged than I thought!" Stryker said.

"We'll be okay as long as you're not flying, Stryker!" Armstrong commented.

Bullets whizzed by and Armstrong returned fire.

The citadel engines shifted and were much louder now.

"All right, she's down, now haul ass!" McKinley shouted.

The men ran out of the base shelter. The gunfire and explosions became more intense.

"Colonel, I was wondering . . . " Stryker inquired.

"Yes, Lieutenant?" Preston replied.

"If ARLAC's pulling Tac Air from the field, where are they?" Stryker wondered.

The jets flying in the distance grew louder as they came closer. The men stopped running and paused for a moment.

"Bogies, four o'clock!!" Thompson cautioned. "That's just drop-off point's CAP scouts, Thompson!" McKinley said.

"No, they're not, sir!" Thompson disagreed.

The jets began to dive for a strafing run.

Stryker hopped into the X-3 and kept the rotor going. Preston said, as he got a face full of wind and water, "Everyone quickly get aboard the chopper. That's an order." The men rushed into the personnel hold and the colonel closed the door.

"Stryker, good thinking," Preston commended.

"Good thing they made this baby bulletproof," Stryker said as they lifted off and bullets bounced off the armor. At that same moment, the MacArthur took off as well, clipped the nose of one of the jets as the platform ascended, flipping a MiG-38 Draco, or Drakes, as the air jockeys call them, backwards, upside down, flipped it end over end, screwing up the pilot's instruments. The pilot immediately had to eject from the aircraft and it crashed into the rock face in the canyon. The platform would provide the cover that the X-3 Cyclone stealth helicopter would need. Synchronizing their watches, this would give Stryker the exact time for extraction, plus the place where they would be extracted from a highly mountainous region, with lush forests and a waterfall, which would give them perfect cover, a place called Kumgangsan. Within Kumgangsan there was Kuryong Falls, about four meters wide and with a drop of seventy-four meters. The falls led to the pond below called Kuryong Lake. From the lake one could climb for seven hundred meters to Kuryong Rock. Here there was a view of a deep valley and several lakes.

9   The Plan

"Let's buy some time for the colonel," the squadron leader said.

"That's an affirmative, squadron leader," said the wingman to the squadron leader as the wingman gave him a salute off his left wing.

"You have a go to engage the enemy," the leader replied.

"Roger, captain. Okay, boys, let's see what ya got," the wingman answered.

"Fox two," the third pilot said as he launched a missile at the incoming Drake fixed-wing aircraft.

The leader fired a barrage of heavy-caliber bullets at the incoming squadron. Several shells ripped through the back part of the canopy, forcing the pilot to punch out. The plane exploded as it hit the ground. Another took hits in the left wing, causing it to tilt to one side and lose altitude, forcing the pilot to eject. The remaining enemy Drake fixed-wing aircraft fired a counterstrike of air-to-air heat-seeking sparrow missiles at the remaining two aircraft squadrons. Outsmarted and outgunned, the ARLAC Skyblazers were ordered back to base by their commanding officers. The planes fired off some flares to divert the inbound missiles. They blew up on impact and the two jets flew an ascending half-loop, followed by a half-roll, or an Immelmann, and then straightened out formation going the opposite direction while hitting the afterburners to escape the North Korean jets.

"Nice flying, delta echo," the squadron leader commented.

"Likewise, captain," said his wingman.

"Not like you. I may be an old geezer, but I still got it."

Meanwhile, back at the heli-platform, ARLAC was being briefed on the plan of action. General Petering was having a nice chat with the Russian Federation's top brass. He was trying to smooth things over after the incident in Georgia, one of Russia's breakaway republics. The colonel came in walking briskly, carrying a leather briefcase, and he was wearing a government wool commando sweater with his officer's bunk hat under one of his star straps. Colonel Wayne Preston was a highly decorated US Army Ranger and helped evacuate US refugees after the North Korean nuclear attack.

Corporal Jake McKinley was a US Marine Sniper and helped with crowd control during the evacuation. Jake earned a sharpshooter's medal for crowd control when two armed thugs tried to loot a grocery store during a food riot.

Sergeant Maxwell Armstrong always had a low tolerance for disagreement, which meant he had a hot temper. He used to be a US Marine Gunnery Sergeant. He helped train soldiers to be the last line of defense against the North Korean Army. To his comrades, he acted tough, but actually on the inside he was a softie.

Major Keith Thompson worked in the US Army's motor pool as a mechanic.

Lieutenant Quinn Dexter was a highly decorated tracker and medic for the US Army with the help of his Cherokee blood and medical training from his grandfather, who was a medicine man. He was able to help lead a platoon of soldiers safely through a minefield.

Lance Corporal Leonid Krychovskiwas also a highly decorated soldier in the Spetsnaz Russian Special Forces.

Finally there was Lieutenant Terry Stryker, who helped a US Army convoy through the Mojave Desert by defending it against an air strike, using his Apache attack helicopter.

These men were hand-picked to go into the Gobi Desert under the cover of darkness wearing ski masks, night-vision goggles, commando weaponry, and C-4 plastic explosives. The weapons would include HK MP-20 submachine guns, the US Army Rangers' standard-issue ceramic knives, which were often made from zirconium oxide and hardly, if ever, needed sharpening, and a garrote. They would insert themselves near the western border of Mongolia and destroy the four nuclear warhead eight-wheeled launcher trucks.

At 2330 that night, Stryker and the crew took off in their prototype stealth helicopter in silent running mode to western Mongolia. Everyone was dressed in black, wearing ski masks, night-vision goggles, and HK MP-20's with silencer/suppressors. Colonel Preston and his men hid behind a hillside. He pointed two fingers at McKinley and Thompson. He held his hand palm down, telling his men to stay low, and put his other hand to his ear. They heard someone speaking in Korean in the distance, so he held his fist above his head, signaling them to check it out. Meanwhile, Dexter and Krychovski went with the colonel to the back of one of the huge eight-wheeled ICBM trucks between two. The colonel held up one finger to his lips as he put the other hand to his ear. They heard louder Korean chatter in the background. Dexter pulled out a screwdriver and began removing a panel off the side of one of the warheads and found the ten-digit keypad followed by a lit number display in red and an enter button. Krychovski, special liaison to the US, pulled out a folded piece of paper and began entering a three-digit number and hit enter. Dexter put the plate back in place and screwed it tight. The number was an override code so that the warhead wouldn't go nuclear. They continued this procedure throughout the night for each missile and C-4 plastic explosive charges on the gas tanks of each truck. The reason there was a Russian liaison assigned to the unit was because the missiles were sold to the North Koreans illegally by the Russians, going against the treaty made by the UN.

According to the Korean layout, there were four guards to each truck; the launchers were assigned to a specific target or geographic location. One was aimed at Russia, another at China, another at the United States, and finally one at central Europe.

At 0445, shortly before dawn, Colonel Preston gave the order to take out the Korean guards. McKinley, who was still high up on the ridge, saw three silhouettes in his green cross-haired sight on his AP88 M-43 Prowler sniper rifle with special armor-piercing titanium-tipped shells. He took the shot! Two crumpled to the ground like a pile of bones. The third scurried away. Two more were taken out on a sand dune. Dexter stabbed one in the back and fired off several shots through his silencer on his HK MP-20 sub-machine gun, killing three. Thompson snagged another with a garrote, while the colonel dodged a few shots from an AK-97 and returned fire with his silenced side arm, killing two. Krychovski rattled off a few shots, killing three with his HK MP-20. A Korean came at Preston with a knife and he held him back, while Preston leaned into him and shot him. Another tried it again but caught a slug in the back of the head from McKinley's sniper rifle as the soldier fell backwards.

"Excellent job, men. Did all that in under fifteen minutes, before sunrise," the colonel commended his men.

"How much time do we have until detonation, Dexter?" Preston asked with a tired and concerned expression on his face.

When he looked up, after looking at his watch, he said, "One hour. On our way back, we have to make a stop," the colonel added. Stryker put down his sun visor on his helmet and started the rotor blades up, as he looked at the sunrise on the horizon of the sand dunes.

"We have to take a detour through the Diamond Mountains and around waterfalls, lagoons, and mineral springs. I owe a friend a favor," the colonel said as he looked up from a photograph of his wife.

When they got there, the colonel, Dexter, and McKinley climbed a partially steep incline of stones up a hill inside a canopy of lush Korean trees with a waterfall going down between the stones. What used to be a vacation spot was now a restricted area by the North Koreans. There were tall and short stones. All of a sudden, shots rang out from a higher ledge of stones. Colonel Preston and his patrol dove for cover behind some stones, thick shrubbery, and vines.

Out of the corner of his eye, Thompson saw an armored scout motorcycle left by one of the snipers. He briefly informed the colonel about the motorcycle as well as the plan he had thought of.

He explained to the colonel that he would head for the Wasteland and warn the Russian army about the Koreans' plan to invade that area. He would then advise Lieutenant Stryker to meet them at the top of a ravine. With the colonel's consent, Major Thompson climbed into the canopy and put on the helmet that was lying in the seat. He hurriedly closed the hatch, turned the key in the ignition, and made off like a bandit.

After a while, he realized that time had passed. Thompson checked in on his radio to let the strike team know of his whereabouts. Upon approaching a Korean checkpoint, Major Thompson sped up his armored motorcycle and smashed through the steel gate, setting off alarms, leaving his pursuers in the dust. Two Hummers chased after him as well as machine-gun fire. Trying to shake his followers on a mountain trail, he then ran one off the road, having it tumble over the side as it burst into flames. Losing the other Hummer in his tracks, Major Thompson then proceeded to his destination of rendezvous. After finally arriving at a Russian base camp, he immediately warned General Strauvinski about the Koreans' plan to invade the Wasteland by attempting to take his army by surprise. General Mikhail Strauvinski was Russia's commanding officer for the main armored division. The major then notified Lieutenant Stryker that Strike Team Zero was ready to pull out and that he should meet them at the top of a ravine.

Meanwhile in the deep forest, Colonel Preston led his patrol out of danger through shrubbery and thick vines. In a clearing they could see a river surrounded by several layers of vegetation going downhill between trees. Next to the river were many ridges of rocks covered with moss. Atop the hill, two Korean scouts, wearing protective armor dragon skin covered suits, including helmets and sun goggles, crouched behind rocks. They loaded their AP88 M-43 Prowler sniping rifles with special armor piercing titanium tipped shells. A split second later, gunshots blazed in the team's direction. Ducking for cover, Corporal McKinley returned fire on the snipers with his sniper rifle. Scoring a critical hit on one of the men, Lieutenant Dexter spun him into a dance of death with one final blow. Aiming his sniper rifle, Corporal McKinley fired another shot at the second man. Unfortunately, he dodged the shot fired at him. Finally Sergeant Armstrong ripped a hand grenade off his battle harness, turned the arming knob and tossed it over the rock behind which the sniper was hiding, thus exploding, and killing him on contact. Now that they were rid of their menacing enemies, the group raced to the top of the ravine. Climbing out of the bushes, they could see Lieutenant Stryker awaiting their arrival in the chopper. They then took off and headed for Kazakhstan.

The wasteland was the stronghold of the Russian Federal territory about to be taken by the Koreans. On the barren desert basin, the X-3 Cyclone helicopter that was carrying Colonel Preston and his special elite tactical commando unit flew over the battlefield. Looking off in the distance, a small convoy consisting of desert-camouflaged Humvees, MBT-51 Scorpion Battle Tanks, and Bradley Fighting Vehicles spotted the small aircraft approaching their vicinity. The Korean ground troops, their antiquated battle tanks, and their armored cars prepared themselves for combat in the realization of what was in store for them. The X-3 chopper fluttered over the scene, as a Korean six-wheeled forest-camouflaged armored car armed with a fifty-caliber anti-aircraft machinegun moved out of the shrubbery. Stryker made evasive maneuvers to be sure to avoid it.

As the chopper swooped over the targeting area, Sergeant Armstrong rattled off a few shots at the ground troops with his door-mounted minigun. Making evasive maneuvers, the chopper avoided several volleys of rockets that were released into the air by a SAM launcher. As they coasted through the sky, Lieutenant Stryker fired rockets out of his rocket pods onto the site. Counting at least two destroyed units, the team searched for a perfect landing pad to get ready for the main assault on the Korean division. After landing, the group got out and found an area to hide out in until they were needed. Waiting for the Koreans to make their next move, the men decided to stay put for the time being. As the opposing forces prepared themselves to engage in combat, Preston motioned his men to take their positions.

As the Koreans moved closer, their armored units began shelling the area. Hunched behind a boulder, McKinley reloaded his assault rifle to get another shot at the troops. From out of the brush came an X-21 Battle

Armor Suit pointing its machine gun at the four men. The suit then spun the chamber on the weapon and directed its fire toward the men. Dodging bullets, the brave commandos dove for cover. McKinley tried to get out of its line of fire but ended up stumbling over a rock, allowing him to be an easy target. As he slowly crawled away from his opponent, the suit struck McKinley's right leg with a volley of shells. This was an extremely danger-ous weapon during the time when the Koreans first developed it. The Russians later stole this design idea and manufactured a similar model. The X-21 model was equipped with a robotic exoskeleton and had armor plating consisting of a standard plasteel alloy. It also had a multiple rocket launcher, which could deploy two missiles to a target. Mounted on its right arm was a 35mm rotary Gatling machine gun. However, the Russians' design had almost identical functions but minor changes were made. This type of armor suit was armed with a laser-guided targeting system linked to the suit's shoulder-mounted recoilless rifle. It also had bionic power jump capability, which was supplied by an attached backpack. Both of these suits' strength was estimated to be able to destroy a single mechanized vehicle. Paying the least bit of attention to what was going on behind him, Major Thompson, on his armored motorcycle, leaped into the soldier's armor suit and knocked it down.

As the ravaged commando crawled out of the burning wreckage, he made a quick effort to get away. Unfortunately, Major Thompson got to him first by gunning him down with his 9mm MAC-17 autopistol. Dexter immediately rushed over to McKinley and prepared a special herbal treat-ment to heal his injuries. Dexter began by removing two dried-up leaves from a pouch that was attached to his belt and proceeded to chant while rubbing them on McKinley's wounds. McKinley could then feel a warm and tingly sensation in his leg as Dexter's hands massaged it. When Dexter took his hands away, the leaves had totally crumbled to powder and the sensation had faded. When he examined the former site of the wound, there was absolutely no trace of a scar.

On the battlefield, Korean troops moved in closer to engage combat with the Russians. Slowly Strike Team Zero moved downhill, spraying the area with machine-gun fire. Men dropped as they were each individ-ually struck with clusters of bullets and blown away by hand grenades.

Looking over his left shoulder, the colonel sighted at least twenty to thirty Korean troops hiking up the side of the ledge. From behind the intersecting hills loomed Lieutenant Stryker in his X-3 Cyclone. Unaware of what was happening behind them, the soldiers had no time to react to the situation. Without warning, Lieutenant Stryker launched mortar shells from the chopper, killing at least half of the unit. The remaining men swung around and drew fire from both the helicopter and Colonel Preston's unit. Some fired back but were unable to survive a second bombardment. Setting the aircraft down once more, Colonel Preston and his team boarded the transport. Cruising over, the crew in the chopper observed the whole field. Burning wrecks, bloody carcasses, and fresh smoky craters were scattered every-where. Up ahead, they could see ground troops running for their very lives but were unsuccessful. Many mechanized units were disabled and strewn across the battlefield like dice tumbled from a giant's fist.

It had been known by many scientists that certain small geographical areas all over the world existed that were mysteriously capable of sustaining life. They especially had to check out the area within the North Korean DMZ. ARLAC desperately needed this area for resettlement, with its rumored fresh supply of uncontaminated water, lush growth, and fertile plains suitable for agriculture. Reconnaissance had to be undertaken to determine the availability of other natural resources such as timber and precious mineral deposits. Also meteorological data had to be collected to understand such basics as rainfall and seasonal changes with any dramatic shifts in temperature. Since the nuclear holocaust, great changes in climate had occurred, because of the disruption of the Earth's atmosphere. The ozone layer, much of which had been lost, left many areas barren deserts while others, ironically, like the Sahara Desert, would now support a large variety of plant life. Although due largely to bizarre mutations from nuclear fallout, this area would not support human life because of contamination. As a result of the nuclear war, the radiation transformed what was once a green, fertile planet into a partially dry, desolate world.

Pushing forty-three years of age, Preston was still rugged enough to carry his six-foot frame confidently through the hardest of missions. Although some of the finer edges of his sharply honed skills had eroded over the past few years, he still possessed a strong body to complement a quick and agile mind, a mind that seemed to work best when under pressure. Decisions had to be made instantly when the only alternative was death. It seemed lately those decisions had to be made more often and they were becoming more difficult to do. Maybe, as Preston thought, he was getting too old for this type of work after nearly twenty years in the service of his once mighty country. Part of the legacy left over from a lost generation.

Millions had perished outright from the firestorms that raged or the tens of millions who died later from radiation poisoning. The community that his father had selected was well planned. Built far to the north in what was known as the Territories, it had not received any blast damage. Sealed botanical domes, huge structures had been constructed for the cultivation of fruits and vegetables; also livestock was grown so that fresh meat could be had. Fresh water was contained in giant underground cisterns so that the supply remained constant. Plenty of timber was available for the building of protective shelters and also for fuel to run generators. Although the power needs of the community were minimal, most lighting being supplied by candles and naturally distilled fuels, some high-voltage electricity was required to run sophisticated decontamination equipment that was absolutely essential to survival. Preston could still recall with a shudder the times as a child when the survivalists would have to remain in their protective shelters sometimes for weeks on end as prevailing winds brought deadly particulate matter raining down on the wilderness. Even when these protective measures and elaborate safeguards were employed to protect the survivors from radiation sickness, people still developed cancer and, in the absence of modern medical care, usually died. The last he heard, there had not been a death due to cancer in three years, though it would surely afflict the colony periodically for generations to come.

Throughout the historical events that he was once put through, Preston often pondered the morbid experiences. During the periods of the North American downfall and the reconstruction of a new country, he donated his time and energy for a noble cause to help rescue the remaining population, after the surprise nuclear attack on the West Coast of the United States. He still remembered the times when people had to live inside protective housing units surrounded by concrete, a steel alloy several feet thick, followed by a layer of lead.

Stryker landed the chopper on a rocky ledge in the canyon with smoke all around him. The six members of the team that weren't on board during the assault got back on. Stryker flew the chopper northwest toward Kazakhstan. The colonel wasn't considered a friend to the others, but he sure acted like one of them by keeping a cool head. When they finally got to Kazakhstan, they saw five people dressed in white lab coats, standing near an abandoned nuclear missile silo.

"Well, Terry, this is the moment you've been waiting for," the colonel said as he pulled out a box made of jade marble from under his seat.

"What's that?" Terry replied to the colonel's statement.

"You're getting promoted just like I said before," he said as he took a medal off the left breast of his sweater.

"Congratulations! You earned it, Colonel. I think I'm getting too old for this sort of thing. It's time for some young blood in the field," Preston said as he pinned the medal to Terry, saluted, and exited the chopper. He slapped the door, signaling Terry to take off, and waved to him.

Master of Peace

1 Origins

On a desert planet at the edge of our universe, billions of light years from Earth, there were two tribes of lizard people living on it. The Sedarians looked more lizard-like, including a tail and dry scales, because of the desert. They also had orange-yellow eyes and two small, scaly fins. The Davonians had one large fin and looked more humanoid, with one big snout. One lizard person in particular was sitting at a red wooden table having a drink at a local café made out of yellow stone. He was thinking about the past and was confused about the future. It had been three hundred years ago to the day since the Great War ended. An elderly rust-colored cloaked figure was sitting at it.

"You're blocking my view!" the cloaked figure said.

"I'm sorry, is this seat taken?"

Another cloaked figure responded. "Who's asking?" the Sedarian replied.

"Perhaps introductions are in order. I'm Garayen Yanx. You must be Aejah Terae, and you knew my mother." He was a tall, young, and slender lad. He had his mother's eyes, no doubt.

"Let's take a walk," Aejah said.

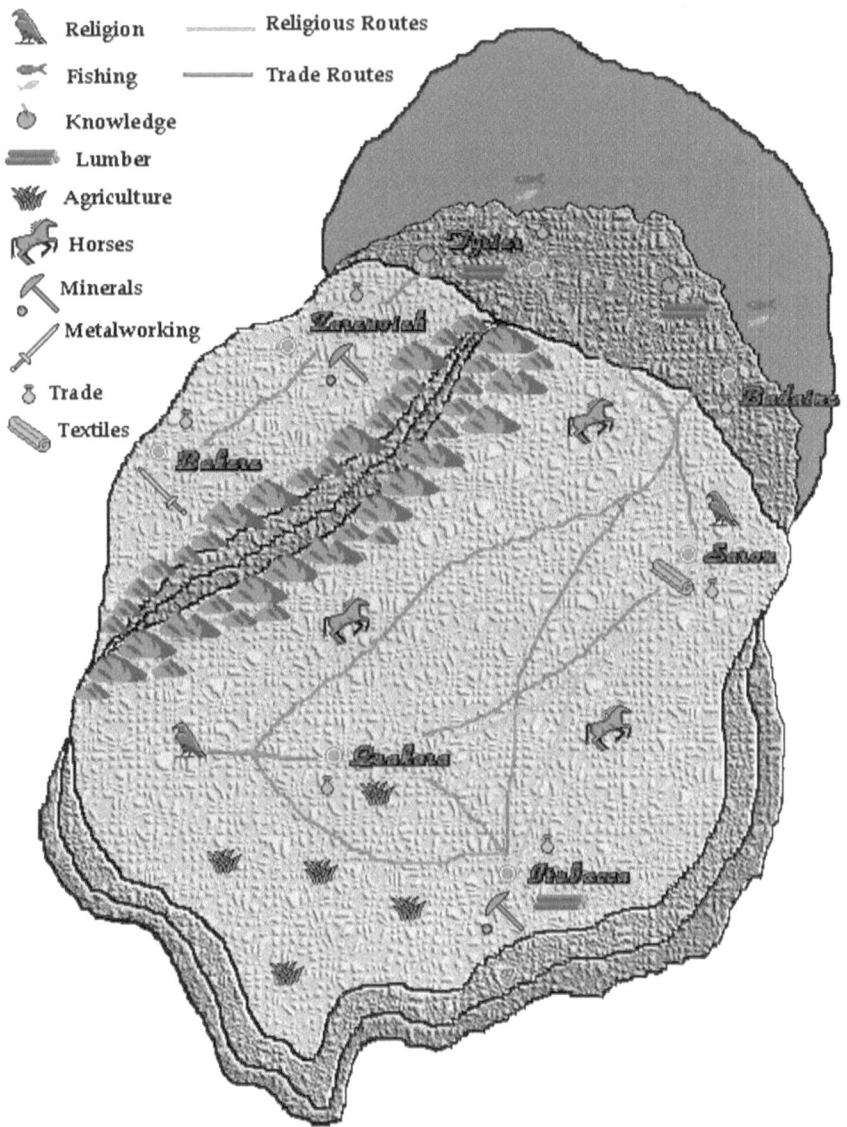

Early that evening, against a magenta sky, Garayen and Aejah rode on the horizon across the blue desert. They rode slowly in single file on horseback, wearing sky-blue robes as if they were Elyzonian monks. "Where are we going?" Garayen asked. "Are we going to stop soon?"

"You will know in due time," said Aejah.

"You agreed to take me to this place. Are we almost there?" Garayen asked.

"Have patience, my friend, patience!" Aejah said. "Just a few more paces and we will be there."

They ascended a sand dune, toward an ancient temple. There were rows of descending steps assembled like a forum in front of two semicircular walls of stone. Between these two curved walls of stone was a large, hollow stone cylinder, through which the sun was shining. As they got off their horses, Aejah spoke.

"My friend, this is why I brought you here! Look at the way the setting sun glows at the right time of day!"

Garayen looked near the horizon and put one hand on his brow to shade his eyes from the intense ball of sunlight blazing through the sun tunnel.

"Is this the only reason you brought me here, to show me this attraction? What is the significance of this particular temple?" Garayen asked.

Aejah spoke, "No, young one, this is not the sole reason why I brought you here! I brought you here because it's your heritage. This temple was a symbol of the ancients' beliefs."

He continued by describing a mural.

"Elyzon, the universal god of peace, created this world long ago and made it what it is today. These people were peaceful and tried to make a living out of what they do best as a culture," Aejah explained, "I'm passing on what is left of my peoples' history to a potential scribe such as you, Garayen, so that we do not lose our precious history. I want you to record what is left of our history, because you will be the next scribe. Your grandfather, mother, and I would have wanted this."

"Why would they want this of me?" Garayen asked. "Wouldn't they rather have me make my own decisions? I would have to give this some thought; after all, it is a lot of responsibility. Where did all the people go if they settled their differences and managed to thrive all these years?"

Aejah spoke again, "Recent generations passed on. Others went with the sky people to seek further enlightenment." Pointing to the sky, he began to explain the various parts of the mural to his apprentice. "The first part of the mural shows Davon, the god of war, overseeing a battle between the Davonians and the Sedarians. The Davonians were another race of people that lived with the Sedarians during times of peace many centuries ago. The only other difference they had besides their physical appearances was their beliefs since that bloody skirmish in the village square in the marketplace." He continued by describing the different ruins and telling the history of his people through his eyes.

"It all began with that food riot in the marketplace. There was a drought that year and the farmers started rationing food. Several Davonians took more than their share and broke the law, inciting a riot. They hunted their most sacred animal, the Dajahrak, the desert lizard, almost to extinction since that bloody skirmish in the marketplace square of the city of Quakara started by the Davonian Laviek, all because he got greedy and wanted more food. That tragic day will forever be burned in our ancestors' skulls.

"It started something like this according to history:"

"All right, line up for your Maujara fruit ration," the farmer said.

Unfortunately, Laviek was first in line. He was wearing a light gray ragged tunic and looked tired and worn out, like he had a hard day's work.

It all started as the farmer handed him his ration. Laviek produced a dagger, held the farmer in a choke hold, and held a knife at his throat.

"Quick! Grab as much fruit as you can carry, before the Sedarians catch you doing it," he said to his fellow Davonians.

"Hey, they're taking more than their share," one Sedarian shouted.

"Stop them!" another shouted.

After that, the Davonians ran off with what they had. A few were captured and put in a lineup by a famous chief, Chief Hakiwon, who wore orange feathers from one of the last of the Giant Vantler birds in the Hall of Chiefs. It was kind of a dark brick hallway lit with torches. On the walls, there were different markings depicting the chief's predecessors. The hall was inside a temple.

"Who started stealing food?"

There was a long silence among them.

"All right, since you all won't explain your actions, you leave me no choice but to banish you all from the Sedarian Mesa forever."

Aejah the elder pointed to an ancient mural depicting the pantheon of deities.

"At one time the Davonians believed in the same religion as the Sedarians did. There were a series of ground quakes, torrential rains, and floods. Our ancestors believed that the gods were punishing them, but actually, our world was changing. The Davonians thought that our two races were destined to destroy each other, and they've believed that ever since, until now.

"On the other hand, their people, the Sedarians, are a people that want to maintain a peaceful lifestyle. Trying to put aside their barbaric tendencies and be more civilized, they are kind to others and not cruel. Their ancestors were at times too quick to judge and took religion too seriously. They have trouble dealing with religious fundamentalists, because they see them as an embarrassment and do not want to face them. The Sedarians see the fundamentalists as a failure within themselves.

"Our Sedarian ancestors wanted to control the Davonians' lifestyle, but they were too stubborn and didn't want to share. Davon was in the image of a half-formed snake and then the other Davonian. He was both cold-hearted and cruel. He wore the armored chest plate of force, the gauntlets of power. He held the spear of fire in one hand and the shield of cruelty in the other. The shield had a Death Crawler on it, a green, spiney poisonous snake.

"The Davonians wanted to take and not give. The Sedarians were a poor, caring people, but they couldn't give what they did not have. Like, for example, borrowing resources like food, water, and building materials and helping each other when in need. The other reason that they fought was the religion adopted by the Davonians—to hate all religions. The Davonians believed that Davon, the god of war, had the Davonian people start the Great War. You see, in order to appease him, the people of Saj Hari had to shed blood or make war with each other as a sacrifice. Davon was angry because the people did not do this when the two peoples were at peace long ago. These two clans, who lived with each other in harmony for eons, were turned against each other. Davon had influenced them to do battle for his benefit, because he wanted to be in total control of this world. What the Davonians did to stay in this mind-set was to have a high priest perform a hypnotizing ritual that makes the people think this way. The priest uses a special amulet to put a hypnotic suggestion into their minds."

Aejah walked over to another wall. He gestured a clawed hand toward the universal god of peace, Elyzon, who raised the mountain range to stop the fighting between the Sedarians and the Davonians. He grew tired of the fact that Davon had the people do his bidding. He created two mountain ranges with a river running between them to divide the people.

"Elyzon was in the reptilian image of our Sedarian ancestors and wore the Eye of Light symbol around his neck. This symbol is a golden halo surrounding a gray stone with a hole in it. The Eye of Light symbolizes good overcoming evil."

"It sounds like this Elyzon was very good to our people," Garayen said.

The elder pointed to another segment in the mural, depicting where Elyzon came from. "Elyzon was born from the sun goddess, Mervaura, Guider of the Enlightened, after the eternal flame was lit. She is shown in the image of a Sedarian wearing an orange gown of warmth and the mask of the sun."

He then moved to an almost incomplete wall. "Davon became furious when Elyzon divided the people, and he enclosed the once fertile grounds with a barren wasteland."

"Doesn't Davon want anyone to have this place?" Garayen asked.

"Well, to tell you the truth, he wanted everyone to suffer for it."

Another part of the mural depicted a map of the mesa where their people once lived.

"The people on the northwest side of the mountain ranges were called Davonians, named after Davon, the war god. The people on the southeast side were my people. The word *Sedar* means a person of the desert."

On another wall, it described in detail the pathway of their people's journey to the afterlife. "Sedarians believed that when they died, their spirits took a journey through the Valley of the Heavens, between the mountains, to a place called the inner world or World of Dreams. The guardian of this world, Saduran, decided if they were worthy to enter. If not, he would send them back up to the surface until it was their time. Saduran, the guardian to the inner world, was just a shadowy spirit of a Sedarian, who was both judgmental and forgiving." He shifted his gaze over to another side of the mural. Aejah explained the afterlife. "The only way they could get to the fertile world was to wait until their spirit traveled there. The Sedarians called it the World of Dreams because, when they slept, they believed their spirit went to the inner world to rejuvenate. The spirit can also travel there when the body dies," Aejah said as he gestured at the different stages of spiritual travel.

He then moved on to the almost complete wall and pointed to the next one. "On this particular wall, Elyzon is summoning the four nature deities to help defend this fertile world from destruction. You know them as Quakara, Keeper of the Ground, who is both gentle and hardworking; Garric, Watcher of the Seed, who is both protective and merciful; Parenzoah, Sentinel of the Water, is both strong and vigilant; Mervaura, Guider of the Enlightened, who is both warm and kind; as well as Elyzon.

"Quakara wore a beige tunic with a brown sash. He also wore the tiara of the fertile ground with a gem in the middle of it resembling the blue desert sand dunes. Garric, the god of fertility, was half reptile and half plant. He wore a tunic and several vines with berries over his shoulders, representing the vegetation and the life-giving fruit that grew upon it. Parenzoah was a female in the image of the Sedarian people and had a fish tail like a mermaid, representing the creatures that lived in the sea. She wore a necklace with a sailing boat attached to it, signifying the sacred fishing boat. She also held the curved-bladed sword of vigilance in one hand and the water pail of refreshing water in the other.

"The only power Elyzon would be able to keep Davon at bay with would be peace, which would weaken Davon. The one reason he would refuse to fight for himself would be out of anger, and that would go against all that he believed in." The mural also depicted Elyzon allowing Garric to sprinkle seeds of the Farranari, or protected plant, onto their world of Saj Hari. It was similar to a tropical tree, but it had flowery magenta leaves instead of green ones.

"The power within these seeds would be to protect the flourishing life. The Sedarians were created by Quakara herself to watch over their world of dreams. Mervaura created a beacon of light, or the sun, to guide them during the course of their lives and not be engulfed by infinite darkness. Along with his attempt to eliminate the world of dreams, Davon made sure this planet suffered. He made it heat up slowly. Davon also had Wishiane, the evil wind spirit of the skies, who was both discretionary and arrogant, creating destructive winds to do Davon's evil biddings. Wishiane was a goddess with a lavender gown and hood with a magenta sash. She had slanted, orange eyes on a shadowy face."

2   A New Kingdom

"**I** believe you will find more answers when you hear a history lesson of when our society flourished and arose from an older kingdom long ago. I think your grandfather would want you to hear this." Aejah spoke of the past society of their ancestors:

"There was a city called Kandurel, which is now Saron, named after a well-known Sedarian ruler, Saron. He was the wealthiest chief of all Sedaria and had many loyal followers. He allowed the Sedarian nation to prosper to what it had become. The one thing that made him well known to the people was that he treated them as equals. Saron's advisors saw that he was unable to lead them into battle; they needed someone who could, so his advisors planned a coup. If he was assassinated, there could be a chance of an uprising, because after all, the people did respect him. Saron was too proud of his people; he did not see what was about to happen. He respected his people as if he was one of them. He was a very kind and caring person and was always willing to lend a hand. All the wealthy wanted was to keep everything to themselves. He was blinded by his vision, an unrealistic view of his people's future. The wealthy felt threatened when one of their own respected the working class. The advisors had control over the government. At the time, if the leader did poorly, they could have him executed. To the advisors, the chief was just a figurehead. During our early days in history, our people used monetary units called trade tokens as our form of currency. For each workday, a Sedarian citizen earned a token a day depending on how productive they were. These were used for bartering in the marketplace. Represented by different icons, each token was used to purchase different things. At the time, they could purchase tools, food, transportation, or necessities like fabric and potted goods." Aejah continued by describing their people's history to his apprentice:

During the time of Saron's rule, their world, Saj Hari, was blooming with fertility. Most Sedarians were vegetarians because of the abundance of plant life. Years later, their people advanced a step further in agriculture and developed a way to irrigate with water by using a method based on valves made out of a bamboo-like plant. This created the Fertile Garden, so we can grow our own food.

The early Sedarians built huts, forts, and tents out of wood and straw, because they could not figure out a way to move heavy stone blocks. The town of Glydruf was a perfect example of the most primitive civilization in Sedarian history, because Glydruf was one of the first villages that Sedarians built.

During his reign, Saron lived in the city of Mervaura, because it had city walls for defense. The Sedarians and Davonians were on uneasy terms during this period in Sedarian history.

Mervaura was more advanced than other cities during this time. They were able to forge weapons. They used the wheel and yellow stone to build sturdier structures.

3 The War Monger

"In the less civilized years after Saron's rule and the coup that Saron's advisors had started, the Sedarian tyrant Hezkro Czban came to power. He dissolved the council of advisors and decided to lead the Sedarian people with an iron fist. He felt his people were weakened by his predecessor, instead of strong and disciplined in preparation for war. He promoted propaganda that made the Sedarian people hate the Davonians even more. He basically had undone what Saron had been teaching his people. Saron taught his people to respect other people's beliefs even if they were different from their own.

"Saron was a very well-known leader amongst the Sedarian people and the many chiefs that ruled the mesa. Czban soon grew to be a mean old tyrant. He walked all over the poor. The three classes were disbanded by Czban for the war. Both the Davonians and the Sedarians became less and less friendly with each other in future years. The Sedarians wanted to adapt their peaceful lifestyle and allow their two cultures to live peacefully. After centuries of living this way, the Sedarians got too strict in their ways and the Davonians needed some breathing room. They were banished from the mesa and this angered the Davonians. At one time, the Davonians and Sedarians lived together in peace. Then there was a food shortage and a riot broke out. Chief Czban eventually had the Sedarian army enslave the poor to build his army. He would abuse his servants to the point of revolting to overthrow his power.

"Czban was angry that the Davonians had more superior weapons while his army had primitive weapons and armor. He did have greater numbers, which made the stakes too high in casualties. He wondered how his people would be able to defeat them. The Sedarians were the exact opposite. They grew more crops than they made weapons. Czban did not like the Davonians and he was stubborn; he felt his own people were weak in military might. He wanted to toughen up his people. He was very mean to his people, which I seem to recall him beating a certain slave boy for his mistakes.

"The slave was dragged by his arms to a wooden pole driven into the ground. They tied his arms around the pole with leather straps, with his back toward the guards. The guards were dressed in the same attire as the chief, only one held a whip, which he proceeded to use on the slave. Slaves and workers were often beaten to death when they didn't do as they were told by their owners. Some were even thrown into a pit of poisonous sand crabs, just like the Davonians did to their prisoners.

"Living conditions were poor, because Czban didn't bother to fix the villages up or maintain them. There were broken-down old wooden shacks, filthy water, and dead carcasses of people and animals lying around.

"The next year, the war started and the Davonians began invading the country. As they marched into Sedaria, the Sedarian soldiers watched them in awe. The Davonians wore a gold samurai-like helmet with its back curled up. They had steel breastplates, face guards, gauntlets, and black boots with gold knee guards. In one hand they held a rectangular shield that had the symbol of their war god, Davon. It had a green, spiney death-crawler snake in an S shape and two diamond-bladed spears crossed behind it. In the other, they carried a double-edged two-handed sword with a spike in the middle on each edge of the blade.

"During the war, houses were burned. Animals and people were killed. Many Sedarian cities were taken from them and then seized. Davonians and Sedarians charged at each other on the battlefield. Bodies fell with weapons in hand as the soldiers struck each other.

"Fighting against the odds, the Sedarians charged on foot toward their foe, the heavily armored Davonians. Blades clashed and soldiers fell onto the battlefield. One Sedarian got slashed in the side of his neck and help-lessly hit the ground with his blade falling out of his hand. Another Sedarian threw a spear only to have it batted away by a Davonian tower shield. He then drew his wedge blade in order to try and slay his attacker. The blow was blocked again by the Davonian's blade. The Sedarian took another swipe and slashed the Davonian's arm. The Davonian gripped his arm in pain, dropping his weapon. While he was distracted by the agony of his fresh wound, the Sedarian warrior ran him through, right between two plates of armor. (This is where the "wedge" blade got its name.) The Sedarian turned to continue engaging the enemy, but never got the chance. He was stabbed from behind and went down. Another Sedarian threw a hunting spear and hit a Davonian square in the neck, propelling him backwards to his death.

"Spears flew through the air from every location on the battlefield. The Davonians used the tactic of making their shields like a turtle shell to deflect any bombardments from spears. Davonians and Sedarians charged at each other, arms raised, holding their blades two-handed. When they got close enough, they slashed and parried their weapons up and down, often switching blades from one hand to another. Sometimes they would block blows using one hand with either a shield or their curved blade. Another Davonian blocked a blow from a Sedarian's wedge blade with his tower shield and swung back and hit a different one in the gut. Two Sedarians took a huge log and used it as a battering ram on the Davonian fortress.

"It was your Uncle Kajir. A young warrior shouted as he had his blade raised. At first there was no answer amongst the dust, the sound of horses' hooves hitting the ground, and blades clanging. Then he heard a voice shout back. Scaz, his loyal second-in-command shouted back. He was just telling Kajir that reinforcements were on the way; Scaz, the skilled swordsman, yelled as he smote a warrior down. Kajir looked up to see clouds of dust coming from the south as he shouted a battle cry to his legions. The troops charged forward as the reinforcements approached the battlefield. Both armies caught the Davonians right in the middle." The elder described further battle tactics as he got up to throw another log on the fire. "We trapped the Davonian army between our two armies."

"That must have been a close call," Garayen said intently.

"Well, it was, but it was before my time. It was close, but too close," Aejah replied.

"How was he able to pull it off?" Garayen asked.

"There was one problem with that maneuver. Czban always waited until the last minute to request reinforcements and that would be his downfall. The Sedarian farming village of Quakara was captured by the Davonians. Czban tried to liberate it, only to find out that the Davonians' weapons were better as well as being outnumbered. Czban and his small army of soldiers rode from the east on their horses to take the village back. When they got close to the village, he ordered his army to dismount, pitch their tents, and make camp. He then wrote a message to send to the city of Itubacca, asking for more reinforcements, sending a rider to deliver it to them.

"The rider returned with a message from the chief scribe. The message read: 'We have none to spare, proceed to the village without them.'

"Czban angrily mounted his steed and went to the village under protest. Unfortunately, Czban was defeated after fifty years of fighting. This left the Sedarian country without a leader, as well as leaving them in anarchy. One day a young Sedarian rose up and decided to form a revolt against their oppressors. He was a good friend of mine too. Some thought it was a setup to be rid of Czban. The Sedarians thought the only way to end the war would be to give the Davonians a formal apology for their leader's actions in exchange for their village. The Davonians were so angered by what had happened over the past fifty years, they said no deal. When the Davonians invaded the mesa during the Two Hundred Year War, the farming village of Quakara was captured and the Sedarian inhabitants were enslaved. This only gave the people limited food supply until fifty years later, when there was a slave revolt, driving the Davonians out. This was what saved the nation soon after Czban was defeated. The Davonians were unable to invade after that, because they were outnumbered. After the first battle, there weren't enough resources to mount another attack."

4 Era of Peace

One afternoon, one hundred and fifty years after Czban had been killed, when Aejah was a young scribe, Aejah often wandered away from the capital city of Saron. Saron was located on the northeast side of the Sedarian mesa. He was contemplating a way to put an end to the senseless fighting, which his people had contributed to long ago. The Sedarian people were going through a difficult phase in history. Aejah knew his people were having trouble gaining control of their primal urges and acting more intelligent and civilized. When Aejah slowly strolled east of the mesa through the bleached white sands, he heard a voice.

"Does life have a purpose?" said a voice in his head.

Aejah looked up and around to see where it was coming from, but he saw no one.

"Who are you? Where are you? Show yourself," he said.

He received no reply to his commands. He unsheathed his wedge blade and gazed around once more.

"No need for that. Answer the question, my friend," the voice said.

"Why are you asking me this?" he demanded as he waved his sword around.

"Put away your weapon and I will tell you."

With curiosity, he slid his blade back into its scabbard.

"Who I am is not important. What I want to do for you is important. I feel your people need help. War is not the answer to your troubles. If you fight, you have no future. Do something that is more meaningful to you than violence," said the voice.

"How did you know this?" he asked.

"I have a way of knowing things," the voice said. "Concentrate on where you are going with your life, not where you have been with it," it answered.

"How do I convince my people?" Aejah inquired.

There was no response after that. He looked around one last time and then headed for home.

"The moral of that story was, it is not always important to know who you are talking to, but it is important to know what they are saying. It is very important to keep your attention on what's happening around you.

"That same day, a chief named Parxis Yanx, who was also a great chief, went out into the Fertile Garden to visit his daughter, Zia.

"The Fertile Garden was an irrigated piece of land that was used for farming. It was planted and grown shortly after the farming village's first attack to reduce our loss if we were attacked during a harvest again.

"Deep in the greenest part of the field, out in the middle of the desert, Zia was picking flowers for the tribe's traditional medicines and ceremonial drugs. Zia was wearing a dark pink gown with short sleeves and a magenta sash around her middle."

"Hello, Father," Zia said with a smile.

"How's my girl doing on this fine day?" he asked as he caressed her shoulders.

"I'm fine, but my bundle of joy leaves one to be desired," she responded.

"I hope you've gathered enough flowers for tomorrow's bazaar festival," Parxis said.

"Don't worry, Father, I've collected plenty," she replied.

"Well, I have to go now; I have a meeting with my advisors. Keep up the good work and I'll see you later," Parxis said as he made his way off of the field.

"Zia was born when her mother started to have complications during labor. After Zia's egg came out, another egg got stuck in the birth canal, trying to come out sideways. They could not save her mother after that, because one of the eggs broke and caused too many internal injuries, which led to her mother's death.

"Strolling through the hot desert, the young scribe thought about what the voice had told him. He knew that it was referring to values of living, but he didn't quite know how to teach this philosophy to his people. All that was important to him was to deter them from fighting. Saron had the right idea, but didn't have the patience. The scribe had to undo all of what Czban had destroyed to teach what Saron had started. That evening, he knelt down on some stuffed cushions in his dimly lit house and began eating a bowl of some mashed Maujara fruit. As he watched the orange sun set in the lavender-colored sky, through his window, he knew that there would be better days for his people. On that thought, he extinguished his everlighter, curled up on the cushions in the corner of his house, and went to sleep."

"What is an everlighter?" Garayen interrupted.

"An everlighter is a wax-coated stick that contains a liquid that glows when lit. This stick was used to provide light at night. This liquid was extracted from a fish that lived in the lake.

"That night, he dreamt of what it might be like to live in peace. He saw his people burning their weapons in a huge bonfire in the village square. He also saw that some were meditating and chanting to spiritual music on a daily basis. Then the sun rose up into the sky behind a temple they were in, as it enlightened their souls.

"The next day, he woke up to a bright sunrise, refreshed and ready to start the day. He ate a hearty morning meal of cooked unfertilized eggs from a Vantler, a fierce bird of prey that lived in the desert, and a flask of Zaeka nectar. After having a nutritious breakfast, he stepped out on the threshold of his yellow-stone brick house, gazed into the sunlight, and took in a deep breath of the lake breeze. The sky was light blue in color, which meant an average weather day. His good friend, Chief Parxis, greeted him as he walked over to talk with him."

"A beautiful sun-gazing day, isn't it?" Parxis spoke in his usual calm way.

"Parxis, what can we do to convince our people that fighting wastes our lives?"

Parxis just stood there pondering his scribe's thought. "Well, my friend, you have to look at it this way. Our people fight for only one thing—their beliefs."

"When they fight, their beliefs do not mean anything, especially when they get themselves killed," the scribe said with despair.

Parxis stood there, looked him straight in the eyes, and said, "You know, you may have something there. Follow me, my friend!"

"Parxis put one arm around his scribe's shoulders and walked with him through the marketplace. As they passed pastel colored shops where merchants peddled their wares, he told Parxis what the voice in the desert had said to him. The shops that they passed had dark pink cloth overhangs attached to them just above the doorway. Some of them were selling fruits and vegetables, while others were selling clothing, hides, and leather goods. The scribe decided to stop at one of the shops and buy a new clay jar for his scrolls. When he asked the shopkeeper how much it was, the shopkeeper held up two clawed fingers. He handed two trade tokens with a ceramic pot and a roll of fabric embossed on them to the merchant. The merchant held them in his fist and nodded to the scribe, thanking him for his patronage. They proceeded through the marketplace. They walked past a small bazaar and listened to the soothing music coming from it. The scribe recognized it as the Greosk spiritual music that he heard in his dreams. This music was formed through three instruments. The first one was a hand drum called a Darmboren. It was basically a wooden ring with some animal hide attached to one side and a wooden ball connected to the rim of it as a counterbalance. The second one was a curved flute out of the same wood cut from their palm trees used for making the boats, only thicker. This instrument was named the Saceoflout. The flute made this sound because the inside had been carved in a corrugated fashion. The third and final sound was also out of wood. He made a crescent-curved base with a hole in the center and used a thin yarn-like material made from the tall, strong grass that grew in the Fertile Garden. This material was used to make the strings for it. This instrument was named the Setre. Originally the instruments weren't meant for religion or spiritual aspirations.

"Where was I? Oh! Yeah! That's right!" he continued.

"Parxis and the scribe turned a corner and saw two Sedarian soldiers out on the village terrace, discussing fighting strategies. Strolling slowly toward them, the scribe quietly spoke to Parxis."

"Where are we going?" the scribe spoke.

"Have patience, my friend, patience," Parxis implored with a whisper. As they approached the two bleached yellow walls, Parxis reassured him. "I understand how you feel. This is the only way we can get through to them."

Upon entering, Parxis greeted the two foot soldiers and asked them to listen to what his scribe had to say. They were wearing leather-studded armor without sleeves, thereby protecting the torso region. The soldiers also had leather-studded shoulder pads, leather loin covers, as well as wrist and shin guards. One soldier had a sheathed wedge blade and the other had a diamond-bladed hunting spear.

"What is your purpose in life?" the scribe asked.

"Why do you ask?" the first soldier said as he brandished his spear.

"It seems to me that you have nothing better to do with your life," the scribe replied.

The second soldier stepped forward, wielding his hunting spear. "At the present time, my purpose in life is to defend our homeland from invaders."

"What if we could find a way to irrigate the land some more and pay tribute each harvest? You wouldn't have to concern yourselves with defending," said the scribe.

"What if they break their promise?" inquired the second soldier.

"They won't. Their food supply would get cut off. You see, war is like this, once you start fighting, it's hard to stop," Parxis interrupted.

"An individual's life can only be used once. You should cherish it for what it is," said the scribe.

The first soldier fidgeted with his sheathed blade. "There are so few, why don't we just kill them all?"

"The Davonians have every right to live and believe as much as we do! Hatred is an eternal fire that will spread evil within all of us," the scribe replied.

"We are not even close to being evil," said the first soldier.

"You're wrong! Hatred leads to violence and that provokes the evil in all of us," the scribe answered.

Parxis stepped in to intervene in the discussion.

"Can't you see what the Davonians are trying to do? They want you to fight! If we go to war, they will lust for more blood. You see, they are more advanced than we are. They have the advantage with their arsenal of weapons lined up for us. If you force them to fight, they will retaliate with increased strength."

The crowd of people that gathered to listen picked up their leader, Parxis, and carried him to the town's square, where he spoke of peaceful harmony amongst his people. The middle and lower classes were very pleased with what they heard. They applauded him in his efforts. Parxis spoke of his scribe's philosophy, which he told the people of Sedaria the day before. He also spoke to the rich about their behavior.

"We need to pool our resources and put aside our differences if we are going to survive this war," Parxis added.

"You people need to understand that in order to get through this thing, we need to work as a team or there will be no riches to enjoy. I'm sure you don't want to be enslaved by the Davonian army."

The town square had an upside-down arched, white stone wall on each side of it, and a white stone pedestal at its heart with a podium as well. The ground had a red cobblestone-covered road. That afternoon, the scribe, Parxis, and the Davonian leader signed a temporary treaty for as long as they had enough food, to end all bloodshed.

5   The Blade of Vyriad

The following morning, the elder began again. "Long ago, there was a tribe of Sedarians known as the Vyriad who were said to have the strongest male and female warriors in all the land. To show their strength, they built these pyramid obelisks. During a time when vegetation had been abundant, there were also these gigantic birds, probably the ancestors of the Vantlers. They were ridden by the bravest of the Vyriad warriors and they carried blades made of the strongest metal known to their people, Zercadion steel. After millennia of wars with the Davonians and famine from the sun's heat during the hot summers, the climate changes had made the gigantic birds extinct and their reign over the skies had ended. The famine eventually killed off most of the strong Vyriads, and the rest of the tribe resettled next to a large lake. If the legend is true, supposedly the last of the forged blades was entombed with the last Vyriad chief. It would bring everlasting peace between the Davonians and the Sedarians to whomever possessed it. It was also said that the formula for forging the blade would be engraved on the blade itself. No one who has ever searched for it has ever returned with it.

"They had dominated most of the waterholes and oases in the area. This prevented the Davonians from getting their share of water. When the giant birds began dying off, the Davonians were able to get a sufficient supply of water other than the lake. Since the Davonians never learned how to build boats, they couldn't cross the lake.

"The scribe had to go on a journey, because it was the Sedarians' only chance of evading another war, because their food stores would not last. He put his hood up as he felt the wind and sand pick up. As he wandered awhile through the storm, he happened to stumble upon a rock. He waited for the storm to pass; when it did, he was able to read the inscription on top of it. It showed Sedarian hieroglyphics depicting a Sedarian stepping on a rock and grabbing a tablet, which rose up, lying flat on the ground. He did just that. The tablet showed a map of an area northwest of the mesa. There was a river that curved around the mesa to the south into a tunnel going northwest and to an oasis before the Vyriad obelisks. There was an area between the oasis and the stones marked as a warning.

"So he picked up the stone tablet and went back to the Glydruf village, to build a Glydra sailing boat; this was back before the sand crab epidemic. The scribe also built a cart to take the boat to the river. He brought it over to the fast-moving current and untied the ropes holding the boat to the cart, except the tether line attached to the front of the boat so the boat didn't float away. He climbed into the boat, cut the rope, and off he went through the tunnel into the underground river. It took him about three days before he got out of the underground river. It flowed up through the oasis and he anchored the boat next to where the obelisks were.

"He found a carved magenta crystal as he walked between the pyramid-like structures. He picked it up and stepped forward. He knelt down when he stumbled upon a carved stone with a hole shaped like the width of the crystal. He slid the crystal into its slot and he heard the sound of stone scraping against stone as he stepped back. Something rose up from the sand that looked like a sarcophagus. The sarcophagus had hieroglyphs in the ancient dialect. It wasn't that difficult to make out. On one side it said something along the lines of 'When peace is finally restored, so will be our people.' He gave the lid a good push and it slid right off.

"What amazed him was that the sarcophagus lid had the Eye of Light inscribed on each side. He pulled the blade out of the Vyriad leader's mummified grasp. He took a brief glimpse of the blade and it had the formula to forge the blade engraved on it, just as the legend said. He concealed it in his cloak and pushed the lid back on the sarcophagus to put him back to rest by pulling the crystal out to lower it. He promised himself to reveal it at the proper time.

"He returned to his boat, kept it anchored, and used the boat's rudder against the current to use the boat as a bridge to cross the river. He crossed the boat bridge, and there were five stones in the sand. The first was the hardest, to see if he was worthy of the blade. The stones were arranged in four points and one in the middle surrounded by sand. The question was, what was underneath the sand? He stepped up onto one of the stones just like the one at the burial site. He immediately did a back flip to the center one before he could get clawed to death. Then a whole bunch of sand crabs tried to climb the stone, but he took a swipe with the Blade of Vyriad and cut their claws off. He dove for a corner and flipped over off that one foot first. That's what made it not so easy.

"Then he wandered past a small stream to an oasis. There was a small pool where he cleaned the blade. Then a hooded figure approached him and he stood ready. The figure threw six crystalline spheres, one at a time, to see how fast he could cut them. One by one, they were split in two."

"Nice, clean cutting, young one" exclaimed the cloaked figure.

"Nice throw," the scribe said.

The cloaked figure applauded and then announced, "The blade is yours! You've proven yourself worthy. Now listen carefully. If you can shatter a Davonian's blade, you're truly worthy."

6   Tribal Banishment

"Parxis had two brothers, Kajir and Grax. Kajir was the captain of the Celestial Knights in the Celestial City of Mervaura, named after the sun goddess. The Celestial Knights acted as police or peacekeepers whenever there was a need for them. Especially when there were renegade Sedarians who disagreed with the treaty and the Davonians themselves who were looking for a reason to start a fight. The Elyzonian believers frowned upon the Celestial Knights' presence if they were around too long, because they didn't like the fact they carried weapons, which was against their religion. The knights took a vow—never fight in aggression, always in defense. My people were living with the Davonians at the time, before trouble started amongst our two peoples. Grax was the founder of the new Davonian religion, which was more brutal than the first. They were supposed to change the religion, but instead made it more evil, no thanks to Grax. Grax did not agree with Parxis's scribe's idea of a peaceful religion, because Grax thought he was taking over their minds and not letting them believe what they wanted to believe. He became defiant and did not wish to participate in it. Grax began to develop his own idea of a religion; this made Parxis not trust his brother. Grax thought since Parxis was older than him that he was trying to dominate him. This was a major embarrassment to Parxis's family. Parxis was really trying to introduce a new style of living, an alternative to fighting. The three brothers were raised differently. Parxis was raised as a leader and to treat his people as equals. Kajir was raised as a fighter. He was trained by his father in the form of sword combat. Grax was the weakest of the three. He was ignored by his father as the weakest of the family. He grew up without a father and someone to look up to.

"The ancients' methods were not sound. When they got tired of negotiating with people, they would banish them. Rather than deal with their problems, they chose to ignore them. They would later come back to haunt them.

"From that day on, Grax became a fanatic in the Davonian occult. He continually performed bloody animal sacrifices much like the one he had just made. He would drink some of the blood during them. He even stole religious artifacts from temples and shrines and burned them in a bonfire. His religion basically expressed hatred toward all peaceful religious beliefs. Parxis never saw Grax do all of these heinous acts, but after he caught Grax stealing several times, he never trusted him again.

"One day, outside the farming village of Quakara, young Grax was hunting for food. Looking over a sand dune, he spied a Dajahrak, or a huge lizard, in the distance. He ducked behind a rock, gripping his hunting spear. When he got a clear view, he threw his spear at its midsection, critically wounding it. He stood up and approached it. Getting nearer, he noticed it choking on its own red blood as it spewed out of its wound and mouth. Finally, it collapsed as it took in its last breath. Grax reached down, picked it up, and brought it back to town. That evening Grax cooked it on an open pit over a fire and feasted upon it, picking the meat off of its bones. The next morning, Grax collected all of its bones and wrapped them in a piece of turquoise cloth. He exited the town gates and trekked to where he had killed it. He knelt down, dug a deep hole with his wedge blade in the sand, and buried the bones. When he was finished, he stood up and recited a prayer that he had written himself. 'Almighty Davon, god of war, bless this sacrifice. We give thanks for providing us with the necessities to ensure our existence. Will that the blood of this sacrificial beast replenish your powers. The fertility of life connects us through this sustenance. Our beliefs are sacred and must never be changed because of the influence of another.'

"Grax did these evil acts because Parxis was picked more qualified to be chief over Grax and Grax was jealous over this," answered Aejah. While stirring and continuing to smoke the aromatic herbs within his blue smoke pipe, Aejah continued without hesitation his storytelling of the Celestial Army and Parxis's brothers:

"Along with Grax, some of the Sedarians wanted peace; and others wanted to fight, because it could be a sign of weakness to have peace, like Czban said. That night, Grax decided to sneak across the Davonian border and make a deal to help them destroy Parxis's peaceful cause. After all, the idea was a part of Parxis. One flaw in Grax's plan would be that he would run out of food making weapons. So he would be forced to take what was left of the Sedarians' food," explained Aejah.

Upon Grax's return, Parxis and the scribe approached him. "Where have you been since sunrise?" Parxis asked with concern, as he crossed his arms.

"I was taking a morning saunter outside the city. Why?" Grax said defensively, as he fidgeted.

"It's hard enough looking after my younger brother and keeping him out of mischief."

"Last night I saw him bringing something into the village," interjected the scribe.

"Grax, you better not do anything that is forbidden amongst our people, or you will be punished severely," Parxis warned sternly. With more than a little skepticism on their minds, Parxis and the scribe walked away after their admonishments to Grax.

"During the early evening, Parxis smelled a foul stench coming from Grax's hut. He peeked inside the doorway and saw, lying in the back corner, skeletons and rotting carcasses of what appeared to be Dajahrak. *I have had enough of his insubordination; if he can't participate in the Elyzonian religion, he can't be a part of our tribe*, Parxis thought with frustration. He sent a servant to summon the scribe in rotation of the shadow."

"When you say 'rotation of the shadow,' what exactly does that mean?" asked Garayen.

"It was what my people used as a unit of measurement for time. Time was measured on a huge stone obelisk in the middle of the town square, which had a sundial near the top of it," said the elder. Aejah continued with his storytelling to his disciple, to detail how Grax was punished:

Praxis told the Scribe, "You were right, Grax is up to something. He had carcasses and skeletons of Dajahrak in his hut."

"I knew it!" the scribe shouted.

"I want you to get a message to the Celestial City. Tell Kajir we need one garrison of Celestial Knights at once," Parxis commanded, as he handed the scribe a piece of parchment.

"Yes, Chief, right away," replied the scribe.

For three risings of the sun, Parxis did not see Grax within one hundred footsteps of the village. On the fourth sunrise, Parxis saw over the sand dunes in the distance the Celestial Knights on horseback. The knights were

Sedarians with golden chest plates and they wore golden helmets that fit the shape of their heads with a fin on top and curved eye slits. They also had on golden knee, shin, and arm guards, and light brown tunics underneath. Some of the beasts were pulling wooden battle wagons and carts carrying equipment. Some of the soldiers were carrying axes mounted on pole-arms. Others were carrying flags with their city emblem on them. The flags were triangular, bright yellow with a bright orange sun, and the sun god's face on it. They all had curved-bladed swords in scabbards on their belts. The Sedarians rode up and over the sand dunes in the distance with the clear blue sky overhead. Upon entering the village gates, Kajir commanded his men to dismount. As he got off his beast, Parxis approached him. Putting a hand on his brother's shoulder, Parxis whispered, to Kajir's disappointment:

"Our brother, the youngest of our clan, has betrayed us. I have not seen him since three risings of the sun. We must find him and banish him from this tribe before the darkened sky."

"According to the law, in preparation for his removal, we must set fire to his hut so we can be rid of his filthy beliefs," Kajir read firmly from a scroll.

Parxis pointed out which hut was Grax's; then Kajir ordered his men to light torches to burn it. One of the knights took two rocks and rubbed them together to spark a fire in some dried grass. This was mounted on a stick of wood to be used as a torch. Parxis and Kajir stood back to watch the flames engulf the evil within the lifeless shack.

"Knights, search the area and find this traitor," Kajir commanded.

Within ten rotations of the shadow, two of the soldiers returned from the search with Grax in chains. When they approached Parxis, they threw Grax to the ground on his knees. His tunic was torn and there was blood coming from his nostrils.

"Sorry about his being messed up like this. He gave us a bit of a brawl before we subdued him," said the lead knight.

"That's okay; he probably brought this upon himself," Parxis said. "Well, Grax, what do you have to say for yourself?"

"I don't have to answer to you or anybody!" Grax said, spitting the words out with insolence. "You can't do anything to me; I'm your younger brother."

"You think, because you're my brother, I can't touch you. Just watch me. For years I have tried to keep the peace within our boundaries and now I have to

The Elyzonian Religion

A peaceful culture of people called Sedarrians adopted a philosophy of life, a reason to exist, a religion. In their language they call it Elyzon, translated to English it is known as the Eye of Light which is defined as positive enlightenment. The Eye of Light signifies positive enlightenment, the center of eternity and a vision of the future. The Sedarrians believe that this way of thinking would insure everlasting peace. Elyzon is also the name of the universal god of peace which they worship. In this philosophy it is said as an individual that it is your job to maintain a quality of life and live it to the fullest. The Eye of Light is sought within your heart as the one true ideal in life, to believe in yourself.

If you believe in this you must ask yourself 2 questions: What are your ideals in life? What do you want out of it?

In order to keep yourself in a positive state of mind, you must chant the sacred words of peace.
Peace, the everlasting moral of life.
Life's query, a reason to exist.
Live the life that was given to you.
Live your own life in the present time.
You only have one chance at life.
Do what is here today.
Look to the horizons for the true belief in life.
Look ahead to the next day, for it is worth living just as the first.
If you live your life in fear, it will not be as meaningful to you.

Always remember to ask yourself the sacred question: Do you have a life?

banish troublemakers like you so that peace is not disrupted. *Family members are not exempt from the law. You see, Grax, there is only one reason why we say things are forbidden. It is for keeping people like you in line. When you go beyond that, you cannot be trusted. After seeing what you practice, I think you belong with the Davonians. Guards, remove him."*

"You'll never get away with this; I'll kill you!" Grax shouted in defiance, his voice echoing throughout the village.

Grax continued to yell as the guards grabbed his arms and dragged him to a holding area. Parxis summoned his scribe and told him to send a message to Dakaron and tell him to prepare to receive an outcast by tomorrow's sunrise.

Bangova ridge on planet Sith

Segniad mountains on planet Xenthos

The next sunrise, several of the knights gathered outside Grax's holding area. Two of them stood on either side of the doorway, playing Darmborens, while two entered the house. The two guards walked out holding Grax by the arms like the previous day. The guards put him in a boat and floated him around the other side of Bangova Ridge, where they handed Grax over to the Davonians who were waiting there.

"Well, it looks like we'll have peace after all," Parxis spoke, as he put an arm on his scribe's shoulder. They looked toward the sun setting on the horizon. A fierce red Vantler bird took off from a branch on a tree stump and bounded for the sun.

The elder storyteller extinguished his pipe. The sun had more than begun to set and dusk was settling on the terrain surrounding Aejah and his young apprentice, Garayen. Aejah spoke gently, "Go to sleep, my friend, and tomorrow I will tell you how Grax got his dark revenge."

Garayen respectfully rolled over in his bedding and went to sleep.

7   Village Raid

"**M**y people wanted peace and all they got was trouble from people who wanted no part of their religion. Their concept was good, but their methodology was not sound and that was their downfall. You can't ignore a problem and expect it to go away. Twenty years later, after Grax's banishment, the village of Quakara went back to its original self again. Except for random attacks by a mysterious band of warriors that originated on the other side of Bangova Ridge, there was relative peace. The winter solstice was coming and the farmers prepared for the harvest in the Fertile Garden. After the harvest, the people of Quakara would take their pilgrimage to the still prosperous capitol city of Saron, where they would spend the winter. Winter was a time when the desert got much cooler and the nights were much longer. The Sands of Blue would return. One morning as Kajir returned to camp from his scouting on his horse, he noticed a dust cloud in the sand dunes coming from the Bangova Ridge, toward the west, heading for the village of Quakara.

"Scaz, looks like trouble, better gather the troops," Kajir said to his second-in-command.

"Go on ahead with ten of the best knights. I'll help pack up the gear," he said in agreement.

Within five rotations of the shadow, the troops were ready, with their flags flapping in the breeze and weapons ready. As Kajir stepped out of his tent, he saw smoke coming from the village.

"Let's move out!" Kajir commanded.

Kajir took at least forty more of his best troops in the camp just to be cautious and they galloped on their horses toward the village of Quakara. Upon arrival, Kajir and his men engaged in a skirmish when they tried to enter the village. The warriors that the knights were fighting galloped through the village, kicking up dust clouds. Blades clanged together, soldiers fell off their horses, houses were set on fire, and of course, people scattered in panic. Many were cut down as they tried to get away. When the warriors were finally chased away and the dust had cleared, the village had dead Sedarian bodies everywhere, and houses were burnt until they were black burnt skeletons. The houses were made of yellow stone, long in length, thin in width, and had slanted wooden roofs. When Chief Parxis and his scribe crawled out of the debris, after the smoke had cleared, they saw Kajir and some of the knights sitting on their horses staring back in disbelief. There were people crying over their fallen loved ones.

"Who were those warriors and where did they come from?" Parxis demanded to know.

"I really wish I knew!" Kajir said with astonishment.

"Kajir, have your men gather up all the bodies and bury them in a mass grave. We will build a memorial in their honor. This was much larger than the first three attacks."

"Did anyone survive the massacre?" Kajir asked as he removed his helmet.

"Only my scribe, me, and ten others who were working in the field this morning," Parxis replied.

"I wonder if Grax was behind this," Kajir said to himself. "Well, we can't have our harvest unless we have enough hands to help finish before sundown. Kajir, can some of your men take several of your battle wagons into the Fertile Garden to finish?"

"I can't see why not!" Kajir said eagerly.

"Then it shall be done," Parxis replied with gratitude. That afternoon the knights worked beside the farmers until the work was done.

He held and looked at his enlightenment medallion—the Eye of Light. Parxis kneeled down after looking at the appalling sight of the ruined village and wept into his palms. "I thought we had a treaty. They've violated it for the last time. I condemn this act on the Davonians," he cried. Parxis spat as he picked up a gold Davonian helmet from a charred body near one of the burning houses.

As Garayen listened to Aejah's tale of a warrior race that originated in the Davonia region, he pondered out loud, "What does this medallion that I wear around my own neck mean?" Garayen held the medallion in his clawed hand. The medallion had an oval-shaped dark gray stone with a gold ring around it and it was attached to a gold chain of beads.

Aejah, hearing Garayen ponder out loud, answered, "This medallion is our universal peace symbol. It is all of what our religion represents. They say if you wear it around your neck, it will help guide you on your quest through life. In other words, you are in control of your own destiny. Grax never understood that. This was a symbol of our religion. Elyzon means the Eye of Light, which is defined as positive enlightenment, the center of eternity, and a vision of the future. That is why Elyzon is the name of our universal god of peace that we worship. In this philosophy, it was said your life is valuable in the light and in all being, whether it is for self or others. It must always be cherished. The Eye of Light was sought within our hearts as the one true ideal in life, to believe in ourselves. My people believed their eyes were the windows to life. This was where the sacred proverb, 'Through one's eye, envision the life,' came from." Aejah's tale continued:

"As Parxis and Kajir walked away to the remaining houses, Parxis told Kajir to take his men back to camp. Parxis also reminded him to take his garrison and head for Saron next light.

"The next day, the survivors held a peace ceremony, in honor of those who perished in the massacre and to bring hope that the killing would stop. The ceremony involved several of the worshippers to climb the steps of the Elyzonian temple. When they got to the altar, they knelt to the high priest and prayed while chanting a sacred prayer. Then they smoked the Blue Smoke Pipe that was curved like their Greosk ceremonial flute."

"How does this special pipe work? Does it have any adverse effects?" Garayen inquired.

"Its concept is fairly easy to understand, and I will explain why." Aejah cleared his throat to begin again. "For instance, my pipe here, like our ancestors', works by way of ventilation. The concept works when the pipe is dipped into a fine blue powder in a small golden dish with a bowl permanently attached to the center. The rim of the pipe's spout has to be thoroughly coated with the blue powder in order for the fumes to get into the vents. The grains of powder have a natural adhesive from the sap of the Farranari plant, which it came from. After the powder has covered the entire surface of the rim, it collects into vent pockets. Then it is ignited with an everlighter. The consumer then inhales three puffs of the smoke for the peace ceremony. No, the inhalant does not cause irreparable harm to the person using it. It actually puts them in a positive state of mind. It is also used as an herbal remedy for curing the sick. The inhalant is called a mind enhancer or Sigra. It is made up of two key components. The mixture is comprised of the pollen of the cup-shaped orange Zaeka flower and the petals of the beautiful pink multi-petal Fuqua flower. It was said that this combination gave the mixture psyche-enhancing properties. This was also said to be the process of chemistry that gave the wise mystic of the desert his psychic powers."

Aejah told of the temple to Garayen.

"The Elyzonian temple had three circular stone slabs stacked on top of each other, stair-stepping up. The stone had a texture of peach speckles. At the top of the temple, there were two semicircular walls on either side with a cylinder in the center as an altar. On the altar were the ceremonial peace pipe and the Book of Elyzon. The people would pass up the front and exit down the back."

"Tell me more of the Farranari plant," implored Garayen.

"The Farranari or the protected plant's resources were used in the Sedarians' ceremonial drugs and medicines from the magenta flowery leaves of this palm-tree-like plant. The seeds from this plant were considered sacred by the Sedarians. Only the wise mystics were allowed to water two of these in front of the shrine of Garric every ten days. A ceremony was performed every time it was watered. A prayer was chanted by the high priest as the mystics paid homage to their god. The shrine had two walls turned inward, giving it a trapezoidal shape, with the widest end facing the steps. It also had two walls on the inner side turned in, forming a triangular shape with the point toward the steps. There were arched doorways on these walls, giving entrance to an altar. Supporting the trapezoid roof were two columns on the outside of this room. This whole structure was made from yellow stone, which was used in many of their other structures."

Aejah then spoke of the pilgrimage and hibernation of the Sedarian people. "During the cool, dry harvesting season, the remaining Sedarians would make their pilgrimage to the capitol city of Sedaria, Saron. The sands of Saj Hari at this time of year had a strange turquoise coloration as a result of our world's axial tilt during the change in seasons. When the hot season came to an end, this side of the planet would turn away from the sun, thus cooling it down and allowing us to hibernate over a certain period of time. Winds began to pick up, making the desert sands look like ocean waves. After their long journey across the desert, my people would hibernate during the winter season in the city of Saron, leaving the farming village of Quakara abandoned until next planting season. Every morning until spring, the Sedarians would worship the sun goddess in their temple for warmth and happiness."

Aejah explained the Peace Ceremony involved with their religion. "My people had also developed, along with their philosophy, a method that kept their positive spirit alive. My people invented a religion along with an exercise that involved playing Greosk, meditative ritual music. It helped them become more aware of their own spirituality. They also believed the more you are aware of the individual that you are, the more you realize how precious life is. The whole concept was to listen to the music, which helped induce a self-hypnotic trance into their subconscious. They meditate by incorporating a series of mind patterns. This is completed in four phases. First, they make their bodies relax. Second, they think of themselves. Third, they think of life. Lastly, they think of their creator. After doing that, they would feel more in contact with their souls. They must then ask themselves two simple questions: What are your ideals in life? What do you want out of it?"

Aejah continued, "On the following day, they began their ritual of worshipping the sun goddess, Mervaura. At sunrise they sat on rows of steps in front of two semicircular walls. Between these two stone walls was a large stone hollow cylinder. They started out by whispering the sacred words from an ancient text as they inhaled and exhaled. As the sun rose, they got a sense of renewal and self-awareness as it shined on their bodies. While meditating, the Sedarians paid homage to the universal god of peace; this was where the Elyzon philosophy originated from. My people, the Sedarians, praised the afterlife as something heavenly. They believed it was the passing of the days and a time to move on. While they did this exercise, they chanted the sacred words from an ancient text as it was written."

Aejah then began to quote from a parchment after it was unrolled. "Chant the sacred words of peace. Peace, the everlasting moral of life, is life's query, a reason to exist. Live the life that was given to you. Live your own life in the present time. You only have one chance at life. Do what is here today. Look to the horizons for the true belief in life and in yourself. Look ahead to the next day, for it is worth living just as the first. If you fear the unknown, your direction will be lost. Go forth and embrace the future. Always remember to ask yourself the sacred question—do you have a life?" Aejah rolled the parchment back up and put it away.

"Why do you ask that question?" Garayen asked.

"Do you have a reason to exist? In life, we all have a reason to live. It is what keeps us going. That is what it means!" Aejah replied.

"Elyzonian monks lived three stages in their lives. The first stage was the primitive mystic; this was when they learned the fundamentals of life. The next stage was called the noble mystic. This was when they looked deep into their souls and sought out one goal in their life and put it to task. The last stage was that of the wise mystic. This was when they had learned all there was to know about life and were ready for the afterlife. When they die, their spirit journeys through the valley of the heavens to the inner world, where the stages start again. This is the stage that I'm at," Aejah explained.

"It is getting late. Let's get some rest. We've got a big day ahead of us tomorrow," Aejah suggested.

"Where are we going?" Garayen wondered.

"We are journeying to a mystical land and one of the greatest natural wonders ever created by the gods," Aejah said with excitement.

Aejah smothered the campfire. They curled up in their bedrolls and drifted off to sleep. That night they dreamed of the dune sea of blue and the sand's glittery appearance. The wandering Elyzonian monks tracked their feet through the sand on their pilgrimage to the city of Saron. Passing the Gloom Tree on the way, they saw its twisted branches hang with desperation and watched the brush's colorful beauty wave in the breeze.

8 The Mystic Land

"The scenery was exactly as I envisioned in the dream I had last night," Garayen said as though he had a revelation.

"They say that this place conjures up dreams," Aejah said with amazement.

He held a blue smoke pipe in one hand and a twisted walking stick in the other. It had a lavender ribbon wrapped around the top of it. He was also wearing a silk lavender robe with a magenta sash.

"My name is Zeblor and it is very nice to meet you. Come! Come! Come inside! We have much to talk about!" Zeblor said with great enthusiasm as he hurried them inside his hut.

As night began to fall and the air had gotten much cooler, Zeblor began to tell tales to his young friends around a fireplace. The flames from the fire flickered, making the shadows dance around the room. Inside the wood and straw hut, the mystic had shelves of powders, liquids, and old medicinal remedies inside jars and bottles. There were also scrolls and books of ancient text on a small wooden table surrounded with pastel-colored pillows.

"Yesterday the village of Quakara was attacked by an unknown race of warriors," Parxis said.

"Are you sure they weren't your once archenemy, the Davonians?" Zeblor asked.

"I'm pretty sure! Although they wore the helmet from one, they weren't wearing the uniform of a Davonian," Parxis thought with searching eyes.

"There is only one way to be sure. Where did these beings come from?" Zeblor came over to Aejah to perform his ritual.

"Aejah, have you ever been to the world of dreams?" Zeblor asked.

"No!" Aejah replied.

"It is time you experienced it," Zeblor said with great enthusiasm.

"It is a place that you can go to only in your mind. Many people who have seen it have described it differently," Zeblor began.

"How do I go there?" Aejah inquired.

"Well, I have to put you in a trance and I will ask you to think about things that you have dreamed about before you traveled to this mystical land," Zeblor instructed.

"Sounds interesting. I think I will try it," Aejah said with excitement.

"Zeblor, you were banished from the tribe for abusing our religious practices and you shouldn't be practicing your methods on my people," Parxis protested.

"Can you think of another way to solve this mystery?" Zeblor asked.

"You must trust me, nothing will go wrong," Zeblor continued.

"Oh! All right! If something happens to him, like those monks that disappeared, there will be severe consequences," Parxis gave in. Parxis finally gave in to Zeblor's psychic trickery, so he thought, because he knew he had a point.

"I only do it if they permit it!" Zeblor reinforced.

Ages ago, a group of Elyzonian monks vanished in the misty part of the blue desert. The monks were on their pilgrimage to the city of Saron for the winter solstice. The journey of the monks led through the glittery Sands of Blue in the Sedarian desert, thus allowing them to vanish from existence until they were found years later. For days there were no traces of bodies where the tracks in the sand had ended. The missing monks were found standing in the middle of the blue desert in a state of ecstasy or a trance. My people believed that the monks had traveled through the world of dreams and were trapped there. I was part of the group at the time and knew where they had disappeared to. According to the prophets, the Sands of Blue were a gateway into this world of dreams. This place is supposedly where the inner world is. They also believed that when they dream, the soul goes to the world of dreams, where it rejuvenates its energy. The Sedarians believed each soul was designated to only one individual life form and was not reused for any other when the body dies. When the body dies, the soul goes to this mystic land. A noble mystic once said that I was capable of telling your fortune or what your life would be like in the afterlife."

There were many things Zeblor was capable of doing, but things like that were beyond his power. "Those who have been found remember their journey into the world of dreams. Most who have traveled there have never returned. Either their fate was chosen for them or they have lost their way. Just relax, Aejah, and take a deep breath," Zeblor instructed.

Aejah closed his eyes and focused mainly on the first thing that came into his mind. Zeblor started to give him subliminal messages.

"Focus on the lavender sky above the Sands of Blue, the warm mist coming off the lake, the Gloom Tree, how its leaves hang in despair, and the crystal obelisks on the open plains of the spirit world. Finally, there is the golden arched doorway leading to the metropolis in the clouds. Welcome to this realm of dreams. Do you see this mystical land in your mind?"

"I see an arched window," said Aejah.

"Go to it and tell me what you see," Zeblor instructed.

Aejah looked out the mystical portal.

"I see a large metallic bird gliding through the air over the Sedarian mesa. It landed east of the Bangova Ridge in our country. I see the same green animal-like warriors, but instead of swords, they are carrying weapons that shoot burning light. I see our people enslaved and being put to work in the mines. I can also see dead bodies of our people lying about. Then the bird flew away," Aejah said with horror in his voice.

Aejah came out of the trance in shock and took an even deeper breath.

"It was the future you saw, Aejah," Zeblor replied.

"Do you know when this will occur?" Aejah wondered. "How do we stop this from happening?" Aejah said, sounding alarmed.

"Aejah, I feel this force is stronger than our race can take on. These warriors are probably Davon's war demons coming to punish our people."

"Let me try to get more insight on this clan," Aejah insisted.

Zeblor began to have a vision and automatically went back into a trance and Parxis and Aejah stared at him in astonishment. Aejah envisioned the temple from which an artifact was stolen and three warriors walking out of it. He was carrying a religious artifact and scornfully ignoring a primitive mystic's pleas.

"What gives you the right to barge into this temple and take anything you wish?" the old monk from the shrine said.

"Get out of our way, old man," the leader of the warring faction said.

"Give me back my sacred vessel," the monk demanded to the war-lord.

"I'm warning you, do not interfere," the lead warrior warned.

"I will not permit you to confiscate it," the old man said as the warrior ripped the statue from his hands.

"Then you shall die, for we have no reason to stand around and be bothered by a peon such as yourself."

Winter Solstice

Having said that, the leader angrily drew his Scourger blade and struck the feeble male down. Horrified by what he had seen, he broke out of the trance and explained it to his guests.

"These people obviously show no mercy to any other." He said it like he had seen a ghost.

"Chief, you must prepare your people for the inevitable. Some horrible events will be happening in the years to come," Zeblor said with concern.

"I told him about some of my projections of the future," said Aejah.

"The blue smoke drug does that; that's why we call it a mind enhancer. It broadens our thought processes. That is why your ancestors banished those who use it excessively, because they didn't understand it. They thought that I was just crazy."

"Zeblor, we'll do what we can and thanks for helping us," Parxis said as he gripped Zeblor's hand with his two.

"Farewell, my friends, and have a pleasant journey," Zeblor said.

Aejah and Parxis exited the hut, said their good-byes, and closed the door. They got on their horses and headed home into the winter sun.

9   The Collaborators

That night, the small group traveled into the northern part of Davonia without alerting the Davonians of their presence. They went all the way to where the northern part of the mountain ridge ended. They then stopped where there had once been a cave, but it had long since collapsed.

"Here we are. Let's set up camp here. I have a long tale to tell you, little one, but not before you get some rest," Aejah said, pointing directly at Garayen. The two of them pitched their tent to shelter them from the cool night air. They all curled up in their bedrolls and were fast asleep.

The next day, they all had a nutritious meal and then Aejah began continuing to tell his story. Aejah told his young student how problems were not taken care of by his ancestors:

"It had been almost thirty years since Grax's banishment. Grax became a disbeliever of many of the religions and preached his hatred of them. He sought revenge and became obsessed with stealing artifacts from various temples and shrines. Those that had any meaningful value to him would be burned in a bonfire. Grax came across the legendary Power Stone he found in the Davonian mines. He gained enough hatred to carry out his campaign of conquest. He formed an army called the Phaetozene, which means, in Davonian, revenge. It is said that a barbaric, demon-like race was summoned from the depths of Davon's underworld to destroy my people and all that they stand for. The warriors were scaled, lizard-like creatures with fins jutting out from the sides of their heads; they had big ears, yellow snake-like eyes, and had five clawed fingers on each hand. They had shiny golden suits of armor and helmets that were curved up in the back. They had curved swords called Scourger Blades. They say the warriors' blades were forged deep within the Keorn mine and were strong enough to cut through even the toughest of stone.

"Deep inside the mountain ridge of Davonia, Grax contemplated a plan with his guild of warlords. They knelt down on one knee and listened to their master as he told how he wanted to destroy the Sedarians and their religion. He picked up a chunk of the magenta crystalline stone he found and both the warlords and Grax stared at it in awe. They say that stone had the power to cut through any material including flesh.

"'Come, my comrades! It is time to perform the conquest ceremony,' roared Grax.

"The warriors stood up from their kneeling positions and followed Grax into the lower chambers. Grax was wearing a ceremonial crimson robe over his battle armor. He approached an altar, which was positioned in front of a pyramid-like structure made out of large stone blocks. A Davonian high priest wearing the same kind of robes as well as headdress stepped out in front of him and placed an amulet around his neck. The amulet was decorated with many colorful jewels that looked as if they were hand-picked from a sunset. He then looked down upon his subjects and preached to them an ancient sermon. It was the very same sermon that he used before he was banished.

"'There must be a way to cut through their line of defense,' Grax whispered in fury as he mounted his horse. 'No one understands the power of the Power Stone more than me. I must use it to destroy Parxis and his religious faction.'

"Upon Grax's return, he went down to the lower chambers of his hideout within the mountain ridge to meditate. After a while, he got up from his meditation position and exited the lower chambers. He entered a chamber to where they forged weapons and drew his sword. He pounded the blade down, had a piece of the stone carved into a gemstone, and mounted it into the hilt. When he was done, he held it up with two hands, caressing the blade with one, and looked at it in admiration. He had his warriors work on their swords all day and night. The next day they prepared for their next raid on Saron. Grax removed his ritual cloak, revealing his Phaetozene armor suit, and unsheathed his sword. He began to address his army as he held out a piece of the crystalline Power Stone in his palm.

"'Together, with these magical blades, we will defeat the Sedarian tribes. We will exclude their peaceful ways and bring in a new order to our land of darkness. They will pay for their insolence. This is the power for which we, the Phaetozene, control and there is nothing they can do to take it away from us,' Grax chanted to his followers. He raised his hand, holding a piece of the Power Stone; he gazed in awe as it glowed.

"Far away, on the northeast side of the Sedarian mesa, the eldest brother of Grax intuited danger, in a dream, for his people in the capitol city of Saron. He knew his premonition could mean only one thing; therefore, early that morning he gathered his people. 'Today, my fellow kinsmen, we are going to start construction on city walls to defend our cause,' Praxis announced to his Sedarian people.

That day, his people wheeled carts to a nearby yellow stone quarry and began cutting stone with chisels and mallets made from a metal alloy extracted from a Keorn stone. They used a pulley-like mechanism with counterweights to lift the blocks of stone once they had cut them. Then they hauled the blocks of stone away in horse-drawn carts. They put them in place to construct the first wall using the same pulley mechanism. By the middle of the day, they had the second wall half-completed. By sundown, they put the finishing touches on the wall and then they put a large stone gate with Keorn metal hinges on the exit.

The Sedarians built a wall to protect their sacred library. It had a large base and two other levels, each a stage smaller than the other. On top, it had an observation tower for astronomers.

It was but a short time later—three rotations of a shadow—on a cloudy and dimly moonlit night that Grax and his small band of warriors headed for the city of Saron for their raid. They galloped on their horses up to the city but were stopped by an eight-foot-high reinforced stone wall. Frustrated with their plan, they turned around and went back to their lair.

10 The Phaetozene Last Stand

"**F**or several ages after Grax's banishment, he disappeared. Not even the Davonians knew where he went. Years later, after my people had discovered the mysterious attacks on the villages, they unveiled Grax's true plan.

"Grax sent out his largest army to destroy the city of Saron. That morning, one of Kajir's scouts spied on Grax's camp from Bangova Ridge, discovering his plans. When he tried to leave the tan mountain ridge via rope suspension bridge and slipped on a rock on his way back up the ledge, he was heard by one of the warriors. That warrior blew the alarm horn loudly. The scout jumped on his horse and urged it to get going. He galloped toward Kajir's camp and was soon followed by a Phaetozene army. In the distance, Kajir could see his scout and a large army of angry warriors following him," Aejah said with excitement. "The suspension bridge was built by the early Davonians many years ago, for trade. Now the Davonian invasion force used it, but the Sedarians swiftly cut off that route. The Sedarians severed the ropes supporting the bridge years after the Davonian conflict. After one hundred years of aggression built up, they lacked the resources necessary to fight. Then the river dried up, making it a valley for the Davonians to travel through, between the mountains, but they remained neutral for centuries.

"'Scaz, round up the knights! Looks like one of my scouts found out Grax's next big plan,' Kajir shouted.

"'I will do so right away, sir!' Scaz said as he scurried off.

"The knights got on their mounts and rode them toward the horizon. The Phaetozene battalion headed for the city of Saron on the east side of the mesa. The Phaetozene decided to change course and go where the lake and the mountain ridge touch towards the west, but they miscalculated the entrance to their country. The Celestial Knights soon followed their adversaries over to the lake. Another Celestial army came up from the south side of the mesa and trapped them. Since the Celestial Knight armies were bigger, the Phaetozene army retreated back across the border. The Celestial Knights all met in the capitol city.

"'Welcome back general,' Kajir said to his long-retired comrade and mentor.

"'It has been a long time, my friend,' said General Bangova, whom the mountain ridge was named after because of that maneuver.

"'Chief Parxis, meet General Fadro Bangova,' Kajir introduced to Parxis.

"'When Kajir was young, Fadro taught the ways of the sword to him and has been Kajir's mentor ever since,' Aejah said to Parxis.

"Parxis patted the aged Sedarian on his right shoulder. 'I've heard so much about you.'

"At daybreak, General Bangova, Kajir, and their armies stood waiting on a sand dune outside the city of Saron. The Phaetozene made their presence known by poking their heads out from the mountainous rock face and stood there, facing the knights. For several rotations of the shadow, they stared at each other. The Phaetozene began to charge toward them and the knights just stood there. When the Phaetozene charged closer, Kajir's army and Bangova's army split and went to either side of the Phaetozene.

"Seeing that they were outnumbered, the Phaetozene retreated back into the mountains again. At that moment, both armies saw a single rider coming from the south. Kajir shouted with excitement, "It's Aejah!"

"'Follow me, my friends, across the Davonian border,' Aejah shouted back while galloping toward the Valley of the Heavens. The Phaetozene horde retreated, and the Celestial armies merged and followed, after Aejah followed the horde into Davonia. When they entered, Davonian soldiers marched cautiously closer. Aejah stepped forward with the Blade of Vyriad in hand. A Davonian warlord charged toward Aejah and Aejah struck the Davonian's blade and it shattered. The Davonian was so stunned by what just happened he dropped the broken blade and backed off. Aejah ran up and jabbed it into the ground. Just as that occurred, it got dark and began to rain. Aejah showed Dakaron that his soil was still fertile. The remainder of the Phaetozene died off years later as a result of overuse of the Power Stone.

"The one lesson that the Sedarian people have learned from this is that, you should never walk away from a problem. You should face it and try to solve it, because if you don't, it will grow into a much larger one and will get harder to solve. That's why exile was never a good solution for prisoners."

11   The Village of Glydruf

At first light, Aejah and Garayen packed up their belongings and journeyed back into their native land. They traveled for a day and a half to Parenzoah Lake, just north of the Sedarian Mesa. They took a Glydra fishing boat down the Saduran River, which was heading for a small fishing village south of the mesa. As the gentle breeze slowly pushed the boat down the river, young Garayen inquired about the boat's workings. Aejah explained that the boat was first invented and built in the village of Glydruf. Larger boats were built once the village became more prosperous. The boat was based on the concept of using a pocket of wind to push it along. It was maneuvered by using a revolving wooden T-rod, forming a steering mechanism, which changed the position of the pocket. The boat itself was curved more in the front and less in the back with a sailing envelope arching halfway in the bow section. Two people were needed to steer the boat, as one person had to stand and hold the T-rod, and the other had to handle the rudder. On the bow of the boat, there was a curved piece of wood to tie the boat at the docks. The boats were made from the wood of a palm tree.

"Are we headed for this village?" Garayen asked.

"Yes, we are!" Aejah answered with glee. "We are going to the exact site where my good friend Chief Parxis passed on."

"What do you know of this village?" Garayen asked.

"At one time the village was very prosperous. Several years ago, we didn't hear from the townsfolk anymore. My people knew of a larger seafaring city that once existed across the river, but it disappeared as well some years ago. Fishing vessels like this one used to trade with the people in that city. It had huge stone structures, elaborate, much like the Celestial City of Mervaura. There were tall towers across the skyline that you could still see from greater distances all around," Aejah said with astonishment. "The village and the city could have had a war and they must have destroyed themselves!

"Ah, yes, at last we have arrived," Aejah said as he stood up and helped direct Garayen on how to steer the boat. As the sun began to descend on the horizon, Garayen maneuvered the boat to the docking area next to the village of Glydruf. Aejah stepped onto the dock. "This was the exact same route that Parxis and I took fifty years ago."

As Aejah stood in the village square, he spoke. "Let me tell you some-thing. What I just told you is what my people have theorized for years, not the actual truth. I want to tell you what Parxis and I discovered just before he died. Parxis was bitten by a poisonous sand crab; its bite is lethal. It was my conclusion that the inhabitants of Glydruf died off from a sand crab epi-demic years after Parxis declared peace amongst my people. It has two small claws, two clawed feet, and a hard exoskeleton shell. During the day, the crab would bury itself underneath the searing sands of the desert and await its meal. It used its tail as a digging tool to accomplish this. Its body is col-ored mostly yellow with patches of red and green. It also has several prickly spines along its claw-arms and legs to break it free from larger predators. The crab has two eyes with adjusting transparent eyelids to help dim its vision when going into the sun and to protect its pupils from the crystalline sand. At night it moves around to seek out a new area. There could be crabs bur-rowed in the ground around here, so watch your step. That morning, I fore-saw that something like this would happen. It had been fifty years since the Phaetozene horde died. Parxis took time to prepare for his kingdom's future. His daughter, Zia, gave birth to you, Garayen—a hopeful for the next scribe and possibly a peaceful future for a whole new generation. After two hun-dred years of fighting, the Davonians decided that they could no longer do a war campaign. Their food and supplies were running low, and since Davonia was a small country, it was difficult to support one. So they made a treaty with the Sedarians and remained neutral from any bloodshed. He had his people build a pyramid-shaped tomb for when he passed on. They used the same masonry methods that my people utilized to build the city walls of Saron. The farming village had been rebuilt and was upgraded to a city with an even larger population. Our people even taught the Davonians how to grow their own food.

"At daybreak, when I came out of my house, I saw the bright shining sun over the southwestern part of the mesa on the horizon. An approaching sandstorm began to smother it with sand. In Mervaura, the guards closed the huge stone gates by having horses pull them shut. People fled to their cham-bers and homes in panic. Before I knew it, it was over. The city was gone. Mervaura, the Celestial City, was the home of the Celestial Knights. It was a place of peace, paradise, harmony, a sanctuary for life, and a citadel for protection. The best-defended fortress against any invading army. Mervaura was named after the sun god, which the Sedarians, my people, worship every sunrise during the winter solstice. The four scout towers connecting the four walls on this citadel had three points on them, one large and two smaller towers. It was used to defend Sedaria against rogue armies coming from the south. The city flourished years after the Phaetozene had passed on. According to history, a blinding flash of sunlight blazed from the west behind the city and Bangova Ridge. Blocking the view of the city, a gust of wind blew sand and debris overhead, and smothered it in a thick cloud of dust. When the sky finally cleared, the city was gone. This posed a great mystery. Some said a terrible sand storm had buried the city. Others said it was the ghost of the Phaetozene that did it. Whatever it was, I saw it as a bad omen. Parxis was awestruck at the sight of it disappearing."

Aejah continued by telling Garayen how Parxis directed his people's future:

"What on Elyzon's world was that?" Parxis shouted. "It disappeared!"
"How did that happen? What of my brother Kajir? Did he survive?"
"We haven't heard anything as of yet," I responded.

After seven rotations of the shadow, Parxis and I sailed down the Saduran River and he discussed with me the future of our people. "What I am about to tell you may be a little unsettling. As you probably already know, I will not be around forever. After all, I'm not immortal like you want to believe. I know some people, like you, have thought of me as a legend. Someone has to follow in my footsteps and carry on the tradition of peace. I want you to have the rights to the religion. After all, it was your idea. I also want you to be the next chief of the tribe."

As I turned my attention to steering the boat, I replied, "Chief, I am honored to be the next hopeful for the throne, but you don't have to do this. You can still go on another ten years, can't you?"

"Aejah, there are still some things you need to understand. I need someone to maintain our peaceful lifestyle. No one understands it more than you do." Parxis put a hand on my shoulder.

"I don't know the first thing about being a ruler. I'm just a scribe."

"The only thing you need to know is to think positively, use your common sense, and do what is right. Observe what is around you, all that is good. Here, I will recite an ancient proverb that one of our prophets once said. Maybe this

will enlighten you." Parxis pulled out a scroll of parchment from his beige tunic and unrolled it. "Sunshine is enlightening to life. It is the warmth of all being. It provides feelings of happiness over time. The feelings will always last from now through tomorrow's ages. It feels like a rush of wind off of the warm dune sea. It is as the joyous sight of the Sands of Blue during the winter solstice. The rising of the sun over the horizons will bring positive energy to your day. The future of time has not been written, only the now exists. Look on tomorrow as if it were an invitation to the pleasure of life. Fear brings darkness and takes the joy out of our days. Treasure the most exotic wonders that may never be recreated." Parxis rolled it back up and put it back in his tunic. "This is what I was trying to tell you. Enjoy your days, because we are living in a dying world, my friend, and I don't know if you will see any more good ones like these."

As I considered his words to me, Parxis patted me on the back. I felt content. "Well, I suppose that's the way it'll have to be then," I said.

"That's the spirit, Aejah! You just needed a little encouragement."

As the sun began to descend on the horizon, we maneuvered the boat to the docking area next to the village of Glydruf. When I started to step off the boat, I noticed something strange about the village. "Where are the inhabitants?" I inquired.

"The place looks deserted," Parxis responded.

That night, Parxis described his memory of Glydruf over a campfire. He told me that this village didn't thrive as much as the other cities did. From what he remembered, Glydruf was primitive. It had tents in the shape of the curved sails on their Glydra boats. The people there hunted wild game for food. Being a remote village, Glydruf didn't have much contact and influence on the cities occupying the mesa.

"How and when did they die?" I asked.

"To be honest with you, Aejah, I really don't know."

Parxis and I crawled into our bedrolls and went to sleep. The next morning as I was getting up, I heard Parxis struggling with something. He was being attacked by one of those poisonous sand crabs. I immediately came to his aid as I drew my wedge blade. I tried to kill it, but it was too fast for me. Before I knew it, the skirmish was over and the crab had crawled away. Parxis immediately sat up and noticed he had green ooze coming from the bite mark on his arm. Parxis fell backwards from his sitting position in shock.

"I feel so cold!" Parxis said as he started to shiver.

"Chief, don't leave me!" I cried in panic, as I knelt down beside my beloved chief.

"You know what to do now, Aejah! My time has come." Parxis grimaced.

"Don't go, chief! Please don't go!" I sobbed. "How could I let this happen? Why? I let you down, Chief. I wasn't quick enough!" I felt guilty.

"Don't say that! It was not your fault! There was nothing you could have done to prevent it," Parxis reassured me.

"Remember what I told you. Go on, my friend." Those were to be Praxis's final words to me. He then took in his last breath and his head rolled to one side.

"It was almost like Parxis knew he was going to die," said Garayen.

"Exactly, he could sense the precise moment that he would pass on," Aejah said. "Our ancestors have been known to have this sense." The Elder, Aejah, continued relating to Garayen the tale of their people's ancestry:

"The next day, Parxis's body was prepared for his burial. All of the organs were removed from the body and it was embalmed with a resin made from some of their ceremonial plants. The body was then covered with a burial shroud and placed in a golden sarcophagus. The sarcophagus was then carried in a horse-drawn cart in a funeral procession to the tomb. On the way there, people would follow the cart or just wave to it and throw flower petals. The sarcophagus was then lowered into a pit, in the center of the pyramid tomb, by way of pulleys.

After all the crowd had left, a young woman entered the yellow-stone pyramid tomb with her newborn son cradled in her arms. She looked down into the pit over the metallic railing and said, 'My dear father, Mother would have been proud of what you did in your life, had she been here to see it. I hope my son follows in your footsteps,' she said as she looked down at her newborn. 'Father, I hope your life in the World of Dreams is a pleasant one,' she added as a tear trickled down her cheek. 'I'm going to miss you, Father. I'll remember you always.'"

Aejah briefly paused with his storytelling. He took in a deep breath and slowly released the air from his lungs with a relaxing sigh. Gazing deep into the eyes and heart of Garayen, Aejah gently declared, "That young woman was Zia, your mother, and the newborn she cradled in her arms was you, Garayen. After your mother bid her good-byes, she walked out the door with you, Garayen, and the entrance was forever sealed with a gigantic stone slab."

The day was nearing an end and so too was Aejah's time with Garayen. As the sun began to set, Aejah decided that it would be a good time to make his exit. "And so Parxis, your grandfather, had left his legacy in my care for future generations to learn and gain wisdom from," Aejah said with heartfelt understanding. Aejah pulled out a scroll of parchment from his beige tunic and unrolled it. "Let this guide you on your way." Aejah handed Garayen a rolled-up parchment with a gold ribbon around it.

"What is it?" Garayen asked.

"It is a proverb of my own. Now that I taught you all I know, it is your job to teach others. I trust you can find your way back to the mesa?" Aejah asked cordially.

"Now that I know how to use the boat, I'm sure I can manage." Garayen nodded with a smile.

"I bid you farewell. I hope you have a bright future ahead of you. My people require my guidance so that they too can have a bright future."

Having said that, Aejah waved and wandered off into the desert haze, where he disappeared into the sunset.

Garayen unrolled the parchment and read the proverb aloud to himself:

"As I wander through the desert sands, I ponder the feelings I have within. The everlasting days of what nature once had—a culture that slowly vanishes over time. The calm winds blow with the silence of nature. The magenta leaves on a Gloom Tree, how they hang in despair against the stillness of the dunes in the desert of blue. The illumination of the lavender sky as the sun sets on the horizon. The peaceful town of people left behind. The renewal of life and a reason to go on are the dreams from the minds of many to the soul of one. As my thoughts gather within my mind, I wander as I search my soul. I continue to leave tracks in the sand, only to find an endless land."

Garayen smiled as he looked up at the horizon, knowing that the future could be made into anything you want it to be.

A Dying World

1 The Height of Technology

Young Cranamar Duraxo sat in his quarters on board the Dreadnaught ship Navoirdic, as he looked at a plan to develop the next ultimate weapon against the Wizorans, a common foe amongst his people.

Cranamar Duraxo

Cranamar's people, the Gaedians, were sea-green in skin pigment, with two long ears, two red and yellow eyes slanting inward that glowed orange when they were in the dark, and two three-fingered, clawed hands. An alien his size was shorter than the average human, and very muscular. The Gaedians' oxygen content of their planet was much like the Sherpa, who lived in the Himalayas. The Sherpa were an ethnic group in northeastern Nepal.

They occupied several high valleys, at altitudes between about eight thousand and thirteen thousand feet high. The thin air up there was the same amount as the Gaedians' atmosphere.

He scanned through his portable console, examining the different features in the layout for a new particle weapon. Cranamar thought, if only his people could have seen the rest of the light spectrum, they might have been able to create a more effective weapon, but he was only able to see as far as infra-red light. The Gaedians had discovered their ability to see infra-red light in the dark, which came with their naturally born nocturnal instincts. Their vision adapted through evolution, to see in the dark because they liked to live in dark places. Going to the surface, they would have gone blind from the sunlight had they not worn sun goggles.

The Gaedians were able to develop laser weapons, small, powerful, and fast enough with this special design. A xenon gas tube connected between two reflective surfaces when stimulated atoms released extra energy in the form of light waves. After bouncing between them many times in the tube, the light waves emerged as a laser beam. Connecting a charged power pack to this apparatus would make a powerful weapon.

Cranamar remembered the time when his people found an unusual mineral that turned out to be very useful. Deep beneath Gaed's rocky surface, young excavators in the mining corps dug diligently at the thick and tough gray Gyrite ore inside the hollowed-out cavern. It was about as thick and tough as iron ore. Nearby in another subterranean mining shaft that had its rocky layers scarred by light wave drills, blast hammers, and rock shearers, Dr. Ingro Shamaji, a kind and caring planetologist, was kneeling in front of what looked like a giant geode. He scanned it with a rock depth analyzer to see what was on the other side of it. He needed to do that in order to determine how thick the exterior was. Some excavators had been injured because they did not accurately measure a large mass of mineral correctly. Excavators needed to keep at least a two-meter distance between themselves and the dig site. Some workers used highly dangerous explosives like Dionium, a highly unstable element. That killed a lot of workers as a result of their negligence. Dr. Shamaji calculated that it was only one meter thick.

A light wave drill was made out of Ecron steel, which was fifty times stronger than the average steel. Ecron steel was made from Gyrite ore,

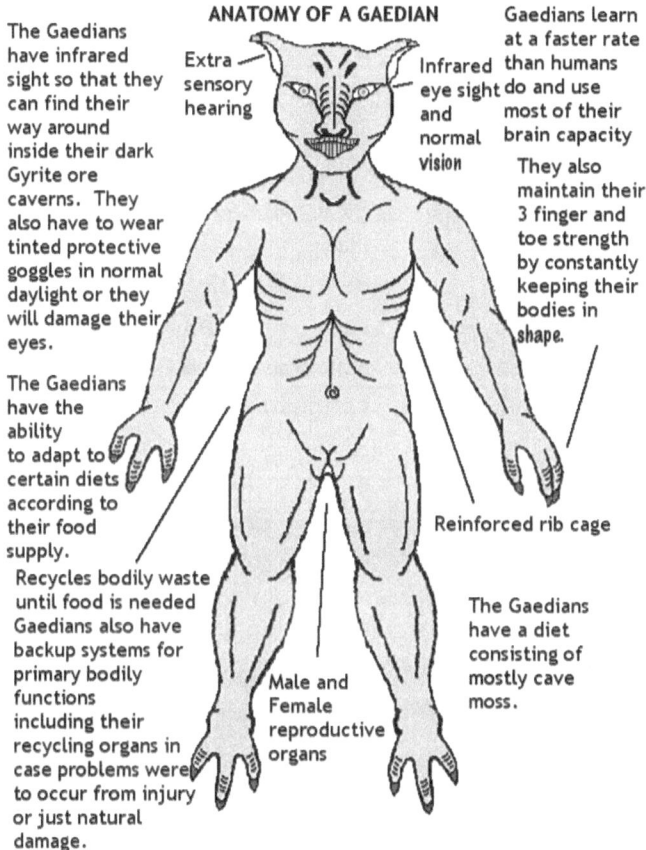

ANATOMY OF A GAEDIAN

The Gaedians have infrared sight so that they can find their way around inside their dark Gyrite ore caverns. They also have to wear tinted protective goggles in normal daylight or they will damage their eyes.

Extra sensory hearing

Infrared eye sight and normal vision

Gaedians learn at a faster rate than humans do and use most of their brain capacity

They also maintain their 3 finger and toe strength by constantly keeping their bodies in shape.

The Gaedians have the ability to adapt to certain diets according to their food supply.

Recycles bodily waste until food is needed Gaedians also have backup systems for primary bodily functions including their recycling organs in case problems were to occur from injury or just natural damage.

Reinforced rib cage

Male and Female reproductive organs

The Gaedians have a diet consisting of mostly cave moss.

which was like iron ore. This metal was used on all of the Gaedians' mining tools. This tool had a cylinder as a base module, accompanied by a ball connected to it, a cylindrical handle going diagonal, and a red button on the end of it. On the side of the base module was another cylindrical handle with an easy-grip handle. This device had an extra-long drill bit on the end of two cylinders, going from smallest to largest on the end of the main module. On the end of the drill bit, there was a laser emitter to help burrow it into thick and tough rock, like Gyrite ore.

A blast hammer was used for shattering unstable pieces of rock by use of sound waves and vibrations. You put it near the rock that you would like to blast, you pressed the button in the back, the piston went down, charged up, and released, sending sound waves vibrating through the thick layers of rock, shattering them in its path. It was thin, L-shaped, metallic, and it had a crook on the black, rubbery handle. The end of the hammer had a sonic vibrator, which looked like an earphone.

A rock shearer was a pneumatic mining tool used for cutting off small pieces of various rock specimens or prying apart rock by use of water pressure to lubricate the blades and help cool them down. It looked like a combination of three things together, a vacuum cleaner, a jack hammer, and kitchen shears. It was metallic and had a hose hooked up to a small tank of water, which a miner carried on his belt.

A rock depth analyzer was used for seeing on the other side of another rock and measuring rock thickness. It had two parts to it, one on either side of the handle, top and bottom. The top had a round-edged, rectangular electronic depth gauge with flashing colorful lights and all those bells and whistles. On the bottom was a magenta light as the sensor to measure the depth. It also had a tan easy-grip handle.

He then entered the previous cavern and called Cranamar over where he was. Cranamar lifted his head up from where he was working to let Dr. Shamaji know where he was. Dr. Shamaji recognized his face with three gray birth marks on his left cheek. Cranamar told his fellow miners that he would be right back, and he picked up his tainted mining spade and stood up to follow Dr. Shamaji to the next cavern. A mining spade was basically a mining tool that was part pickax and part shovel. The blade was horizontal, like a pickax, and the inner part near the handle was flat and wide. The blade would come out to a point. It looked almost like a hoe.

Dr. Shamaji whispered in his ear. "I want you to witness a new discovery," he said with excitement.

As a young excavator, Cranamar didn't have a lot of knowledge to go on as far as minerals were concerned. Ingro had his son, Gozra, and Cranamar dig with rock shearers to start an opening in order to see what was inside. After opening, Dr. Shamaji was awestruck with what he saw. There were whitish transparent glowing crystals inside. He called over a few other workers and they helped him open it up a little wider. Cranamar was the first to enter the gigantic geode. Still holding his slightly tainted mining spade, Cranamar cut loose a sample of the crystals for Dr. Shamaji. From that day on, the Gaedians took technology to new heights.

Most crystals found back on Earth were used as semi-conductors in computers using a form of energy called Piezoelectricity. This form of energy

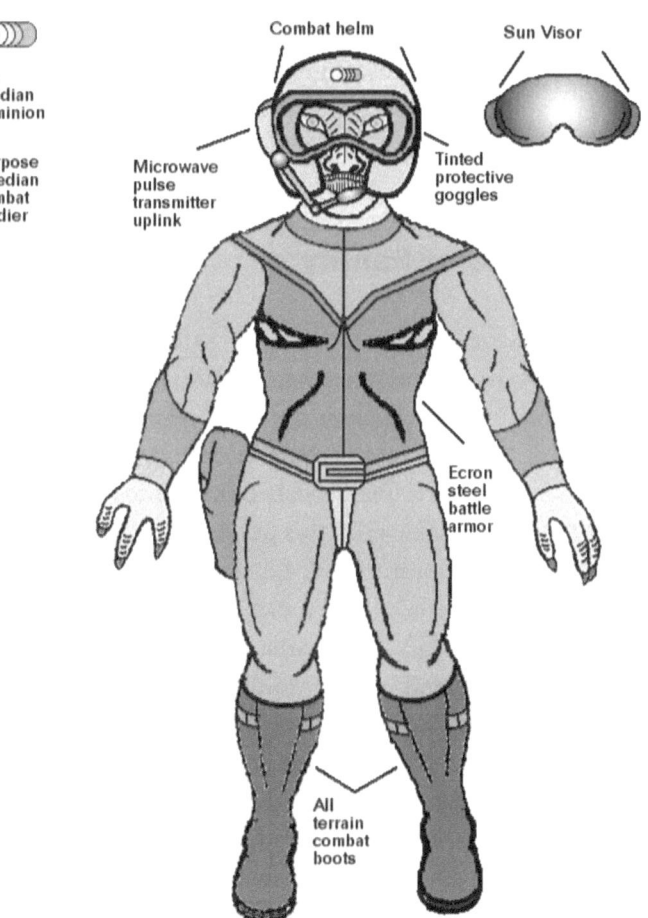

Combat helm

Sun Visor

the gaedian dominion

All Purpose Gaedian combat soldier

Microwave pulse transmitter uplink

Tinted protective goggles

Ecron steel battle armor

All terrain combat boots

required pressure to create it. The only drawback to this was that it wore on the crystal by stretching it out and compressing it until it shattered. The Gaedians utilized three types of crystals in their technology, Ceronium, Zeornium, and Kazium. Unlike the average crystals, these three forms of crystals contained a natural energy emanating from them. Ceronium had a mild energy source that was used in the Gaedians' computers. It was transparent with patches of white shaped in a cubic form. Zeonium had a dangerous level of radiation that was used in the Gaedians' space cruiser reactors. It was housed in a specially lined containment to prevent radiation leakage. It was transparent and magenta-colored in the monoclinic form. The monoclinic system had three unequal axes, two of which were not at right angles. The third made a right angle to the plane of the other two, as in orthoclase, gypsum, micas, augite, epidote, and hornblende. Kazium was in more of a hexagonal shape. The hexagonal system had three equal axes at 120 degree angles. Kazium was used for faster-than-light travel.

2   The Purpose of Family

Gozra Kavex was rescued by Dr. Shamaji during a raid back when the Wizorans started a civil war between them and the Gaedians. (The Wizorans were the Gaedians' brother race on the same planet for several Chrono-periods until after the Wizorans became more savage and began attacking the Gaedians. The Gaedians finally pushed them into barges and launched the Wizorans into space. They did this because they were sub-intelligent, more animal-like, and couldn't think for themselves.) Gozra's father was killed when a WF-7 Deceptor (a Wizoran three-person scout ship) strafed his home up near the surface. Dr. Shamaji was kind, caring, and thoughtful. He devoted his love and wisdom to the unfortunate. He taught these traits to those he took in, to care for, over several Chrono-periods. He was a great young visionary who invented the vows of maturity, because it helped point the offspring in the right direction. It gave them some sense of purpose in their lives, allowing them to have placement, meaning, and values in the circle of life. Gozra wanted to keep the people alive and feeling good, by becoming a positive idealist and one day changing the way his planet thought about life. He wanted them never to fear their enemy, never fight again, never to worry about their resource supply, and to have a beautiful place to live. He knew that he was far from his dream and it would take awhile before it could actually happen.

Thinking back to when his father, Narsis (Nars) Duraxo, a tactical combat officer, was around, Cranamar remembered the times he had with him as an assistant tactical combat officer for the Gaedian Interstellar Assault Force or the GIAF. His father disappeared on the outskirts of the desert moon, Saj Hari, many Chrono-periods ago. The entire planet of Gaed was on an invader watch because the Wizorans had returned after eight years of banishment from their home planet. The Gaedians had to take immediate precautions to ensure protection for their planet in order to drive the

Wizorans back. Evasive action had to be taken, otherwise the planet might be jeopardized. Nars was on a routine training mission for interstellar combat. He was being trained in one of their new long-range fighters, the Warpstar-1. He was practicing a quick reentry on Saj Hari when a thruster went out. He lost total control of it, burying him alive in the sand somewhere on Saj Hari. Shocked by what he heard, Cranamar put his head into his hands and started crying over it. "I hardly knew him," he sobbed. Dr. Shamaji put a gentle hand on Cranamar's shoulder and softly told him, "I'll raise you like my own son."

When Cranamar was about nine Chrono-periods or years of age, his father hardly had time for him. Judging from the crisis at the time, his father's expertise and skills were needed in order to defend the Gaedians' home world, yet Cranamar was too young to understand this. Dr. Shamaji knew that this was not the way for offspring to learn. Cranamar had to be cared for with or without his father. Ingro began to teach Cranamar the fundamentals of survival, so that he would begin to understand why his father was never around for him. Cranamar's father cared more for others than his own kin. This was the main reason why Cranamar was upset with him. Cranamar hardly knew his father, because Nars was too involved in his work to become a tactical combat officer.

Unfortunately, as a result of Nars's disappearance, Cranamar had to live with Dr. Shamaji since he was too young to live on his own. He had to wait until he was officially an adult (about thirteen in Earth years), to be in the Gaedian Legions. Before entering the Gaedian Legion Academy, Cranamar had to join the Mining Corps, in order to learn about their planet. There was so much work to do on their planet that every inhabitant had to get involved. He then had to join the Gaedian Legions. It was instated to defend their home planet from the Wizoran Empire. There, Cranamar met his best friend, Vepron Zuva, who encouraged Cranamar and helped him whenever he was in need. Vepron was like the brother Cranamar never had.

One parent gave birth to and raised a child to a mature age. The Gaedians were semi-reptilian and one person laid a transparent jelly-like membrane that contained a Gaedian embryo unlike the average Earth reptile. The Gaedians' brother race was more than a quarter reptilian; that's why the Wizorans' skin was darker. The reason most Gaedians were addressed as he or him was because they were more known for their male characteristics such as their brute strength and animal aggression. They also had a feminine side to themselves, which involved extreme love to their own kind, unlike the human male that exerted the opposite. Humans expressed too much hatred amongst themselves, which was considered a very negative survival instinct according to Gaedian philosophy. They believed it was better to love rather than express anger to others. Caring about one another and making sure that others lived a fairly equal lifespan was a better method of survival. When a young Gaedian reached maturity (thirteen years of age in human years), a ceremony was performed for the coming of that age. Both father and son were present during it. The son recited a short list of vows to the father, while holding his hand in the form of the harmony hand gesture. With a thumb and finger touching and pointer finger raised.

1. Protect our planet whenever it was threatened.
2. Share our wisdom and affection with only the trustworthy.
3. Treat your own kind as if they were family.
4. Preserve life, don't destroy it.
5. Fight on the defensive, never on the offensive.

When it was completed, the son was presented with a ribbon sash and a pin symbolizing their planet's unity, initiating him as a cadet. This meant he was officially an adult and held a responsibility to protect the planet.

3   The Invasion

The Gaedians built planetary perimeter defense stations in the planet's upper atmosphere. They hovered in the sky by way of anti-gravitational devices that Dr. Shamaji developed. Particles called magnetrons were used against particles called gravitons. They used particle beams of mag-netrons to neutralize gravitons. This in effect made things lighter in weight. They originally were used in this manner to prove his scientific theory, that someday they would be used for terraforming other worlds. Without them, it would leave the Gaedians helpless. Gaed had five of these stations located in its upper atmosphere. They had the capability of warning the planet's surface of any invaders. These stations used three forms of defense: they used force field barriers that blocked incoming bombardments, they could launch combat vessels to divert enemy fire, and used both station-mounted xenon and mega light wave cannons. The stations were metallic and had two circular bases from smallest to largest, going up. In the center, there was a long cylinder for a command tower and a tinted dome on top. There were four rectangular boxes on each side of the cylinder as launching bays for the fighters. The fighters were X-4 Starhawks; they had elongated, streamlined bodies with lime-green and dark turquoise markings for identification purposes. There was one pivoting gunnery pod on either side of the ship where the reentry wings were. They also had engine covers that sloped outward just like the Deceptor and it had a gap underneath the rear for better maneuverability during combat.

The stations weren't the only defense the Gaedians had. They also had xenon canons mounted on the highest mountain peaks of their planet. They were long cylinders mounted on top of rectangular gunnery stations and flat rectangular blast plates on either side of the end of the guns' barrels. These blocked incoming laser fire, so that it was harder for the Wizorans to damage the guns.

Cranamar thought back to when their planet took a real beating during the first invasion of their home planet since eight Chrono-periods ago. His father was an astrogator for the GIAF and Cranamar was a weapons engineer. A weapons engineer's job was to make sure weapons were working properly and determine if they needed repairs. If there were design flaws, it was his job to correct them. The Wizorans had sent down several DS-30 dropship detachments from the main ships. They were metallic and boxy-looking with many areas that looked like they would unfold to reveal some feature. They had two adjustable blast covers above the engines to protect them when they were not in use. It had hatches underneath them that opened up to lower two sets of treads and two off-road wheels. Looking on his view screen, Nars could see that an attack was imminent. He then alerted the Field Commando Unit of the situation at hand. They said they would get right on it and send to the surface sky sweepers. Field commandos, dressed in their blue uniforms, body armor, tinted goggles, and helmets, entered an elevated platform and the leader of the group pressed the button to make it go up. When they got there, the troops scattered on

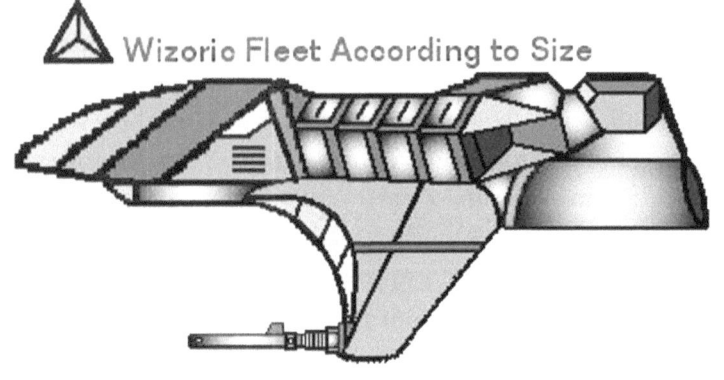

Wizoric Fleet According to Size

Name: W.E.V. Nexus
Class: Battlecruiser

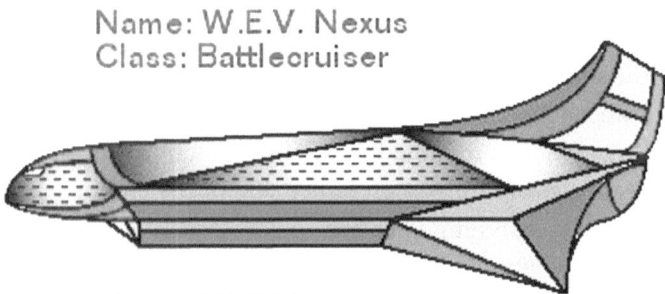

Name: W.E.V. azom
Class: Mining freighter

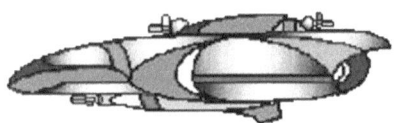

Name: WF-7 Deceptor
Class: Combat Vessel

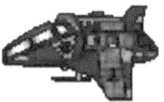

Name: WF-20 Interceptor
Class: Fighter

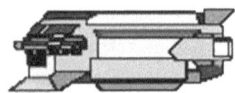

the surface to find a position. The rocky surface was magenta, dark purple, and gray. There were flat, almost smoothed-out mesas and canyons in between them, some deep and some shallow. The sky was light pink in color. The commandos knelt down on one knee and loaded their weapons with rockets from their metallic backpacks. One of them spotted one of the transports on his sight and put a lock on it. He pressed down on the triggering mechanism and the two-winged rocket flew out of the chamber, plunging itself into one of the dropships' hull, and exploded it on impact. Rockets flew through the air, hitting their targets, and shrapnel speckled the rocky surface of the planet. Beams of light waves struck the surface, killing several commandos and disturbing rock formations.

The battle continued overnight. Guns blazed and explosions ignited the sky. Cranamar was called to repair station three's two main gun batteries, because without them, the station would not be at full combat capability. Looking on his green, glowing tactical scanner screen, Cranamar could see according to the wire-frame computer animated objects that a Wizoran WEV Nexus battle cruiser had disengaged its attack on the second perimeter station and proceeded to head toward the severely damaged station that he was on. This ship was long and curved on top, chrome covered, and it had cubic storage areas overlapping each other on the sides of it, in the back. It had two wings swept forward with a big gun underneath each tip. In the front it had decorative lines slanting toward the back, like gills. The command module had the characteristics of an animal's backbone. It also had two slanted rocket engines. As their station fired at the oncoming craft, the ship fired back as a ball of fire emerged from their scopes. The turret had stopped firing on the ship. Foreseeing his station's imminent destruction, Cranamar hastily left his combat terminal and raced to repair the gun turret. He ran through an already open doorway, down long dark chrome hallways, and turned the corner, where he came to a large blast door. He pressed the open switch and the door slowly pushed itself open. When the door opened wide enough for him, Cranamar decided not to wait for it and proceeded to the gunnery platform. As he entered, he spotted the robotic programming controls. He opened a small metal box on the control panel and pressed the emergency power shut-off button. It appeared that the gun's wires overloaded as a result of a direct hit.

Cranamar went down the long, dark chrome hallway to a storage room. Using his metallic access clearance card, he placed the red strip in the box's slot on the wall next to the door. After granting him access, the door automatically slid open on the track. To his right in the dark storage area, he saw tool containers. He picked one up. The door closed behind him, and he pressed the button on the locking mechanism on the wall and the door sealed shut. He took the maintenance tool from his belt and removed the fasteners holding the control panel on. A maintenance tool was a multipurpose tool that ran on a neutron power cell, used for repairing many types of machinery including mining tools. It looked almost like a battery-powered screwdriver. Cranamar snipped off the burnt ends with a wire cutter and took a spare set and attached them with something resembling a soldering iron. He sealed the access panel and tightened the fasteners back up with his maintenance tool. Cranamar then initiated a code sequence to reset the system controls, by flicking switches.

The gun powered itself up and began firing blasts of laser fire at the WEV Nexus. The streams of laser fire struck one of the engines of the vessel, like a miner would do to a rock. Fiery metal chunks flew and fell into the air. The ship tilted to one side. The command module caught fire and crashed into the force field, exploded into a ball of flames. Cranamar raced back up to his battle station to witness his progress. Sitting down at his terminal, he saw a gigantic fireball in the sky and scraps of metal flying everywhere.

"Whew! That was close," Cranamar sighed.

"We've had worse battles than this one, believe me," Vepron said with sympathy.

Cranamar looked on his view screen and saw the Wizorans' ships and war machines fleeing away from the planet. "That time they caught us off guard," Gozra said.

"You sure know how to fix things, Cranamar," Vepron said with happiness.

4   Stolen Technologies

Glancing up from his terminal for a moment, Cranamar remembered the time when a Wizoran spy infiltrated the facility on Planet Gaed where they had been conducting light ray experiments. The spy stole a copy of the exact layout for the new light wave concentrator that Cranamar was looking over. The Gaedians were able to change the formula and design of this weapon, years later. The Wizorans used a crystal instead of xenon gas, which was originally going to be the Gaedians' design. Cranamar and weapons officer Vepron Zuva chased after him away from the Gaedian system into the Karil Nebula in an LR-77 Gladiator scout ship. The Gaedians found out in a flame test that iodine and bromine in a gaseous form made a magenta color. They were also able to decide that ionized hydrogen gave the nebula electromagnetic properties. The ship was elongated, dark in color, and covered with shiny Ecron steel armor plating. Its huge, bulky size made this ship look brute, mean, and capable of taking a beating in rough combat. The LR-77 Gladiator's command module was mounted on top of its body. It had three rocket engines, one in back and two on the sides. It also had two main mega cannons in the front sides and two rotating gun turret pods, one in front of the command module and one in back of it. It was an older model, but it sure could take a lot of punishment.

Cranamar visualized himself for the first time, sitting in the pilot's seat of the LR-77 Gladiator. While preparing for launch, Cranamar could hear the security alarms blaring and see lights flashing outside the ship in the hangar. Alert of the situation, Cranamar knew that if he did not stop the spy, the Wizorans might get the upper hand. Knowing this, Cranamar proceeded to strap himself in while the main officer spoke with central control. Cranamar put on his protective goggles and placed his combat helmet upon his head, tucking his long ears safely inside. The other two officers that were with him seated themselves as well. After going over their routine checklist, Central Control finally gave the okay. Without hesitation, Cranamar pressed the launch engagement button. The crew braced themselves while the craft picked itself up and rocketed out of the launching bay into the void of space. Specifically with this design, it was much easier to change speed and direction by way of vectors using maneuverable retro-rockets underneath the craft. Through the crosshair holo-display, the weapons officer could see a combat vessel thrusting toward the nebula, but he couldn't make out what model. The weapons officer flicked a switch on his laser targeting system and multicolored lights blinked on and off to let him know it was ready to fire. "Almost in range," the officer shouted. When he finally lined up his target, Cranamar lost control of the ship and the weapons officer misfired, skimming the edge of one of the enemy's engines, releasing a ball of fiery exhaust. As a result of the nebula's unstable conditions, the enemy ship went spiraling into it, breaking up the ship's structure in the process. The magenta-colored gases spiraled inward, just as the enemy ship did. Observing the craft from his console, Cranamar blacked out. A few hours later, their ship was recovered. Unfortunately one other crew member was killed when it spun out of control. When the ship entered the nebula, it distorted the gases and created a chemical reaction between the ship's skin and the gases that made electromagnetic waves within the nebula, screwing up the navigator's console.

Cranamar woke up in an infirmary on a foam-like bed covered with a thermal blanket, because the caverns were damp and cold. He was greeted by Vepron, one of the officers who was with him during the chase. "These ships were not designed to withstand the electromagnetic field of that nebula. The Wizorans must have come up with some sort of reflector that would prevent their instruments from getting messed up," Vepron spoke with concern. "I just heard that the information the Wizorans stole was unfortunately retrieved," he said.

"No thanks to the disturbance in the nebula, I got this nasty bump on my head. How did he do it? I can't believe this. His ship was destroyed," Cranamar complained as he rubbed his bandaged brow.

"I'll show you how he did it. Follow me. Dr. Shamaji just found out," said Vepron.

"Our Artificial Brain picked up a microwave transmission." Cranamar immediately climbed out of bed, dressed himself, and accompanied his comrade to the main computer room. They walked down narrow corridors

Dr. Ingro Shamaji
Planetologist

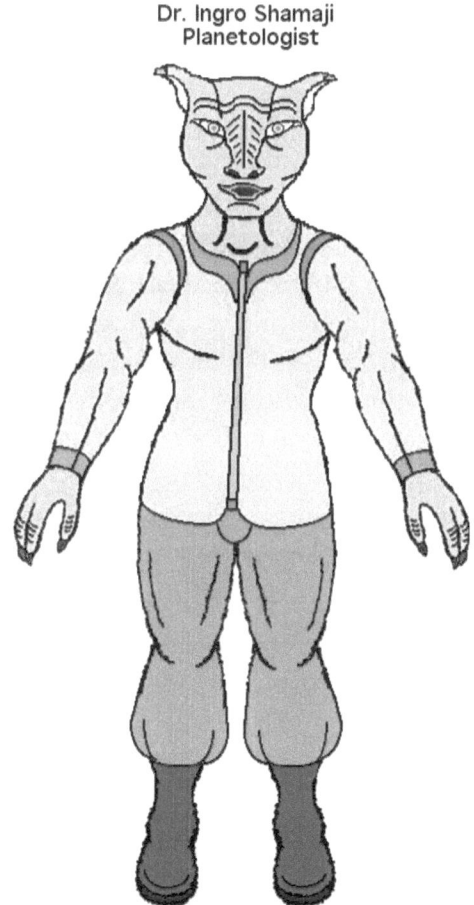

of an old Gyrite ore mining cavern, turning corners until they reached the room. Upon entering Dr. Shamaji's work area, Cranamar pressed the open button and the metallic door opened electronically.

"Come in, my friend, I haven't seen you for a while. What can I do for you?" Ingro spoke as he put his portable console down on his work area.

"You know that ship we were chasing? Could you show me where the transmission came from, that the Micro Pulse Uplink picked up?"

"Sure," Ingro said with a smile. Ingro motioned Cranamar toward a doorway opposite of the one they'd entered.

"I'll see you later," Vepron said while patting Cranamar on the shoulder and departed the room. Cranamar and Ingro entered the main computer room as Ingro turned on the lighting. Before them was an enormous screen on top of a rectangular central processor. The processor had lights that would blink on and off as it processed information. Ingro pressed a button on the side of the processor and a control panel folded out. He fingered several buttons to activate its main processor and a layout of a spacecraft appeared on the screen in front of a green grid box. It showed a top view and a side view of the ship they were pursuing. It was streamlined, dark in color; it had several dimly colored, curved-like racing stripes for identification purposes. It also had two engines in back, and a fin between two engine hoods. It had two visible sitting areas, one on top and one in front. The WF-7 Deceptor also had two long mega cannons underneath it and two rotating gun turret pods, one in front of the upper cockpit and one behind. It was evil-looking and designed to go fast.

"The transmission came from this device here." Ingro pointed to a box outlined in green with a green line pointing to the device on the ship. "The device was a microwave pulse transmitter," Ingro said with enthusiasm.

5   The Protectors

Back on Earth, it had always been man's dream to travel the stars, but the only way they could was by traveling at the speed of light. Many physicists said it was impossible to travel at the speed of light, and the only way to travel was to convert subatomic particles in matter, into waves and back again. A Gaedian scientist named Dr. Ingro Shamaji found a way to make it possible. They were able to invent a machine that would isolate the particles and waves and transport people to worlds as far away as one million light years. He found crystals with subatomic particles that fluctuated from their original form into waves. Due to its extremely high molecular weight, this crystal could excite matter outside when energized. When a test subject was placed in a protective chamber with the device connected to it, the Gaedian scientists were able to focus the energy once the subject was transformed into electromagnetic waves. Exciting electron oscillation through higher and lower subatomic energy shells and synchronizing through the crystal, the energy could be concentrated and transmitted to a designated location. Calculations must be made in order to determine distance and time allowed for energy to generate a subject into particle form at the destination. Gyrite ore was the only material capable of containing the crystals without having them fluctuate.

They were able to make light speed acceleration travel possible by using two power rods and two brace rods connected to a Kazium crystalline core supported by a circular metal frame and two metal columns. This contraption eventually became the first stable method of traveling at the speed of light. This device was then made bigger for ships to go into. It is now known as the "Hypergate." For starters, the device was put on board a GDV-32 transport ship. In order to use it, the ship had to travel great distances with its crew in suspended animation to get close enough to its destination. The ship was dark blue with purple and greenish-yellow markings on its tail. It also had a cockpit with a tinted canopy as well as a small tinted bubble on top. It was almost shaped like a banana, but it looked kind of like a military cargo plane back on Earth and it was the same size of it too. It was originally built with three engines, but the prototype could only have one, because it needed room for the light speed acceleration generators under the wings.

It was only used during a universal emergency, when sentient lifeforms were threatened. The Gaedians mainly used it to help preserve other alien cultures that they admired and could learn from. The prototype Hypergate system failed twice and two volunteer test subjects were lost during the experiments. The device was originally designed to be used as an infiltration device to be used against the Wizorans during their invasions every five Chrono-periods, which the people on Gaed called a year. Dr. Ingro Shamaji, a Gaedian planetologist, decided against having it used for war-like purposes and used it in a more peaceful and practical manner. Dr. Shamaji experimented with his theory by housing a Kazium crystal in a specimen container and connecting it to a generator inside a protective chamber. The two risks involved with this form of travel were that matter could be lost during transportation and a subject could be lost on an unknown world without perfected tracking. During transportation, molecular structures of matter were literally being pulled through space. The matter was drawn into the gateway as energy particles and was transported to its destination. The coordinates where the Hypergate would be located created tremors once a gateway had been opened. These tremors came from the forced isolation of these particles. It was never perfected as a result of the experiments, which made it virtually an unstable method of travel. Research was done on this form of travel and Gaedian scientists eventually developed a light speed accelerator for spacecraft. Some Gaedian travelers described the experience as flying through a tunnel of light.

The Gaedians admired the human race's fascination with integrated circuitry for years. Cybernetics had been the Gaedians' favorite pastime since the Wizorans were banished. When the Wizorans first invaded Saj Hari, it was five Chrono-periods after they were banished from Gaed. The height of the Gaedians' technological build-up began back when the Sedarians on planet Saj Hari were thriving. Gaedian circuitry was almost similar to human microchips, but it was a little different in material. The Gaedians used a special conductive crystal instead of silicon in their maze of wires.

Other than cybernetics, the only cultural qualities admired in the human race were their spiritual beliefs, like the Native American spiritual cultures. The only thing that they disliked the most was humans' obsession with rage and violence. The rage came from people who didn't take responsibility for their actions. People were not raised to respect other lives. They didn't realize once a life was taken, it could not be replaced. Also when one culture disagreed with other ones' beliefs, the opposing side started fighting because of it. That was a very negative and destructive behavior that solved nothing and it would be better off for both sides to negotiate terms.

This just infuriated more people and incited another violent confrontation. War and revenge was a continuous cycle that was infinite and would not stop until someone intervened with the situation with an alternate solution to anger and hatred.

The Gaedians looked for positive qualities in other cultures that they admired and hadn't had time to discover in themselves. On the other hand, the Gaedians found some sense of purpose with their technological knowledge to protect other cultures that they admired and possibly gain allies. Other ancient alien cultures that were in jeopardy needed help to continue positive traditional rituals to make life worth living. Ever since the Wizorans started raising their young with no respect for their brother race, the Gaedians knew they had to protect their own kind. The Gaedians believed that when their planet was created, there was only one giant mass of life, and that separated to form opposites of every one form of life. The Wizorans and the Gaedians were the perfect example of this effect. But instead of male and female, it was good and evil. Unfortunately the Supreme Being failed to put more advanced intelligence into the Wizorans' minds. The Wizorans had the mental equivalent of a barbaric animal. The one thing the Wizorans lacked was the love and gratitude for life and other individuals. They had no mental capacity to think for themselves. As a result, the Gaedians had more in their own mind to make their lives more enjoyable and have some sense of purpose. The Gaedians built their civilization as far advanced as they could, that the Wizorans hardly caught up with the electronic age. The Wizorans stole the Gaedians' technological ideals because they were too incompetent to develop their own.

The Gaedians' ancestors who lived on the planet Patoa long ago had advanced further than them. They developed technology beyond average human capability that they actually had time to integrate art and culture into their society. The Wizorans' behavior obtained racist, destructive, and disrespectful qualities. On the other hand, the Gaedians had a positive attitude, which they gave to the Sedarian religion, and felt indebted to their side of the universe, to protect other lifeforms from danger.

The four primary cultures admired were the Patoans, Sedarians, Native Americans, and ancient Egyptians. They admired the Patoans for their incorporation of cultural design into technology and architecture. The

Gaedians admired the Sedarians and they were appreciated for their positive enlightenment philosophy, the Native Americans for their spiritual religion, and the ancient Egyptians for their preservation of life after death. Unfortunately, the Patoans died out as a result of an ice storm on their planet, but their utopian ideals lived on. The Sedarians were spared after the Wizorans invaded Saj Hari, Chrono-periods ago. The Gaedians were able to intercede with their plan and attacked the Wizorans' fleeing vessels, rescuing the Sedarian prisoners. Dr. Ingro Shamaji, a savior, was able to preserve one member of a Pueblo Southwestern Native American tribe in a transparent suspended animation tube as well as other cultural symbols. Hundreds of years before the pilgrims and Spaniards discovered America, the Gaedians were able to transport the one member of the tribe to Planet Gaed. They did the same for an ancient Egyptian and some of their artifacts like papyrus writings, pottery, and other craftwork. The Gaedians also kept a record archive of each and every cultural specimen.

The Gaedians had the capability to watch over certain alien cultures that they admired and could learn from. The Gaedians and Wizorans were once in unity and had now gone their separate ways. The Wizorans believed in the pleasure of misery and suffering and the Gaedians believed in preserving and protecting life.

6   The Mine War

Looking through his crystal collection of samples that he'd gathered over the years, Cranamar remembered the gruesome times he had as a miner, deep within the dark caverns of Gaed's rocky layers. He also could recall the time when the dreaded mine wars started the battle between the two races on his planet. When the Wizorans and the Gaedians first discovered that their planet had an abundance of minerals, the Wizorans got greedy and wanted total control of the mines and all of the minerals. The tragedy began during the first eclipse of the Gaedians' three moons, when as many as twenty-five Gaedian miners were shot and killed by a squad of Wizoran shock troops. The troops discharged several streams of Plasma Stream Projector beams as they stormed the depths of Gaedian mine shafts, killing ten excavators in the process. Shelves of rock exploded as laser beams struck them, releasing slabs of it and burying workers on impact. This incident brought mineral production to a halt, infuriating many. The Gaedian high council was outraged by this act and demanded troops to be dispatched at once to protect their workers. The council believed that the Wizorans started this in order to force the Gaedians off the planet by terrorizing them. Cranamar was one of the first in command of the operation to respond to a terrorism threat in a primary mining rail shaft.

Cranamar, Gozra, and Vepron were the first to check it out. The Gaedian high council suspected sabotage and advised them to be cautious when entering. The three young cadets took an elevated platform to the top. The primary mine shaft artery started in an external cavern near the surface. Cranamar was the first to enter with his volt rifle raised, walking softly around the twisted and curved mouth of the cave. They all wore their light blue helmets with cyberlinks on the side, their protective goggles up on their helmets, filtration masks to filter out harmful particles and deadly gases, along with their light blue uniforms and shiny Ecron steel body armor. A cyberlink was a special device to help improve aim accuracy on a gun. Cranamar signaled Gozra to his right and Vepron to the left.

The young cadets went their separate ways down the shafts. He saw bodies of dead Gaedian miners lying around. Some were crushed or buried alive by heavy boulders of dark gray Gyrite ore. He also saw tipped-over and wrecked mineral transports, with rocks scattered about. Without warning, plasma fire rang out behind him.

"Rattatatat!" He heard a sound from a shaft behind him.

"Help me! Cranamar, help! They've got me surrounded!" Gozra shouted as he returned fire from his volt rifle.

Sharp electrical bursts of energy lit up the caverns.

"Hang on, I'm coming!" Cranamar yelled as he turned around and picked up his pace. When he got to the end of the shaft that branched off from the main one, he turned the corner and saw Gozra crouched up against the wall with his rifle raised. A Wizoran shock troop stepped into a shaft of bright light holding a rocket rifle. The first actual contact since they were banished eight Chrono-periods ago. The rocket rifle was basically a slanted shaft attached to a stock and it had two handles with a clip in between. The

Wizoran had a closed-in helmet with a dark sun visor; it looked like a moto-cross helmet back on earth. It had a mask and a cyberlink sight on the side of his helmet. He had on his usual dark blue uniform and yellow vertical-striped armband and the same kind of knee boots the Gaedians had. On his chest he had the Wizoran empire insignia on his left lapel. It depicted a yellow triangle outlined in bold black and the triangle was divided into three sections. Its meaning was unknown. The shock troop pulled back on the arming bolt and fired several rounds of rocket ammunition into Gozra's chest, spewing his blood all over. Outraged by what he saw, Cranamar clicked the arming switch on his weapon and pulled back on the trigger, releasing several electrical streams of violet light waves out of the emitter. The shots hit him in both the head and chest, completely encircling his body in electrical energy, overpowering him. Suddenly three Wizoran shock troops jumped down from rocky ledges of the mine and opened fire on him. Luck-ily he was able to dodge their fire. He immediately radioed Vepron for assis-tance while miniature rockets zinged and whizzed by his head. He radioed back telling Cranamar that he was on his way. Cranamar set his weapon to a higher power setting and fired at two of the troopers. One got knocked off his feet and the other one got thrown against the shaft wall. The shots left the Wizorans' bodies convulsing, leaving burn marks on their uniforms and sometimes searing their reptilian flesh. Vepron came charging in, firing his weapon at the highest setting, before they could get a clear shot at Cranamar. Both Cranamar and Vepron shot repeated blasts at the remaining three troops, throwing them to the ground. Cranamar rushed over to Gozra and quickly removed his mask and chest plate. The shots punctured his vital organs and yellow blood splattered all over his chest. Cranamar looked up and saw Gozra was still conscious. Yellow blood had spewed out the sides of his mouth as a result of internal injuries.

"Gozra, everything is going to be all right."

"It's too late, Cranamar, the shells went right through me," he said as he coughed up more blood.

"You were right, we really did have worse situations than this," he said with a smile. Gozra's eyes rolled back into his head as his smile faded into a cold stare. After that, his head slumped to his left shoulder. Cranamar put his head into his hands and mourned Gozra's death.

Rocket ammunition was used in a weapon that fired miniature rockets by use of a pneumatic-driven piston. When the piston was released, compressed air escaped out of the shell casing and the miniature rocket could travel 425 meters before it reached its target until it exploded at point-blank range. When it was fired, four wings opened up and the shell was launched out of the firing chamber. When the shell finally hit its target, it made a small explosion, scattering shards of metal shrapnel. Even with the tiny razor-sharp wings, it could cause a maximum amount of damage. This caused even more damage than the average bullet used during the late twenty-first century. These shells were normally used for armor piercing. Usually any rocket-type weapon could hold fifty to one hundred round clips of these shells.

7   The Future

The next sunrise, the Gaedian high council had a meeting in the council chambers concerning the future of their planet. A large metal door opened in the dimly lit chamber. Five tall Gaedian figures entered and sat at a cobalt-blue semicircular conference table with five tall light blue swiveling chairs, which included adjustable headrests. The table also had built-in consoles on the surface and three Holo-lamps embedded in the ceiling. There was Fadaren Kadril, leader of the Gaedian Dominion, wearing a light blue gown covering his original uniform. It was decorated with gold epaulets on his shoulders; on his left lapel he had a pin of the Gaedian insignia. It was depicting a bright yellow sun and the three known planets eclipsing it. This was representing unity between their world and the other two, Saj Hari and Patoa. On his right lapel he had a bright red sash going diagonal down to his left hip; pinned to it he had his war medals. He also wore dark gray boots with gold trim lining the top of them. Fadaren fought in the war over Patoa with the Wizorans long before the Patoans' extinction. It involved only five squadrons of fighters under Fadaren's command. He later retired from the GIAF to become a leader to his people.

Then there was Quan Dakier, chief of Mining Corps Operations. He wore basically the same decorations, but instead of an insignia pin, he had a patch on his gown, depicting a mining spade and a crystal crossing each other.

Lagril Tazod, administrator of the Gaedian Legion Academy, had the same as Fadaren's only he had more medals on his sash. He was a commandant in the legion, back when the Wizorans were raising havoc, but he grew tired of fighting when they left the planet and became an advisor instead.

Next there was Pato Shagrok, head of the Coalition for Lifeform Preservation. Pato was known for her feminine characteristics more than the general population and she cared about living things more than anything. Her patch showed a person crouched into a ball surrounded by a glowing yellow field.

Finally there was Dr. Ingro Shamaji, director of Planetology and Scientific Studies. He wore his lab coat and it had a patch on his left lapel depicting the planet Gaed and five major stars used for guidance to help Gaedian explorers find their way home. Dr. Shamaji both amazed and boggled the minds of his people with his theories and discoveries over several Chronoperiods. His Light Speed Accelerator, anti-gravity module, and light wave theories had kept them ahead of the Wizorans' primitive technology.

"I have called you all here today to discuss our planet's future," said Fadaren.

"It has been eight hundred thousand Chrono-periods since we first mined it. Since the last invasion our brother race attempted. Our planet cannot withstand another invasion like that again or the subterranean caverns below the surface will collapse. How soon will the Wizorans attempt another, Lagril?"

"Right now it is hard to say. Sometimes they attack within three Chrono-periods, sometimes five, and there really is no set pattern," Lagril replied honestly, as he made figurative gestures.

"Quan, how long until we are totally depleted of mineral resources?" Fadaren said as he pointed to him.

"I would say we have about twenty years left. We only have enough zygate gas to make one journey within our orbital system and enough Ceronium to construct two hundred thousand more control circuits. We have enough Dionium to blow a hole in a Gyrite ore wall nine hundred meters wide and five hundred meters deep, and we have enough Ecron steel to cover an entire hull of a Navoirdic Dreadnought (a spacecraft as big as ten football fields). Finally, we have plenty of Zeonium crystals to power five thousand of our subterranean generators."

"Doctor, how soon can you start working on a terraforming project for the planet Patoa?" Fadaren said as he glanced over at Ingro.

"Well, I don't know. The furthest I have ever gone is my anti-grav devices. I really don't know if my theory on altering gravitational fields will work. I really haven't built any such device that could do the job. I would guess fifty years at the most."

"That's not good enough, Doctor. We need the project completed within twenty, before our time on this planet is up. I want you to continue your research on this and I want current reports when you can get them to me. Also, Commandant, I want those perimeter defense shields up every sundown, night, and sunrise, since the Wizorans choose to attack at those periods of time. This meeting is adjourned." Fadaren stood up from his seat, expressed the harmony sign with his hand, allowed his advisors to do the same, and they all headed out the door. The last person out touched a crystal on the dark gray wall and the lights went out.

"That's not good enough, you need to do better," Ingro muttered under his breath as he sat down at his worktable.

"How am I supposed to do it in twenty Chrono-periods when we don't have all of the technology?" he asked himself as Cranamar walked in, covered in yellow blood, carrying his helmet in one hand.

"What's wrong, my friend?" he said as he turned to face Cranamar.

"I don't know how to break this to you, Doctor! Gozra was killed in that rail shaft today. I'm sorry; there was nothing I could do for him."

Ingro just broke down in tears. "My son, dead!" he said as he cried on Cranamar's left shoulder.

"Gozra was like a brother to me, a close friend, and now he's gone." Cranamar sobbed as he wiped his nose on his sleeve. That experience was too tragic for Cranamar to handle. It brought a fire of rage upon his soul. That kind of feeling would tarnish everything his people believed in, because revenge was a hateful feeling.

The next day, Cranamar, Ingro, Vepron, and all of the people including the leader and his advisors gathered for a farewell ceremony, honoring the dead. Gozra's body was lying on a stone table covered entirely with a crimson velvet-like cloth, outlined with a gold trim, and the gold Gaedian insignia with the three eclipses of their planet embroidered in the middle of the cloth.

"People, friends, and fellow family members, welcome!" Fadaren spoke from a high ledge down to a deep canyon where his people gathered.

"Today is a day of mourning for a fallen comrade, the son of Modaren Kavex and Dr. Ingro Shamaji. Gozra, idealist, visionary, and dreamer, who always wanted to see things change in our time, a change for the good, a change for the better, and a change for the future. Tomorrow we must move on and start anew. He will be missed but not forgotten. Let this tragedy be a renewal for ourselves to start fresh again. We will try our best to fulfill his dream of a new way of life. His loss has enraged a lot of people and I can understand that. It was a senseless act of violence by a barbarian who is a less-than-intelligent lifeform. The only way they can be stopped is by eliminating them entirely out of existence.

"Right now we must focus ourselves on making a better tomorrow and move on with our lives. Let us leave our friend in peace and bid him farewell on his journey through the final stages of life. Let the essence of his body leave our beloved family and rest for the duration of another life. My people, may tomorrow's days be joyful and everlasting from here to eternity. I thank you and bless your forthcoming days."

8 The Spacefortress

It had been ten years since Gozra was killed. Cranamar helped pick the pieces up from his people's loss and moved on with the future. Later that year, Cranamar used his defense expertise and helped supervise the construction of the first spacefortress, his people's first stepping stone to a new home world and beyond.

Cranamar climbed up a ladder made out of Ecron steel bars inside a triangular-shaped maintenance tube. Cranamar remembered when he helped his people put together this fortress, in pressure suits, especially this section of it. Utilizing the waste material from fusion reaction, intense gravitational fields could be generated. When he got to the top, an automatic door shaped like the maintenance tube opened up, and Cranamar climbed out into a little cubicle. This room was sterile white with a relief grid on the walls and ceiling. He pressed a hexagonal green button on the wall on his left, which lit up when he pressed it. A panel opened up on the same wall next to the button. Underneath it were four quadrants of rectangular powder-blue buttons and a circular green scope with a grid on it in the center of them. He tapped them each four times and then another three, making a total of seven taps. On the scope, some words typed themselves on it in his language, telling him that he had just initiated the code to activate the defense systems on the fortress. Cranamar pressed the green button again and the panel closed. Cranamar opened a rectangular double-toothed door lock handle to the left of this wall and he walked down a narrow hallway. The walls had the same look as the cubicle. It was shaped the same way as the maintenance tube, but was large enough to walk through. The floors were covered with circular gray rubbery foot grips. They did not design the hallways with ceilings, just slanted walls.

On his way through, he turned a corner and saw Dr. Shamaji and stopped to talk to him.

"Cranamar, it is good to see you! How have you been these days?"

"I'm just trying to focus on work and not dwell on the past," Cranamar said with a somber voice. The doctor noticed Cranamar didn't feel much like talking. He understood. Some memories were hard to let go of.

"Well, I'm just finishing up a few maintenance and security checks on the station. I never thought I'd see you up here," Cranamar said as he smiled and put a hand on his hip.

"Well, most of us are up here now because our leader ordered us to transfer to the station, in case of another Wizoran invasion. He said it is much safer here because of the new force fields we installed. You helped me design them, remember?" Dr. Shamaji said to Cranamar as he patted him on the back.

"I have to leave the station for a while, but I'll be back in a few days. I have to help finish with the evacuation." Dr. Shamaji tapped Cranamar on the right shoulder and went down the way Cranamar came. Cranamar continued on to the main generator.

He turned a corner in the hallway and proceeded to a room that had no walls, just plexiglass-like windows for walls instead. The sliding automatic doors were designed to fit into cutouts in the walls. He peeked through one of the windows and put a hand over his brow to get a better view. He saw a revolving top-shaped generator with a green glowing band around the center of it and he could hear pulsing vibrations coming from it. It was inside a protective transparent cylindrical chamber surrounded by control consoles with blinking colorful lights. There were people inside the room outside the chamber wearing protective white suits, almost like rain coats or plastic bags. Cranamar entered a small alcove next to the room. He slipped on one of the suits that were hanging inside an open metal locker next to the wall, fastened sideways shield-shaped buckles, and opened a door similar to the one in the cubicle with a lock on it. He entered and the door sealed itself behind him. He stopped to talk to one of the maintenance personnel, who was holding a data tablet and writing implement.

"How is the current on the plasma today?" Cranamar asked the technician.

"It's doing fine now. Dr. Shamaji's idea of using the micro pulses instead of vidcom frequencies worked." The technician spoke with confidence.

Cranamar jumped in, "Also, the reactor gave you more power when we used the plasma from the liquified Zeonium crystals. Keep up the good work and I'll update the doctor on your progress," Cranamar said proudly as he walked over to look at the generator and departed the facility. In the alcove, Cranamar slipped out of his suit. As he left the room, he had a positive feeling within him.

The Gaedians were able to perfect fusion reaction by putting together this apparatus. Poloidal magnets housed the plasma. Toroidal field magnets were making plasma hotter than the core of the sun. Central Solenoid magnets helped generate heat as well. The Gaedians used the super-irradiated Zeonium crystals and turned them into a gas or plasma, and they used their stored energy. Ions and electrons in plasma were made to move more and the product was heat. In a fusion reactor, it was trying to increase particle motion, speed of particles, or number of particles moving. They were trying to move a positive ion one direction and negative electrons the other. The final output was plasma heat to generate steam and the steam was the energy. The sun's core was at least ten million degrees Kelvin. They needed the heat from the plasma to be two hundred fifty million degrees Kelvin for a fusion reaction. The reactor should be at least twenty-five times hotter than the sun.

Cranamar left the room and turned right, heading for the maintenance lift at the end of the corridor. He opened the small door on the one-person lift and entered. On the control panel in front of him, there were multicolored lights and buttons. He pressed the one labeled "down" and the lift engaged itself, slowly making its descent. On the way down, Cranamar thought about how the future of his people's existence had gotten better instead of bleak. They now had the upper hand in technology over the Wizorans. They had nothing to fear from them and now they could begin the healing process. He finally reached the bottom and opened the door to get out. He walked down a long hallway where he entered the hangar bay. There were X-4 Starhawk fighters and transport ships. The transport ships were elongated like the fighters, only bigger. Where the wings should be, there was a gray cylinder that looked like a jet turbine attached to a wing-shaped metal plate. Cranamar saw his friend Vepron bent over in one of the fighters with the tinted canopy open.

"Hey there, buddy, whatcha up to?" Cranamar spoke with a smile.

"I'm repairing the gun control telemetry system for the turrets."

"You should have asked me. I would have been happy to help," Cranamar said eagerly as he pulled out his maintenance tool. He climbed into the two-seated cockpit with Vepron and Vepron sat in the seat next to Cranamar. Cranamar loosened some of the fasteners where the maintenance plate was for the gunner control. He removed a burnt-out circuit, replacing it with a new one. He also rerouted some of the wiring so that it wouldn't short out again.

"There, how's that?"

"Nice work, thanks, pal," Vepron said with gratitude.

"I hear that two Chrono-periods from now, we are going on a mining mission together," Vepron said with excitement.

"Where exactly are we taking the mission to?" Cranamar questioned.

"We are going to the planet Xenthos to mine a new mineral!"

"Isn't that planet too hot for us?" Cranamar said with a little bit of skepticism in his voice.

"Dr. Shamaji is going to send another probe down to the surface to get some samples of its atmosphere and soil composition," Vepron said with optimism.

"When is he going to do this?" Cranamar asked.

"He will send another probe at the beginning of the next Chrono-period. He's working on it right now."

"Let's see how he's doing," Cranamar said as he closed the canopy.

Cranamar initiated a systems check on the weapons and ignition systems. He communicated with the command center and they gave the all clear. He pressed the starter button to fire up the engines. The huge door in the hangar opened. All the air escaped and Cranamar disengaged the magnetic stabilizer that held the ship in place. He pressed the thruster button and he maneuvered the ship so that he wouldn't crash into the other ships. He departed the fortress and he watched on the monitor as the station disappeared from view. There were several stations and some were still under construction. The Gaedians had to dismantle some of the ships in their fleet to build these enormous structures. This particular station had four flat rectangular solar panels, one wider than that in the middle with rounded edges, and one on the bottom a little smaller than the wide one. On top of the flat cylinder, there was a turquoise-tinted dome with white lines crosshatched into a surrounding network. Just below the small cylinder were gun turrets. The small cylinder had four doors, one on each side. That was where the hangar and/or docking bay was. Other stations had geodesic spheres attached at random by Ecron steel rods. It also had antennae and transmitters all over it, the same as the top of the primary station. The ship just glided into the atmosphere and it began to heat up underneath it because of friction from the atmosphere. The ship flew down to the surface and landed on a platform with its struts planted firmly on the ground. Cranamar flicked the switch to open the canopy and they got out.

They stepped on a larger platform than the one-person lift surrounded by a guard rail and it was suspended over a shallow canyon. Vepron pressed the down button and the platform lowered itself to the bottom. They stepped off and Vepron took out his security access card and ran it across a slot on a metal box next to the door and the automatic door opened. When the door closed behind them, Cranamar and Vepron continued down a long corridor to Dr. Shamaji's lab. Cranamar opened the door and entered.

"Doctor, how is the progress on the Xenthos probe coming?" Cranamar asked anxiously.

"It looks like we're going to have to put that on hold for a while. Our leader has just informed me that the Wizorans are headed for Saj Hari, which puts our planet at a symbiotic universal emergency. He has ordered Cranamar and Vepron to take two GDV-57 Maximus carriers, four GDV-99 Navoirdic Dreadnoughts, three GDV-22 Krytha cruisers, and one DST-8 Planetary Explorer frigate and intercept them. Vepron, you have to stay behind and help organize an attack force, because they may attempt another invasion if this mission is successful," Ingro said in a frenzy. Vepron made the harmony sign and departed Dr. Shamaji's work cubicle.

"Well, I better get suited up and I'll see you on board the Navoirdic," Cranamar said with enthusiasm. It had been a long time since the Gaedians had a rescue mission like this one. They were about to get their first taste of action since the Wizorans' insurrection.

9   The Sky People

The years after Parxis's death, the Sedarians experienced their first close-up view of the enormous bird in Aejah's spiritual journey. In the blackened sky of Saj Hari, a huge, elongated metallic bird with brightly colored markings and flashing lights approached the edge of the mesa and hovered slowly until it reached the ground. This event was observed by a Sedarian farmer working in the fields that night. At sunrise, three young Sedarians looked in disbelief over a dune, a distance from the aircraft. They saw what seemed to be huge mechanical wagons moving about and a gathering of crew members outside the ship. Looking up from the horizon was a metallic bird. They ran back to their village shouting, "The sky people! The sky people are coming!" They told the rest of the villagers what they had seen. They described what they saw to Aejah, who told the others. Aejah's advisers explained to him in his primary chambers how big a threat these creatures could become. After what he saw in his dream quest years ago, he feared the worst.

"My lord, I know this disturbs you, but you must understand that if this race is as powerful as you say, we must take cover. Be careful what you say. We don't want to create a panic. Perhaps it's Elyzon coming to warn us of Davon's evil deeds."

"Very well, I will inform my people."

Unfortunately, the advice given was not enough to help the Sedarians. The weapons that these creatures were carrying would be too powerful for them. A small group of these alien beings known throughout the universe as Wizorans noticed the small village nearby. One, assumed to be the leader by its decorations on its dark blue and gold trim uniform, turned around with its back to the mountain and looked up from a crouched position. It growled with hostility in its native tongue and pointed one of its clawed fingers in the village's direction. These creatures were the same as the Phaetozene that died off years ago.

Some of these soldiers invaded the village and beat the helpless and terrified Sedarians to the ground with the butt ends of their rifles. The soldiers who attacked them had on the same kind of uniform that the leader had, except the decorations. They were wearing dark blue helmets with light blue plating, a sun visor, and a face mask with ventilation slits. It also had a cyberlink sight on the side, hooked up to a microprocessor toward the back. They were wearing boots, almost like the ones that the Phaetozene wore. The boots had yellow boot straps coming from around the ankles. Some of the Sedarians were even shot, as a result of their resistance. They were then whipped by a nerve-deadening buzz of electrical cable-like whips to get their loyalty. Next they were apprehended as the guards slapped on these electronic cuff-like devices on their wrists. Finally they were roughly hauled inside the ship, where they were never seen again.

The rest of the villagers got word from what the scouts observed behind a distant dune during that time. One was shot dead trying to sneak away from the site; the other two escaped with minor injuries to bring the villagers this information. The Wizorans had no regard for life forms who had a different point of view from their own and felt that they could come and go as they pleased and do whatever they wanted to. The Wizorans' treatment of the Sedarians was the equivalent of Grax's Phaetozene warriors years ago. Few Sedarians remained in hiding until the Wizorans left. When they did, the Gaedians, their brother race, followed their trail to Saj Hari and picked up the survivors of the Wizorans' raid. They took time to examine the situation and care for the wounded and injured.

The Sedarians' culture was made into a culture that had potential. The Gaedians had admired them for that and vowed to protect them from their brother race. When the Gaedians first landed on Saj Hari, the Wizorans' small fleet got caught in a battle with the much larger Gaedian fleet when it arrived. The bird, where the enslaved Sedarians were taken, was captured by the Gaedians. They were then released from their jailers and taken to one of the Gaedian spacefortresses orbiting their home planet. This was the only way to insure the Sedarians' safety.

The Wizoran fleet was comprised of two WEV-63 Gondien mining freighters and four WEV-87 Nexus battleships. In the Gaedian fleet there were two GDV-75 Maximus carriers, four GDV-99 Navoirdic Dreadnoughts, three GDV-20 Coriden cruisers, and one DST-8 Planetary Explorer frigate. A battle cruiser was about ten jumbo jets long and a freighter was about half of that. The freighter was elongated, thin, metallic, and looked like a bird or a jumbo jet, only bigger. It also had fluorescent-colored markings. This ship was long and curved on top, chrome covered, and it had cubic storage areas overlapping each other on either side of it, in the back. It had two wings swept forward with a big gun underneath each tip. In the front, it had decorative lines slanting toward the back, like gills. The command module had the characteristics of the articulation of an animal's backbone. It also had two slanted thruster engines. A carrier's size was equal to three aircraft carriers in length. It was kind of box-like with slits for windows and rocket engines on it. A Dreadnaught's size was larger than five Empire State buildings lying on their sides. It looked like several globs of mercury squashed together also with slits and engines. A cruiser's size was larger than three aircraft carriers stacked on their sides. One of these are a few of the largest of Earth's structures, the former mentioned being the larger. It was metallic and looked almost like the space shuttle back on Earth. A frigate's size was equal to the Dreadnaught's. It had a dome-like nose on it, a radar dish, two box engines. It also had slits, and was box-like, the same as the carrier.

The Wizorans saw that they were no match for the Gaedian fleet and tried to outrun them anyway. The battleships took evasive maneuvers and broke away from their formation. One of them got hit on the underbelly and was sent hurtling into space. Two of them used an overhead attack pattern head on and disabled one of the Dreadnaught's weapon systems. Its side was blackened and scarred from the damage across the bow. Another battleship was hit in the back by one of the Dreadnaught's cannons. It then collided with another, leaving pieces of metallic junk floating in space. Knowing that they were outnumbered, the second freighter and the two remaining battleships decided to flee the battle. The Wizorans were on Saj Hari approximately seven days. The day they left, the Wizorans' freighter made a loud boom when it activated its thrusters to lift it out of the atmosphere. This of course got the Davonians' attention and made them conjure up a plan. A small group of Davonians made their way up the rocky ridge and peered over the side of it. The expressions on their faces explained how surprised they were. Scattered all over the mesa were charred skeletal remains and debris.

The Davonians were now the soul sentient beings of their planet. Drakor, the captain of the guard, was enraged with the fact that his people were banished from the Sedarian land and it was time they reclaimed it. The thing that angered him the most was that the Davonian people had as much a right to the mesa as the Sedarians did. Also, the Sedarians had more land east of the mesa and the Davonians had a small strip to the west. Drakor decided to organize a party to reclaim their homeland. One night, Drakor led his party of followers to take control over the land and replenish its life. Because Drakor had the power and loyalty of the Davonian army, he could enforce his belief with the people any way he saw fit, regardless of what their leader said.

The Gaedians sent their field commando unit inside the captured mining vessel to release the captives. They wore their light blue helmets with a cyberlink on the side. They wore protective goggles on their helmets, filtration masks to filter out harmful particles and deadly gases, along with their light blue uniforms, and shiny Ecron steel body armor chest plates. A group of nine slowly sneaked along the narrow metallic hallways of the mining freighter. As they saw Wizoran guards dressed in their navy blue uniforms, armored motocross-like helmets, and knee boots, they shot them on sight. The Gaedians used a Tazer-like weapon that shot medium or high quantities of purple electric neutron waves to kill or stun their victims.

Guards got shocked from their positions and thrown against the walls of the corridor.

When the area was secure, they proceeded to the next level, via the servodraulic lift. The same event occurred as before, when they first entered the craft. They blew the electronic sliding door off the track with Dionium detonators from a distance. A young cadet named Cranamar Duraxo led his commandos into the metallic holding chamber. He was the first to enter and remove the electronic shackles from the ragged-clothed Sedarrians. Two Wizoran guards jumped into the doorway and shot a blast of beams at two of the commandos with their two-handled rifles; they turned red just like the beams and disintegrated. Cranamar pulled out his rocket pistol he had taken from one of the Wizorans years ago and pulled the trigger. The piston charged up and two shots rocketed out of the chamber, hitting the guards in the chests. Yellow blood splattered all over and the bodies fell to the floor. The commandos scurried the freed captives to the docked Dreadnaught vessel and the ship released its docking mechanism, leaving the freighter to float helplessly in space.

"Commander, fire two mega cannon beams into that vessel and dispose of it," the Gaedian captain said as he pointed to the viewing scope. It was circular and had flashing red, yellow, green, and orange lights to the left and to the right sides of the dark console. There were also similarly colored buttons blinking on and off. A metallic ball-like gun pod on the ship's deck pivoted to where the freighter was and fired two blasts of beams that literally cut it in half and sent it spinning off into the darkness of space.

These masked, sea-green-skinned creatures hauled the liberated Sedarians into a small room. They were standing on a shiny black floor with tiny white speckles. The cubicle they were in seemed rather dark blue and dimly lit. To their left was a convex wall in the shape of the ship, with a rectangular curved window. There they waited until three of the unmasked green aliens walked in and stood in front of some sort of white screen. They had two long ears, two red and yellow eyes slanting inward that glowed orange when they were in the dark, two three-fingered, clawed hands, were about the Sedarians' height, and very muscular. The aliens were wearing light blue uniforms decorated with fiery-red sashes, golden-outlined shoulder pads, and insignia pins with golden circles overlapping three semicircles. Two of the aliens spoke amongst themselves in a jargon they could not understand. One of the aliens assumed to be the leader stepped forward and put one of its three-fingered clawed hands on one of the Sedarians' foreheads. When he did this, the aliens were then able to speak the Sedarians' hissing tongue. He spoke to the lead Sedarian.

"Hello, my name is Dr. Ingro Shamaji. I'm sorry if we startled you. We got here just in time. We would have lost you for good had we left you in the hands of those animals."

"My name is Garayen Yanx and these are my friends," he said in a non-offensive manner.

"I know that this is going to be hard for you to accept. We cannot return you to your planet."

"May I ask why?" Garayen said with concern.

"This may be difficult for you to understand." Ingro walked over to Garayen and put one of his three-fingered hands on Garayen's muscular shoulder. He spoke with depth and honesty.

"Your planet is dying. With it goes ours and we have to make a new world for ourselves." Ingro walked over to one of the ship's portals and glanced at his magenta-colored rocky home world.

"We've all learned our lesson about destroying the planets we live on and now it is time to move on with life," Ingro said with happiness.

"You see, we have both influenced and admired your culture for many centuries," Ingro said as he turned to face Garayen.

"What do you mean dying? We knew we were living on a dying planet for many centuries. What makes you think it is going to get any worse?"

"Your planet is slowly heating up and it has about eighty years of breathable air left."

"What do you mean by influenced?" Garayen questioned as he walked over to Ingro.

"We knew your people had potential. We did not want your culture to waste it, like many that I've seen," Ingro said with despair.

Ingro placed a hand on Garayen's shoulder again and said, "Violence and disorder are not the solution to life's problems, and you must find peace. I think it is time we all learn to live in an equal environment," Ingro said with a grin.

Garayen had a need to know why.

"Why couldn't you let our civilization run its course?"

"You needed something to motivate your lives," Ingro said with advanced knowledge.

"I really meant it when I said we admire your culture," he calmly said with passion.

"Thank you for helping us. We couldn't have done it without your encouragement."

"It looks like we are going to have a wonderful future together," Ingro said to Garayen as they faced the window looking out into space.

10   Mission to Xenthos

It had been two years since the Gaedians took their first step to finding a new home. Now the Gaedians would brief the chosen specialists on what would decide their fate. That morning, Fadaren Kadril, leader of the Gaedian Dominion, Quan Dakier, chief of Mining Corps Operations, and Dr. Ingro Shamaji, director of Planetology and Scientific Studies accompanied Weapons Engineer Cranamar Duraxo and Structural Engineer Vepron Zuva into the gray briefing room. They would be involved in the mining mission to planet Xenthos, second planet from the sun or the Vorex star. The room had a curved, C-shaped countertop, almost like the ones in a news media station back on Earth. This was where the three present council members sat and Cranamar and Vepron sat in floor-mounted chairs in front of the large desk.

"I've gathered you all here to discuss the objective of this mission," Fadaren said to the group.

"Dr. Shamaji will brief you on the statistics and progress of the probe sent to Xenthos. Doctor," Fadaren gave the floor to the doctor.

"We found some interesting facts on what is supposed to be a very hot planet. What has caused its tremendously high temperatures is the mixture of hydrogen, methane, and sulfur in its atmosphere. This created the greenhouse effect, letting sunlight in but not letting heat out, because of its thick clouds. The core on Xenthos is at least five hundred degrees hot. Its surface composition is made of nickel-iron, zinc, and sulfur. The surface gravity is one point twenty-five compared to our gravity, which is one. A day there is one hundred and eighty of our days and a year is two hundred and seventy of our days. It's also twelve times our planet's mass. What is so interesting is that most of the surface is covered with Chivon dust and there are argon gas vents just beneath it, keeping the surface cool. I have devised a special insulated pressure suit, which has a thick coating of Chivon dust woven into the fabric on the exterior, which has proven to be virtually heat resistant. The planet's atmosphere can make it heat up, but these suits should protect you from the extreme heat. You will be mining Xenthos's surface approximately seven of our days, because we cannot risk your lives any longer than that. The climate changes too often too fast for you to be down there for that length of time. Quan Dakier, chief of Mining Corps Operations, will brief you on the landing procedure. Quan." The doctor turned the discussion over to the chief.

"Thanks, Doctor," Quan said before he proceeded. "I will now show you the equipment that you will be using on this mission."

The deep-voiced Quan stood up and walked behind Cranamar and Vepron to switch on a large data tablet or view screen. He then proceeded to pull out a small pen-sized metallic cylinder and he switched it on and there was a red dot of laser light emanating from it. Cranamar and Vepron turned their seats around to look at what the chief was showing them.

Quan touched a liquid crystal button on the screen below an empty green grid on a black background and a picture of what looked like a pickup truck with treads appeared. This was the same type of grid as the one on the artificial brain that Dr. Shamaji showed Cranamar. The vehicle had a sloped front and windshield. There was a loading ramp in back and tool compartments on either side of the bed with a dumping capability.

"This is the vehicle you will use on this mission. It is the Terrain Trak-four. It is capable of climbing a hill of over sixty degrees of angle. It also has a carrying capacity of over three-quarter tons of loads. Anyone have any questions? Okay, on to the next one." He tapped the liquid crystal arrow at the bottom of the screen and the picture changed. It showed another treaded vehicle that appeared to look like a bulldozer back on Earth, only it was box-shaped and blue. It had a digging mechanism on the front of it and a laser on the end of a robotic arm on top of the vehicle.

"This is a captured Wizoran mining vehicle, which they left on Saj Hari after they enslaved the Sedarians. This is one of several in our possession. It cannot climb as high as the Terrain Trak-four, but it is good at digging, quite deep, in fact. The xenon laser drill can dig into rock five hundred thirty-two meters deep. Any further questions before we continue? Let's move on, shall we?" Quan tapped it again and it did the same as before. The screen showed what looked like a double-treaded army transport vehicle from Earth with a gun turret and two adjustable blast covers above the engines in the back to protect them just like the Wizorans' DS-30 drop-ships. It was larger than the other two mining vehicles, because it needed to make room for them.

"This is the Armored Trak-one. It can carry a load more than half its size. It can descend against a planet's gravity as well as drive just like the Wizorans' vehicle. The mining vehicles I just showed you can be used with the transport ship or this vehicle. You will still use the same mining tools that you've used over the years. The last thing you will be using on this mission is a vacuum hose that will attach to either the transport ship or the Armored Trak-one to suck up any minerals found. Are there any more questions? Fadaren, I give you the floor."

"Dr. Shamaji will go along with you to monitor your progress and to make sure you are in good health. If there are any last-minute questions, feel free to ask them. If not, then I will allow you to proceed with your mission. I now consider this discussion closed." Fadaren and the rest of the council members stood up and made their way out the door. Vepron and Cranamar stood up also, after the council had left the room.

Cranamar turned and looked at Vepron from the corner of his eye and said, "Why did they pick you for this mission?"

"Mineral expert; I have more Chrono-periods' experience than you," Vepron said to Cranamar as he headed out the door. Cranamar shook his head and made a disgusted grimace as he stomped his foot. Cranamar followed his best friend down the long, dark gray Gyrite ore hallway.

"Hey! Wait up!" Cranamar shouted as he tried to keep up.

"You never told me why they picked you," Vepron said with a smile, as they walked next to each other.

"It's kind of an odd job for me. They thought since I had a machinery and servodraulics background that I would be good at making sure the mining vehicles are running okay," Cranamar said as one side of his brow and mouth went up.

"That's not an odd job; I think you would be great at it," Vepron said to his buddy as he patted him on the back while they continued walking down the corridor.

Cranamar rode up on the maintenance lift to the surface, contemplating a question he had asked himself. He had wondered why the Wizorans did not attack his people during a time that left them so vulnerable, like now. That question he could not answer for himself. When he got close enough to the top, he stepped off before the lift could reach it. Cranamar wore his light blue flight suit, dark gray gear harness, dark gray rough-terrain boots, and carried his briefcase-shaped canvas bag, which contained some of his belongings. He walked over to the flight hangar carved into the rock formation and saw Vepron standing next to the dark blue transport ship with the back ramp down.

"Where is Dr. Shamaji?" Cranamar said, surprised.

"Oh! He's already onboard the Dreadnought Navoirdic. He decided to go on ahead of us because he wanted to make sure everything was in order before we got there. Are you all ready to go? We just have to load the rest of the supplies first and then we can head up there," Vepron said with enthusiasm as he checked out his data tablet. Cranamar stood there as he watched the hover loaders carry the metallic cases of supplies onboard the transport. When they backed away, Cranamar and Vepron walked up the ramp and the ramp raised itself to close. Inside, Cranamar strapped himself in with a restraint harness as Vepron did the same. The interior looked very much like a C-130 cargo plane, only more sophisticated. It had straps and nets hanging from the walls and ceiling. The cockpit had four seats with steps in between them and the cockpit. Out of the tinted canopy, they could see a lot of activity going on in space. There were Dreadnoughts, a captured Wizoran freighter, cruisers, fighters, planetary explorer craft, carriers, scouts, and transports. The Wizoran freighter looked almost like a bird or an enlarged jumbo jet with dark fluorescent markings on it.

The small ship entered the landing bay, as the larger ship blinked its white guidance lights. When they were finally in, the two large, curved doors sealed and pressurized. They could see the enormous landing bay, with many transport ships, scouts, and fighters as well as the many decks on either side of the fighters and an elevator directly in front. The back door or ramp opened and lowered itself. The box-like hover loader was waiting outside the loading platform to unload the cargo. Cranamar had been onboard the Navoirdic before, back when the first invasion started, but he was too young to remember; he was only six Chrono-periods old. He had to go onboard because his father had to be there. As Cranamar and Vepron departed the craft, they could hear the dull rumble of the Dreadnought's engines. Dr. Shamaji and the captain were there to greet them.

"Cranamar, I'd like you to meet Captain Zurka."

The captain nodded with a smile. He was wearing a light blue cap with their three-star eclipse insignia and he was wearing a light blue uniform with a reddish-orange sash and a closed golden collar. He was also wearing shiny dress boots. Captain Zurka had been around for a while, since the banishment of the Wizorans. Seeing as the Gaedians aged slower than humans, he looked pretty good aside from a slightly wrinkled brow.

"It's nice to meet you, sir." Cranamar nodded.

"Don't I know you?" The captain smirked.

"I'm not sure," Cranamar said with modesty.

"Are you Nars's son?"

"That's right!" Cranamar responded.

"Cranamar, we're going to prep you, Vepron, and myself, along with some other miners for hyper-sleep, because it is going to take two Chrono-periods' time to get to Xenthos," Dr. Shamaji said as he looked over his data tablet.

The doctor put one hand on Cranamar's shoulder and they walked to the cargo lift to get to the sleep chambers. The captain and Vepron soon followed them. On the way up, Ingro went over the specifics of the mission and the plans of the mining machinery. When they got to the tenth deck, the lift stopped and they got off. They walked down a long, metallic hallway, turned several corners, and Dr. Shamaji pulled out his metallic access card to open the triangular automatic door. After that he punched a five-button sequence code to enter. The door slid open to reveal a powder-blue room with a computation console on their left and a row of beds with a half-transparent cylinder covering them. Some had Gaedians with their eyes closed, dressed in light blue jumpsuits, and some were empty. The room was cool feeling and the hyper-sleep chambers made a humming noise like a refrigerator.

"Shall we proceed?" the doctor said with enthusiasm.

That night, Cranamar removed his terrain boots, slipped out of his flight suit, revealing his light blue jumpsuit. As he sat down on the side of his chamber, Ingro walked in to check on him.

"All set for our long journey?" the doctor said to Cranamar as he helped him into his chamber.

"I guess I'll be seeing you in a couple of years, my friend," he said as he closed the hatch.

The doctor pressed a button to pressurize it and set the temperature, breath rate, and heart rate for deep space travel. Cranamar closed his eyes and dreamt of his future. In his dream, Cranamar saw an alien spacecraft, one he had never seen before. It had wings like a bird and it was stream-lined. It was white in color and there were two engines. It glided slowly through space toward the Gaedian star system. It had five crew members of a lifeform different from his. Their skeletal structures were of different forms and skin pigments unlike each other. Focusing on what planet these creatures came from, he was horrified by the sight he saw. Their atmosphere was almost depleted of oxygen, and in its place were extremely filthy pollutants and gases unbreathable to most lifeforms. Vegetation was mostly wiped out as a result of over-farming. He was astonished with the fact that these lifeforms were transforming their planet into something that looked like the Gaedians' planet and that frightened him the most.

Two years later, Cranamar, Vepron, and Ingro, in their light blue robotic exoskeleton pressure suits, carrying their helmets under one arm, took the cargo lift down to the flight deck after they gathered their necessities. When it reached the bottom, they all headed for the Armored Trak-one. The enormous treaded vehicle was parked next to a transport ship with both the side airlock doors and back cargo door open. It sat on a huge metallic platform mounted in the center of the flight deck's floor. Some of the flight crew were guiding the Terrain Trak-four in as the flight crew drove it up the ramped cargo door, as well as the captured Wizoran mining vehicle. They

climbed into the Armored Trak-one, sitting down next to ten other excavators in their pressure suits without helmets on. The interior of the transport was very much like the transport ship, only more box-shaped. Some
workers held mining spades and a few others had light wave drills, rock
shearers, blast hammers, and vibrating saws.

A vibrating saw was used for cutting softer rock beneath the thick
Gyrite ore. The crystalline-toothed blade vibrated, allowing it to cut. This
tool was different than the standard power saw humans were used to. It had
a handle that was curved toward the front with a guard on the front to protect against the blade. It had a primary rectangular metallic module that
housed the electric motor inside that vibrated the blade.

The vehicles were parked in back of the huge dropship transport and
the excavators between the pilot's cabin and the mining vehicles. The two
airlock doors closed, as well as the cargo door, pressurizing the cabin in
the process. The pilot and copilot sat in a closed-in cabin with a pressure
door facing the crew. The platform lowered the vehicle down into a compartment beneath the forward hull of the Dreadnought. Clamps reached
out and held the dropship from the fore and aft sections, as the platform
lowered to the exterior doors. Both sets of treads turned on their sides and
slid into shafts underneath the vehicle and little doors sealed them inside.
The barrel of the gun turret was already folded up like a telescope with a
protective dust cover over it. The exterior material of this particular vehicle was specifically made heat-resistant like the pressure suits as well as the
mining vehicles. It was also equipped with anti-grav devices on the bottom of it, to help the dropship escape the planet's heavy gravity. The blast
covers on the engines folded up to reveal them. The pilot pressed several
buttons and checked his systems. While doing that, the main command
center onboard the Navoirdic communicated with the dropship.

"Armored-Trak-one, you are cleared for drop launch."

The outer doors opened up to reveal the depths of space with the
orange-red planet of Xenthos below. It had a yellowish haze surrounding
its edges; this was its sulfuric unbreathable atmosphere. It was too hot and
dry to make sulfuric clouds, which would make sulfuric acid rain like on
planet Venus in the Milky Way galaxy. The pilot counted back from five
and then pressed the ignition button. The engines fired up and the clamps
released the craft. It descended first with its bottom toward the planet and

then went nose first, accelerating faster and faster. It entered the planet's atmosphere and streaks of fire lined its path. The cabin rattled and shattered as the vehicle traveled into the hellfires. When it finally came close to the surface, it hovered for a moment with its jets on the bottom of the dropship and gently set down as it extended its treads.

The excavators inside the dropship unstrapped themselves and gathered their gear. They helped each other with their space helmets and adjusted their air conditioners. Some of the excavators climbed into the vehicles and started their electric motors. The pilot announced to prepare for departure and he released the cargo door. As it opened up, a strong gust of hot, dusty wind blew in. The two mining vehicles drove out of the dropship, leaving dust tracks behind in Xenthos's soil. Cranamar looked around and saw a yellowish-orange haze in the sky and a reddish-brown dirt landscape like on planet Mars. The ground was soft but firm enough to stand on. Vepron used his radiation scanner to find traces of extreme heat.

A radiation scanner was used for measuring radiation through several layers of rock. It had a magenta-striped pyramid-shaped sensor connected to a cylindrical-shaped handle. The bottom had a rounded circular end to it with an on/off switch on the handle.

"Cranamar, in some places it's hotter than others, so we better get this job done in a few days, because it could get worse," Vepron said with concern.

In the meantime, Cranamar pulled out his rock depth analyzer and pointed it toward a rock formation that was taller than him. This one was eighty-five feet thick. That was perfect for digging to look for precious minerals.

"Hey, Vepron, come over here!" Cranamar shouted into his helmet communicator.

Vepron handed Cranamar a mining spade and Cranamar began digging into the rock, but it was too tough to penetrate.

"Tell Javox to bring a light wave drill."

Javox slowly came over to Cranamar, because of Xenthos's slightly heavy gravity. Cranamar put one hand on the button and the other on the handle and began drilling. It bored through the rock as it cracked and partially fell apart. He paused for a moment to look at what was inside.

He saw the hard and silvery white metal of nickel-iron in the rock. Vepron and Javox used their mining spades to dig out the mineral and some workers brought over a dark metallic bin with two handles on it. An excavator came over with a rock shearer and the Terrain Track-four soon followed. The worker used the shearer to pry the rock open and found no other minerals. Cranamar, Vepron, Javox, and the other worker went over to an even larger rock, but it was thinner than the last one. They dug well into the night with their mining equipment.

The next day they hauled a load of minerals into the cargo hold. The pilot launched a small satellite into orbit so that they could communicate with the ship above using their micro-pulse uplink. A satellite needed to be sent, because Xenthos's thick atmosphere created too much interference. The satellite was a metallic cylinder attached to a metal ball with two antennae and blue flashing lights on top of it. The pilot communicated with the ship and asked to have five freight rocket pods sent down to them. That afternoon, five pods were jettisoned from the Navoirdic and soared down to Xenthos's surface. When they touched down on their landing struts, two doors automatically opened on top. The pods were metallic and cylinder-shaped with two engines sprouting out of each side of the back on a flat cone connected to the cylinder. The Terrain Track-four began dumping loads of minerals into the pods to be delivered back to the ship. That night, the excavation crew slept inside the dropship. Suddenly, they felt a rumble and then the radiation alarms went off. Cranamar looked on the view monitor to see what it was. It was a flare from the Vorex star. The pilot immediately pressed a button and a geodesic dome came out of a compartment on top of the transport and began unfolding. The dome was made out of a special alloy to protect them from the radiation. Cranamar looked on the monitor again and saw the flare's plume and the tip of it had distorted it and dissipated its energy in Xenthos's heated atmosphere.

"That was close!" Cranamar said as he wiped his brow. They heard squawks and static from their uplink; they could barely make it out.

"Navoirdic to Xenthos 12, come in, Xenthos! I repeat, Navoirdic to Xenthos 12, come in, Xenthos! Our home world just informed us that you'll have to prepare to journey back home in two days. A Wizoran invasion force is coming soon and we must return at once," Dr. Shamaji said.

"How many more days away is the invasion force?" the pilot asked with concern.

"Thirty days!" the doctor replied.

"Tell them to defend it as long as possible; we'll be there as soon as we can," Vepron said as he grabbed the communicator.

"Understood. Navoirdic will be advised. Over and out!" the doctor signed off.

"It looks like we're going to have to get busy, on the double," Cranamar said with disappointment.

"Come on, let's move!" Vepron said as he clapped his hands together.

Cranamar finally got his answer as to the whereabouts of the Wizorans. It didn't really help his situation any or make it any better.

The workers put their helmets on and gathered their equipment. The pilot closed his pressure door and opened the inner airlock door. They stepped in two at a time, the door closed, and the outer door opened. Cranamar opened a compartment on the outside of the vehicle and pulled out a beige corrugated vacuum hose and flicked the on switch. He sucked up some Chivon dust that might be clogging the hover jets underneath the transport. Plus it gave them some more dust samples. He then turned it off and put the hose back, closing the compartment.

Xenthos only had one mineral that was really important to the Gaedians and that was nickel-iron. Sulfur and zinc were no use to them. Sulfur they didn't really use and zinc was too weak of a metal for the Gaedians to use. The nickel-iron could be used for reinforcing their Ecron steel alloys.

The Terrain Track-four loaded the last of the nickel-iron into the last available pod. The workers pressed buttons on each of the pods to close their doors, pulled levers to unfold the launch ramps, and detached them. They opened up panels on the sides of the pods and pressed a button that said launch on it. There were five red lights below that counted back from five and then they closed their panels. The engines fired up and they blasted off, escaping the planet's heavy gravity. When they left the planet and were clear of gravitational forces, the engines shut off. The Navoirdic coasted over the pods and picked them up with a robotic grappling arm, closing the cargo doors that came out on the bottom of the ship. The two mining vehicles drove into the cargo hold and the door closed. The miners put their tools away in compartments inside the dropship. The workers then removed their helmets, sat down, and strapped themselves in. They then began to rest for their trip back to the ship.

The next day, the pilot fired up the hover jets and activated the anti-grav devices. The craft shook and rattled as it made its ascent. When it escaped its atmosphere and gravity, it pointed its nose up and rocketed toward the launching bay doors as they opened. It slowly drifted in, landed on its platform, and the huge doors closed. The cargo door opened and the dirty and tainted vehicles backed out and drove to their designated parking spots between ships. When Cranamar, Vepron, and the excavators finally came out of the dropship, the cargo door closed. An officer approached Vepron and Cranamar.

"Captain Zurka wants you to report to the bridge right away."

Vepron and Cranamar hurried to the cargo lift and immediately took it to the top. The bridge was located at the top of the ship and in the center of it. When they got to the top floor, they departed it and walked down a long, wide corridor to the end of it. At that far end, there was a wide, tri-angular door. Cranamar walked up to it and touched the control to open it. They walked through a control room with open doorways and turned a corner, where there was another triangular door. This one had a metal box with a keypad on it instead of a button. Cranamar pulled out his access key-card and ran it through a slot on the top just like the other security doors he used and the door slid open. They saw many computer consoles with bright, colorful lights blinking on and off underneath some slits for portals looking out into space. Standing in front of the gray view screen were Dr. Shamaji and Captain Zurka. The doctor turned around with a concerned face.

"It doesn't look good for our home world, Cranamar," the doctor said as a tear trickled down his right cheek.

"What can we do?" Cranamar said as he felt helpless.

The captain turned around and put a clawed hand on Cranamar's left shoulder.

"Without this ship, which is used mainly as a blockade vessel, the planet is literally defenseless. The perimeter defense stations and the space-fortresses are our only hope. In the meantime, our people are going to begin the evacuation."

"Where are we supposed to go?" Cranamar questioned.

The doctor pulled a transparent rectangle of crystal with microcircuits inside from his lab coat pocket.

"This is where we will go," he said to Cranamar as he placed it in a slot underneath a monitor on a blackened background.

It showed a computer simulation of the frozen planet of Patoa on a black background. Then four round, metallic orbs with lights and circuitry on them moved simultaneously over four points of the planet. A green grid covered the planet and then the ice melted, thus forming clouds. Then it showed the planets Gaed and Saj Hari with Patoa as the fifth planet from the Vorex star. Patoa moved from fifth planet to fourth, right next to Saj Hari and Gaed side by side, filling in the large gap between them.

"You mean, you can actually move planets with those orbs?" Cranamar said with amazement.

"Yes, we can. You see, by altering the planet's gravitational fields and moving it to the correct position in the solar system, we can adjust its climate and create a breathable atmosphere. These devices, which are known as Planetary Shift Modules, or PSMs, are orb-shaped, in order to simulate the planet's gravity. Normally, we can't do this with any ordinary planet, because it could disrupt the other planets' gravity if their distance from the sun is not exactly right. It also can't be used on a very hot world, because there are no elements to be released and used as an atmosphere. If we move it, it would become a dead planet without an atmosphere. Gaed won't lose its atmosphere or gravity, because it has enough mass to maintain it and the planet will not allow its atmosphere to escape into space. There you have it. Are there any further questions?" the doctor said with an open mind.

"Won't we have trouble breathing on this planet, because of it having more oxygen content?" Vepron said with interest.

"You will at first, but after you have breathed it for so many years, you'll get used to it. After all, it will be better for us, because our planet is losing its plant life and will no longer have any oxygen in our atmosphere. Many of our people will test in enviro-chambers first after it is terraformed, to get used to it. Any further questions? If not, then let's move on," the doctor said as he took his crystal bar out of the slot.

"What about all of your research back on our home world?" Cranamar said with curiosity.

Dr. Shamaji lifted a flap on his lab coat and opened a box on his belt and put the bar on terraforming away. The box contained seven more crystal bars.

"I'm never without them. Ever since that spy stole the plans to that new laser weapon, I haven't trusted myself or the Wizorans," Ingro said reassuringly.

"We'll let you, Vepron, and the excavators get some rest in hyper-sleep. You'll only have to stay in the chambers half of what it took to get here. You and Vepron have to go on ahead of us to coordinate the attack. We'll wake you when we get there. You and Vepron can go get prepared and I'll be back to set your chambers," Dr. Shamaji said as he saw them off.

"Captain, let's head home!"

The captain walked over to the middle of the room and sat in his navy blue leathery swivel chair. He gave the order and the rumble of the thrusters engaged.

11   Doomed World

From a distance, the captain saw the Wizoran fleet of freighters, WF-7 Deceptors, WEV Nexuses, WF-20 Interceptors, and dropships amassing for an assault on Gaed. The Interceptor was dark brown with two tail wings and two side wings. The fighter looked almost like a hawk and it was highly maneuverable in combat. It had two seats in it, one for the astrogator and one for the weapons officer. It also had two landing skis, particle beam blasters in front of each side wing, and two thrusters in back. The sides of the ship looked kind of boxy, like the dropship. This fighter was not seen very often by the Gaedians. Some speculated that it was used in mostly covert missions. They might never know its true usage; only the Wizorans knew. The Gaedians did know that it was not another one of their stolen technologies.

The Gaedian fleet was hiding on the far side of their planet.

The captain had to hide his vessel behind the desert planet of Saj Hari so that they didn't get spotted by the Wizorans. A strike by the entire armada would completely destroy the Navoirdic. It was tough but not that tough.

Cranamar lay in his hyper-sleep chamber, groggy and blurry-eyed from his long hibernation of only one year. Dr. Shamaji sat at his bedside waiting for Cranamar to get awake.

"Cranamar, wake up!" the doctor said softly.

"Go away! Give me another year's rest," he grumbled as he rolled over.

"Come on! It's time," Dr. Shamaji said as he laid out Cranamar's astrogator suit and helmet.

The suit was dark turquoise with yellowish-green armor plates in some spots. There was a brown strap on the left shoulder as well as a metal clasp on the left arm. The helmet looked like a bird's head, with breathing slits in the mouth area. The visor had two ovals connected, was shiny and a little bit tinted. The boots were yellowish-gold and had kneepads. The strap was for his oxygen mixture in case his ship got damaged beyond repair. He also had gloves that fastened to his suit.

"Oh! All right, I'm coming!" Cranamar said with frustration. He sat up and turned, sitting on the bedside. He rubbed his eyes, squinted a bit, and slowly opened them. He grabbed his astrogator suit, slipped it on, as well as his boots. He then picked up his helmet and put it under one arm.

"How close are we to the Wizoran fleet?" Cranamar inquired.

"We are about a year away from them, but with your fighter, a few days," Ingro informed him.

"How much of a difference can that be?" Cranamar wondered.

"Well, because it is smaller, it can go faster," Ingro said as he headed for the door.

"Are you ready to go?" Ingro said.

"Let's go for it!" Cranamar said with confidence.

"Vepron's already on the flight deck getting your fighter ready."

The doctor pressed the button and the door slid open. Cranamar turned the corner and walked down the long hallway to the cargo lift. He pressed the down button and it lowered to the flight deck. He stepped off and ran to his fighter with helmet in hand. There were other astrogators in flight gear, preparing their ships for launch, as well. The canopy was open on his and Vepron was adjusting the vector control on the control panel when he looked up to see where Cranamar was.

"Hey there, buddy! How's it going?" Cranamar said with recognition.

"Seeing as we're about to go into battle, I don't think things are good at this time," Vepron stated.

"I'm only glad to see ya. Nothing major is necessary," Cranamar explained to Vepron.

"Come on! Climb in!" Vepron said anxiously.

Cranamar stepped through the mess of hoses and mist left over from the Zygate gas line. He climbed up the ladder leading to the pilot's seat, flicked a few operations controls, and pulled the servodraulic lever that closed the cockpit. He pressed the engine firing button and the engines and retros test fired. With the jets running, they both placed their attack helmets on their heads, safely tucking their ears inside. They pulled down their tinted goggles, positioned their chin straps, and lowered their micro pulse uplinks to mouth level. They then helped each other connect their oxygen tanks and strapped themselves in. Cranamar then pressed the firing button for the retro rockets and pulled the lever to draw the landing gear in. As he put his hands on the control sticks, he clicked the orange thruster switches on them. This launched the ship out of the bay and into the vacuum of space. The other ships soon followed.

They soared at top speed in formation for several days behind the planet of Saj Hari, heading for the far side of their world. In thirty days they were able to travel safely to the rest of the fleet without being detected. They approached the lit-up landing bay of the GDV Maximus, a carrier, and they each landed one by one into the upside-down trapezoidal-shaped mouth of the bay. They landed in the large hangar deck of the enormous carrier and allowed their ships to refuel as the astrogators were briefed on their tactical plan. They entered what looked like a lecture hall with chairs and desks descending toward a darkened holo-display screen and glass-like desktop where the tactical specialist sat. Cranamar and Vepron sat down and placed their helmets on their desks as well as others who entered.

"Is everyone seated? If so, then we can begin," the specialist said as he switched on the display.

"All right, here's the situation. The Wizoran fleet is on the far side of our planet, amassing for an attack," he said as he pointed to the simulation of the Wizoran fleet compared to theirs on the opposite side of the planet.

"We must send our fighters over our upper atmosphere and surprise their fleet. We will also send two GDV-22 Krytha cruisers to help evacuate the planet and provide cover fire. Any further questions?" The screen showed their planet with a squadron of their fighters drawing arcs over the top of it with the two cruisers, one on either side of them.

"How are we going to get close enough to the fleet without getting totally obliterated?" Javox said with concern.

"That is a very good question," the specialist said.

"The only way you can do that is by allowing the Wolfraider-1s to get close enough to launch their concussion warheads at the larger ships and that will give you enough time." The screen then showed a light blue ship that was wishbone-shaped with two engines and a three-crew-member cockpit. It also had small side wings, a gun in front of each of the engines, and a rocket underneath each of them. The nose of the ship was flattened and there was a circular door on each side of it. This ship was only in the experimental stages but in working condition.

"Any further questions?" the specialist said with enthusiasm.

"May your mission be a successful one."

The pilots all departed the forum and took a lift to the hangar deck. There were the light blue Wolfraider-1s, green X-four Starhawks, and navy blue transport ships parked on either side of the hangar next to the walls. Cranamar climbed up the access ladder, and just before he got to the top, he turned to look at the Wolfraider as he held on to one of the rungs. He had his doubts about that ship. Ever since his father had disappeared, he feared and questioned the safety features on it, whether it would get his people through the battle or they would go down as they took hits.

"Cranamar, is there something wrong?" Vepron said as he held his helmet with both hands while sitting in the gunner's seat.

"What? Oh! I'm sorry, what did you say?" he replied.

"You seem to be a little preoccupied right now. Are you feeling okay?" Vepron said with concern.

"Nothing, I'm fine!" Cranamar snapped.

"Look, I know how you feel about that ship, but we need all the help we can get. Doubting its performance is not going to bring your father back. Now let's go!" Vepron said as he set Cranamar straight.

"You're right! Come on, we got a war to fight!" Cranamar said in better spirits.

"That's the spirit!" Vepron said with enthusiasm.

Vepron put on his helmet as Cranamar climbed into the cockpit. After preparing themselves, Cranamar closed the canopy. They both flicked switches and pressed buttons as the engines started up. The entire squadron of ships hovered and lined up with the launch chute. One by one, they blasted into the chute, picking up speed as they went. The squadron of eighty-two fighters departed the large tube and lined up in formation while in flight.

The Wolfraiders glided overhead and the Krytha cruisers soon followed with their gun turrets poised. The fighters skimmed over the atmosphere of the purple planet of Gaed with the cruisers and Wolfraiders surrounding them to provide cover fire. As soon as they got to the far side of the planet, the fighters broke formation and scattered, as well as the larger ships. The Wizoran fighter squadron of brown ships chased after the Gaedian fighters in a frenzy of red laser fire. Ships exploded, chunks of metal scattered, and fireballs lightened the darkness of space. Blue lasers came out of the emitters from Gaedian gun turrets and destroyed several Wizoran fighters in the process. Cranamar noticed on his Tactron display that three WEV Nexuses broke away from the attack and began to enter the atmosphere. The perimeter defense stations reacted with bolts of blue lasers as they tried penetrating their thick armor. One station exploded, showering the sky with huge pieces of shrapnel. Cranamar and another astrogator piloted their craft into their planet's atmosphere where those battle cruisers went. He could see through his cross-hairs on his Tactron combat holo-display that two Interceptor fighters flew overhead, passing the Gaedians by.

"Almost in range, just a few more meters," he said to himself.

Running out of options and time, Vepron readied his firing stick.

"All right, I got you now," he growled. He pressed his left thumb down on the blaster turret positioning switch and the gun turrets automatically moved to forward combat position. He then squeezed the orange trigger button, firing repeated beams of light wave blasts. The guns were synchronized so when used with telemetry, they could move the guns with the stick. Vepron targeted one of the two ship's engines and squeezed the orange button in front of his telemetry stick. There was a bright orange, smoking fireball and the large ship turned away, drifting nose first into a canyon. The metal hulk crashed and exploded into pieces of shrapnel. The two fighters glided over the large ships and came around for another pass. Red beams of light came out of the big cannons of the Nexus and missed their designated targets. The two fighters came at the cruiser, one on either side of it, and fired multiple blasts. Cranamar flew his ship at the forward hull of the Nexus in a frontal attack pattern head on and Vepron fired right into the command module. The front of it burst into flames and the nose went down. With the ship on fire, it tipped to one side and plunged itself into a rock face.

With two perimeter defense stations severely damaged, Wizoran dropships were deployed. Four of them had already landed and two had positioned their rocket racks at the mountain guns. They fired four SG X05 (ship-to-ground) rockets and the guns exploded, sending debris down to the bottom. Cranamar flew his fighter down to the surface and landed it with the landing struts out.

"Come on, we've got to get out of here before those dropships find us," Cranamar said as he unstrapped himself and took his helmet off.

Vepron looked at Cranamar and drew his rocket pistol. Cranamar looked back, pulled out his, and pulled back on the piston armament bolt. The pistol looked like the average firearm, only it had a slanted handle and an almost cylindrical barrel, except for the end, which was closed in a bit and curved.

Cranamar popped open the canopy and they both climbed out. "Meet back here in one hour. If I'm not back by that time, leave without me. That is an order, Lieutenant. It's too dangerous out here," Cranamar commanded as he bent his arm to point his gun up.

"What are we doing down here anyway?" Vepron wondered.

"We are here to provide any help with the evacuation that might be needed," Cranamar said.

"What about the ship?" Vepron said with concern.

"Don't worry about it. They won't find it," Cranamar said with confidence.

Cranamar entered a dark, empty cavern, holding his gun up with two hands and walking softly to be aware of intruders. He quietly moved through the dampness as water dripped from the stalactites. He could feel vibrations in the floor of the cave from incoming bombardments outside. The fragile crystalline stalactites and stalagmites developed over millions of years of time were slowly being shattered in a matter of milliseconds. He creeped along the darkened, empty hallways as bits of rock debris crumbled to the floor. He stumbled as larger chunks tried to cave in the whole corridor.

Down where it was lighter, Cranamar saw a doorway being blasted open by two Wizoran space troopers. They wore standard spacesuits made out of dark brown material resembling velour. The helmets looked almost like a fighter pilot's helmet back on Earth, complete with a silvery-tinted visor, helmet radio, and oxygen hoses connected to a respirator control box. The troopers also had terrain boots with shin guards and a device that overloaded their suits' systems and destroyed the body with suit and all in order to prevent their enemy from capturing them. They would prefer not to be interrogated and reveal their secret operations to the Gaedians. They held their two-handled rifles with flared barrel ends and they had a disintegration setting.

Cranamar hid around the corner with his pistol raised. When they finally kicked the door open, Cranamar turned and pointed his pistol with two hands at the intruders.

"Stop or I'll shoot!" Cranamar shouted angrily.

One of them raised a weapon and Cranamar fired off two rounds into the trooper's chest. He flipped backwards from the impact of the small rockets. He then fired one toward the other trooper, missing him as he scurried out the way he came in. Cranamar walked swiftly toward the body and slid the trooper's gun away with his foot. He knelt down on one knee and lifted the trooper's visor, releasing a hiss of oxygen. The green, scaly Wizoran was coughing up yellow blood out of its fanged mouth. It had entirely different facial features than the Gaedians. There were fins jutting out from its cheeks. It also had big ears, yellow, snake-like eyes, and it had five clawed fingers on each hand, unlike the Gaedians.

"You people are pathetic! What do you expect to gain from this?" Cranamar said as he grabbed the Wizoran by the lapels of his uniform.

"Every last thing you value!" he said as he spit yellow blood in Cranamar's face.

"Your people killed one of my best friends!" he yelled as he wiped the blood off his cheek.

"Your people are so smart it makes us look mindless," the Wizoran said as he choked on his blood.

"You're just jealous," Cranamar gloated.

"We hate your kind and everything you stand for!" he snarled.

"You're killing innocent people! How does that make you feel?" Cranamar said as he shook the trooper by the lapels.

"Numb!" He laughed out loud as he clicked a red switch on his leg.

Cranamar quickly bent down to try and shut it off, but it wouldn't.

"It's too late!" the Wizoran chuckled.

Cranamar growled as he let go of the trooper's uniform. He looked down on the cave's floor and saw the other trooper's hand blaster. It looked like a .357 Magnum of ancient Earth with a handle guard on it. He grabbed it and ran like the wind. The trooper laughed louder and louder as Cranamar hustled down the hallway. He ran farther down the corridor and turned a corner. At that moment, the device exploded, leaving a dust cloud in its wake. Cranamar peeked around the corner and noticed that the hallway was sealed off. He turned around and proceeded down the hall toward his leader's chambers. The doorway had collapsed and the room looked dead. He cleared some of the debris to make a path for himself. He saw his leader pinned under a piece of the cave's ceiling. His yellow blood was splattered all over his chest, arms, and the rock.

"Cranamar, help me!" Fadaren cried.

Cranamar went over, moved a piece of Fadaren's dented and twisted metal desk, and tried to lift the huge chunk of rock that was crushing his leader. He tried as he might to budge it, but couldn't. He grabbed a loose metal rod that held the ceiling up and attempted to use it as a lever on the stone slab. He moved it just enough to push it off Fadaren's chest. Fadaren lay on the floor, coughing up blood, with his light blue uniform soaked in it.

"Come on! We've got to get you out of here," Cranamar said softly.

"You go on without me! I'll only slow your escape," Fadaren said with labored breathing.

"I'm not going to leave you!" Cranamar sobbed.

"Cranamar, you must understand that we don't live forever. My time is up. Go on now! It's time for you to start your future," Fadaren insisted. His face remained plain and his eyes rolled back into his head as he passed on.

Cranamar looked up with a tear on his cheek and got up off his knees. He holstered his rocket pistol and raised the hand blaster. Upon leaving, he felt another impact tremor and the ceiling in his leader's chambers gave way. He scurried down the hallway while small rocks and debris showered over him. He rushed down the corridor as fast as he could, where he finally saw daylight at the end of it. He lowered his sun goggles and continued through the walkway until he reached the end. A ramp of Gyrite ore formation led to the outside, where he proceeded.

Outside, he saw the enormous Krytha cruiser almost in the shape of a jumbo jet but ten times the size. At the bottom of it, there was a loading ramp with many Gaedian citizens going up it. Over a hilltop, Cranamar saw a garrison of Wizoran shock troops approaching the cruiser. They had on dark blue and gold trim uniforms and they wore terrain boots. They were wearing dark blue helmets with yellow plating, a sun visor, a face mask with ventilation slits, and their ears sticking out of the top. The helmet also had a cyberlink sight on the side, hooked up to a microprocessor toward the back. A platoon of Gaedian troopers went over to intercept them. Their uniforms were similar to the Wizorans', only a lighter shade of blue and yellow trim. Their helmets were dark turquoise and they wore sun goggles. They had their clan's insignia of the three eclipsed Gaedian moons on their sleeves and they wore Ecron steel body armor on their chests. Their rifles were quite larger than the Wizorans'. The weapon was kind of a combination of an Earth assault rifle and a carbine with just a frame for a stock and a handle guard.

Red and blue laser bolts flew from both directions. Some soldiers fell, while others kept charging. One of the shock troops attempted to attack the civilians, but Cranamar dropped his rocket pistol and grabbed a hand blaster. He managed to hit the trooper with a few bolts of laser fire.

His body flew backwards and flopped down like a rag doll, while his gun fell and broke into several pieces.

Two more broke off from the assault and charged at the ship, firing multiple blasts of red laser fire. Cranamar heard a shout from behind him and Vepron came running with his rocket pistol raised. Five miniature rockets flew out of the chamber and two struck one soldier in both the chest and arm. He fired two more with deadly accuracy as a laser bolt grazed Vepron's left shoulder; he winced in pain when it passed. They went right through the soldier's visor, squirting yellow blood all over his helmet. His body slumped down like the others and there was smoke coming from all the troopers' wounds. The rest of the shock troops had been killed by the field commando unit.

"Is that all of them?" Vepron asked Cranamar.

"That's all for now!" Cranamar replied.

"Good, let's get the rest of our people onboard before there are any more," Vepron said anxiously.

They both stood there with their weapons raised as they looked side to side for shock troops. When they finally loaded the last person onboard, Cranamar and Vepron motioned toward the ramp as it was closing. When they got halfway up it, Cranamar said something to Vepron. He put a hand on Vepron's right shoulder and said, "Our leader is dead."

"What happened?" Vepron said with concern.

"A piece of the cave's ceiling came down on top of him," Cranamar explained. "By the way, what happened to our fighter?" Cranamar asked.

"It was destroyed when I returned to it," Vepron clarified as he gave Cranamar a dirty look.

The two of them entered the ship and departed the sunken platform. The ship was much smaller than the Navoirdic, because it was used for transporting large numbers of people for an exodus. Cranamar and Vepron entered a large cargo bay where the decks of the ship were outlined with railings. They stepped onto a cargo lift and took it to the bridge at the top.

When they got to the top, they proceeded down a long hallway to the very end, straight ahead. When they got there, there was a door, which Cranamar proceeded to access using his access card. He slid his access card across the top of the control box and entered a three-digit code. The door opened and revealed a lift that led to the bridge. Cranamar and Vepron got in and the door closed. The lift automatically rose to the top without even giving it a destination. The door then opened, uncovering the semicircular bridge with a railing just below a large view screen straight ahead. There were control consoles to the left and right of the command center. Dr. Shamaji stood behind the railing staring beyond their planet's atmosphere. Cranamar and Vepron walked over to him and they stood on either side of him.

"We're just about out of our atmosphere," Ingro said without making eye contact.

"How many more ships are coming, besides us?" Cranamar wondered.

"Two more are coming!" Ingro replied.

One Krytha cruiser glided away from the planet's surface with one trailing close behind it. Laser fire broke out behind them as a squadron of the brown Interceptors chased after the cruisers. One of the three engines on the trailing cruiser went out as it took a hit. Two of the gun pods on the belly of the ship turned toward the back of the cruiser and returned fire. Five of the chasing fighters exploded on impact as the targeting lasers struck them. As the cruiser sustained some damage, the ship started tipping to one side because of the unbalance in the engines. It finally lost its altitude and dove down, nose first into the rocky surface of Gaed. The damaged hulk exploded as it hit the rocky surface of the planet, leaving a small mushroom cloud.

The other cruiser hightailed it out of there with minimal damage. Now that the perimeter defense stations were destroyed, the gigantic Nexus battle cruisers began firing on Gaed. Red beams of lasers came out of their large mega cannons, causing several direct hits on the planet's surface. Then the subterranean caverns collapsed, creating immense fiery explosions on the rocky planet of Gaed, sending a shockwave beyond their solar system and into space as chunks of rock floated away with it. Cranamar felt the rumble of the tremendous concussion blast against the hull of the ship as he hung on to the front railing. Bits of rocks and debris clattered on the ship's metal plating as the ship struggled to stay on course. When it had passed, Cranamar and Ingro gasped in relief.

"Whew! That was a close one!" Cranamar said at ease.

"I thought it was going to take us with it!" Vepron said.

"Where are we going to go now?" Cranamar said as he looked up at the doctor.

"Don't worry, Cranamar! In thirty Chrono-periods, that will be our new home," he said as he pointed to the planet Patoa out the ship's porthole. Ingro turned to face Cranamar and said, "While you were gone on Xenthos and in your hyper-sleep chamber, I was able to calculate a method to terraform Patoa using my anti-gravity theory. It's complicated, but I think I can make it work.

"It's time to move on and look to the future. You must forget our home world, Cranamar, because it isn't our home anymore. You knew the time would come sooner or later, and it has," Ingro said with faith.

Ingro put his clawed hand on Cranamar's shoulder and they both stared at the planet Patoa as the sun shined on its crystalline icy exterior. The Wizoran fleet retreated to the far side of Gaed and disappeared from sight.

12　Making Contact

It had been ten years since the destruction of the Gaedians' home world, and they had just begun rebuilding what was left of their civilization. During those years, Dr. Shamaji worked on completing his terraforming theory, but there was much more work to be done before. The Wizorans had regrouped at the edge of the galaxy to refuel and plan their next assault. It would be years before the Wizorans could begin another attack on the Gaedians after taking a beating from them during the invasion. The Gaedians considered themselves lucky since the Wizorans' last invasion, considering that was one of their most vulnerable times.

"Cranamar, it's time!" Ingro said with compassion. Cranamar set his portable console down after reminiscing about his planet's struggles and triumphs during the last decades of his youth.

Cranamar and Dr. Shamaji, in their powder-blue flight suits, walked to the circular airlock where the test ship for a light speed accelerator was docked. Looking in the room, Cranamar saw the dark blue curved wall and the skylight overhead looking out into the stars.

"Take one last look, because this might not be here when you get back," the doctor said as he looked into Cranamar's eyes.

"Why won't it be here when I get back?" Cranamar questioned.

"You see, Cranamar, it's time to begin a whole new generation of our people," the doctor explained. "We may be gone for almost one hundred trillion years before we return. While we are traveling the speed of light, people back home may have been born and passed away during our trip. Those are the risks when using this means of transportation," the doctor clarified.

"What about Vepron and Captain Zurka?" Cranamar asked.

"Vepron will be going along, because I know he's your best friend. Captain Zurka will stay behind. He's seen better days, I'm afraid, and besides, his body could not withstand being put under suspended animation for the amount of time we're going to be gone," the doctor enlightened Cranamar.

"I know we are testing the accelerator, but where exactly are we going with it?" Cranamar wondered.

"We are going to help develop a whole new generation of rare life-forms, especially the supreme ones, and bring back samples. There is a small portion of species threatened by extinction that we need to save," the doctor elaborated.

"What is this place?" Cranamar said with curiosity.

"It is known by the primary inhabitants as Earth," Ingro told Cranamar. "Enough questions! We have work to do," the doctor said without hesitation.

They entered the airlock's circular doorway and then entered the transport ship. This ship's interior was much different than the other transport ships'. It had a cargo hold with a specimen pod, three hyper-sleep chambers, and a cockpit with two seats facing the tinted canopy.

"Welcome aboard, Commander! The course has been programmed into the computer," Vepron said upon greeting.

"It's time to get into our chambers. The ship will activate the accelerator when we are in our chambers and it will stop at our destination. The chambers will automatically open when we get there," the doctor explained to Cranamar and Vepron.

"Closing airlocks and retracting docking tube," Vepron said as he pressed a button on the command console.

All three of them climbed into their chambers and the hatches closed, activating the life support systems and the light speed accelerator. The engines engaged to give the ship a boost and then there was a flash of white light coming from the accelerator. The ship slowly coasted away and began gaining speed as it opened up a hole in space and went faster than light, through the portal. The hole closed up and disappeared from sight.

The Gaedians were able to make their multiversal travel device into an engine form by placing two Kazium crystals on a spacecraft and exciting the entire vessel; unidirectional travel in a ship could be achieved. By changing phase of crystal excitation and the relative position of the crystals to each other, guidance and velocity could be controlled. By utilizing harmonic sidebands, velocities in multiples of light speed were attained. Dr. Shamaji made it possible to literally create a tunnel in space and shorten the distance between two points by half.

They traveled googols of parsecs, as generations of Gaedians came and went. (A googol is a number with a one followed by one hundred zeros. One parsec is 30,857,000,000,000 km or 19,174,000,000,000 mi. One parsec equals 3.26 light-years in human terms.)

Cranamar, Vepron, and the doctor were automatically awakened by the ship's artificial brain. Trying to get awake, they each ate a nutritious meal and began their duties. Cranamar readied the short-range teleportation device to take them to the surface of Earth in Central America. The Gaedians salvaged the old version of the light speed acceleration device after developing the light speed accelerator. They altered the old device to transport at short range from ship to planet, rather than by rocket pod. The rocket pod method of travel was difficult to accomplish, because calculations for vectors in propulsion had to be precise. This had to be done or the small craft could run out of fuel and drift off into space.

A blue shower of sparkly light materialized on the planet. Cranamar, Vepron, and the doctor were in the Esquinas Forest in southern Costa Rica, one of the last protected lowland tropical rainforests on the Pacific coast of what use to be Central America. They were in a clearing in the center of what was left of the national park declared by the Costa Rican presidency. A long time ago, funds had to be raised to buy the land and preserve it from further deforestation. Now, as a result of their lack of funds and Costa Rica being a somewhat poor country, logging had to proceed because the industries were needed to maintain their economy. They clear-cut this large habitat as result of the slash-and-burn farming and logging. What was left of this forest was now endangered because of the industries.

"Cranamar, we have come because this forest is precious to all living things, including us, and we are going to take it back with us. We are going to start a new life. This lifestyle will have no violence and no environmental destruction. We'll finally have time for a culture of our own, that's if the Wizorans don't return." The doctor spoke with great awe as he explained his vision to Cranamar and Vepron.

In order to bring something with such an enormous diversity of life-forms back home with them, the Gaedians had to use a method called molecular reduction. It involved slowing down electron orbits in atoms, in order to shrink the size of molecular structures. The theory was, if you slowed down anything that orbited, such as a planet in space, it would eventually move in closer and somewhat compress together. The only other way to transport something this large would be to use a ship twice the cargo's size. A bigger ship could not do the job, because it needed to be small in order to travel at the speed of light. The Gaedians had to perfect a way to allow more mass, such as a larger ship, to travel in this fashion. They believed it to be unstable when it involved more mass, especially when traveling at speeds faster than light.

Ingro scanned the area for any humans and found none nearby. Vepron and Cranamar set down a large metallic box with some sort of emitter array attached to it and several multicolored buttons on top of the box. The doctor had them aim it at the remaining forest as he directed them using an electronic transit or surveying device. When he gave the signal to begin compression, Cranamar pressed a button and the emitters lit up, charging their coils. Then he pressed one to focus the beam and the device energized the forest as it was reduced and sent up to their ship. Dr. Shamaji took a look at the barren wasteland of what used to be a large rainforest and imagined it full of foliage and various forms of life, such as insects, furry mammals, flowers, and amphibians. The once blue sky was now brownish-yellow with a haze of pollution. Then the doctor handed Vepron a crystalline cube.

"Dr. Shamaji! What is this?" Vepron asked.

"Think of it as a portal into the future, my friend," said the doctor.

"In order for these people to understand, they must learn our ways!" the doctor defined more clearly as he took the cube from Vepron's hand.

"Why would you want to explain this to humans? They wouldn't understand the meaning of our intentions!" Cranamar blurted out.

"Cranamar, my boy, perhaps when you are older, you'll see it more clearly," Ingro said with a chuckle.

"I guess you're right! Maybe when I'm older I'll understand it better," Cranamar sighed.

"After all, you are forgetting, Vepron is older than you!" Ingro added.

"Stick with me, my friend, and you'll learn something," Vepron said as he put an arm around Cranamar's back.

Ingro gave the cube back to Vepron and said, "I believe you know what to do with this."

Vepron nodded and knelt down to bury it in the Costa Rican soil. They each looked around one last time and decided to leave this almost dead planet. Ingro looked down at his hand and tapped a few buttons on a small, flat control almost like a remote control. The blue light surrounded them again and they disappeared from sight.

All three of them stared at the tiny version of the Costa Rican rainforest in the specimen jar.

"Soon, my friends, you will see this in a larger size. But not until several years from now." Ingro smiled.

Cranamar and Vepron climbed back into their hyper-sleep chambers as Dr. Shamaji programmed their course to head back home into the ship's artificial brain. He eventually climbed into his hyper-sleep chamber. The ship slowly turned around and opened a tunnel in space as it zipped through in a flash of light.

13   The Galactic Patrol

Eighty years had passed since the destruction of the Gaedians' home world. Their enemy, the Wizorans, thought that all would be lost for the Gaedians and that their technology would be for the taking. The Wizoran Empire had been broken up into a smaller faction called the Marauders that conducted raids on supply freighters that traversed between Terran and Gaedian colonies. No Terran had ever seen a Wizoran face-to-face and lived to tell about it. When the Wizorans raided the freighters, they stole the contents and then destroyed the ship. One day, one such event occurred. The station was monitoring an ore transfer from a freighter when the chief monitor felt a shake in the station like something hit it. Then there was what sounded like a muffled explosion. The freighter was adrift on one of the monitor screens. Meanwhile, on planet Xanthu, a Wizoran named Torack, a primary leader to his people, attempted to escape during the transfer. A WF-20 Interceptor shaped like a falcon took its grappling claws and punctured the side of the freighter's hull. The cockpit of the Interceptor opened up and the two pilots got out in their spacesuits. One of them grabbed a bulkhead and placed a charge on the main cargo hold and released himself from the ship. The charge blew out the atmosphere, allowing them to enter. They gathered up the ore with a suction bag and allowed it to float out into space. One of them remained in the ship upon killing the pilot. The Wizoran steered the ship over to where it would pick up ore. He stuffed a spacesuit into the ore expeller as the expeller rotated back in. Torack hurriedly got into the spacesuit and got into the expeller to leave the prison. The damaged freighter and the Interceptor along with the ore left through the Hypergate. The most precious resource the Wizorans had been after was Gyrite ore, because Ecron steel was made from it. Ecron steel was one of the strongest metal alloys ever made on this side of the universe. Since Gyrite ore was in short supply as a result of the Gaedians' home world's destruction, these were trying times.

Several centuries before the mine war and before Cranamar was born, the Wizorans were banished to the barren blue moon of Xanthu. The moon was used as a penal colony before they were banished to it. The Wizorans started trouble by not working together with the Gaedians on gathering resources for all their people. Quan Dakier, chief of Mining Corps Operations, discovered that there was a deficiency in minerals. The Wizorans were stealing some of the minerals that the Gaedians were mining and hiding stockpiles of them. The Wizorans also enslaved some of the mining workers to help them perform this devious act. From then on, the Wizorans were sent to Xanthu. They did not wish to use their knowledge to survive on their own, and instead, they wanted all the work done for them. The Gaedians had to rely upon slave labor from the Wizoran prisoners in order to speed up production. The moon of Xanthu was also rich in Gyrite ore. After mining the precious mineral, the prisoners put it into a shipping container and it was picked up by the freighter by use of a grappling arm. Security had to be very tight during the transfer operation to prevent a prison break. However, it was ironic that the very ore the Wizorans were trying to steal, they were being forced to dig up as punishment.

At the present time, the Gaedians were in the process of building dispursal domes for greenhouse gases on the frozen moon of Patoa, which had a slightly thin atmosphere. A small orbiting station had been monitoring its progress. Construction could be difficult when building materials were in short supply. Xanthu had an orbiting monitor station as well, but this one controled a force shield surrounding the moon to deter escapees. The steel shortage had been so bad it had affected the building and repairing of ships.

Cranamar had now been promoted to commander of weapons engineering detail. During these times of struggle, Cranamar had to keep his crew up to speed on the maintenance checks to make sure all defense systems were operational and ready for an imminent attack. It would take at least twenty more Chrono-periods before Patoa was ready for habitation and it had been already at least eighty. Since their home world's destruction, the surviving refugees had to live aboard orbiting spacecraft or habitat domes on Patoa until their new world was complete.

The Gaedian people had spent most of their lives fighting and running from the Wizorans, with no time for developing a culture of their own. Before the Gaedians could actually build structures on Patoa, they had to have the Gaedian planetary engineers develop some spherical devices that were capable of altering orbits in comets or asteroids by manipulating gravity wells. These devices would have to be embedded into the rock. With the proper trajectory, they directed comets at the poles of Patoa. The dry ice and the permafrost would boil away, adding its mass to the atmosphere. The carbon dioxide in the dry ice and the permafrost would increase the greenhouse gases. Since Patoa's atmosphere was almost devoid of breatheable air, this would make it habitable again.

For the time being, a special task force was assembled by Fadaren Kadril, leader of the Gaedian Dominion. It was called the Galactic Patrol and its job was to make sure the supply freighters got between planets safely without them getting raided by the Marauders. Since there was quite a distance between the Gaed planetary debris field and Patoa, the patrol had to keep a watchful eye out for pirates.

"This is Commander Duraxo; I am ready to initiate launch sequence," a voice came over the microwave pulse uplink.

"Begin filling fuel tanks with Zygate gas mixture."

"Securing airlocks now," transmission squabble came back.

Cranamar flicked on several switches and pressed many buttons as he heard the whine of the long-range booster engines powering up. Going out on routine patrols to guard the transport freighters coming from Xanthu from Wizoran attacks was always business as usual for Cranamar. This mission wasn't like the normal missions he was used to. According to Gaedian intelligence, somewhere beyond the Vorex system, the Wizorans might be rearming again since the war ended over eighty years ago. Worst-case scenario, the Wizoran pirates, or Marauders, as they were called, would attack the Gaedians now, when they were most vulnerable, rebuilding their habitat. This would be a scouting mission but not like the ones he was use to.

For the time being, the only means of long-distance space travel would be through a series of gates close to the speed of light. The superconductivity of the Ceronium had enough power to operate the gate even though it was only being used for their computers in the past and even now. The Gaedians called it the Hypergate; it was only being run by a small cube of the Ceronium crystalline element. The gate basically made a shortcut between star systems. The technology for the light speed accelerator was still in the experimental stages and was at least a century away from being at full-time use.

After one full day of work, an unidentified vessel was detected by the Xanthu penal colony monitoring station. Just as the last transport freighter prepared to dock with the habitat dome on the planet Patoa, the Gaedian communication officer received a transmission. The micro-pulse transmitter picked up a signal of an unidentified spacecraft approaching.

"Unidentified spacecraft, please identify youself."

There was no response. He repeated the communication. There was still no answer. A moment later, there was a vibration coming from outside the station and then there was a muffled explosion. When the officer was able to get a visual of what was happening, he saw a transport freighter adrift on the vidcom. It must have had its engines disabled by someone or something. A ship that looked like a WF-7 Deceptor was dragging the freighter in tow, helpless, by a bright blue beam from the bottom of the craft. The fastest the Gaedians could respond to the problem was sending Commander Duraxo after the ship. Their new long-range experimental and modified-from-the-original-craft, the X-4, had long-range engines that ran on the Zygate gas mixture and could run on it for almost eight hours. The freighter was dragged to its intended destination, through the Hypergate.

Meanwhile, on Xanthu, three Wizorans were mounting an escape plan. Torack, the leader of the unit, found a way to modulate a device using salvaged parts smuggled in from his damaged ship, before he was captured. The way it worked was, it operated like the microwave pulse transmitter. The force field sealing the mining shaft off so that no one tried to escape could be turned on or off by finding the right frequency. Between Natorg and Varx, they decided at night during the freight transfer would be best. They sat in the tunnel where the freighter would make its pickup. When security turned the field off in this sector, they would make their move. Supposedly their device they made would expand the opening in the field if successful. They had friends on the outside who had been trying to help them from time to time unsuccessfully. Their friends were fully aware of when they were successful to make their move.

When the alarm sounded to warn the inhabitants of the airlock opening, Torack turned the dial all the way to the left and slightly right, disabling the one sector of the force field. When the door finally opened, a cylinder rotated within a cylinder to dump the ore into the freighter. The three prisoners climbed into the freight container. Then the outside cylinder rotated back inside the ship. The Wizoran ship and the freighter in tow were headed for the Hypergate. When Cranamar saw this on his screen, he made a transmission to the monitoring station.

"This is X-4 leader on patrol. There is an intruder in your sector. Is there any ship that can assist?" Cranamar spoke over the vidcom.

"Ah! That's a negative. There are no ships available. Looks like you're on your own with this one," the night shift station operator said.

"Has the planetary debris field been cleared of all necessary mineral deposits?"

"According to our long-range scans, there's barely enough to fill a crater. Not worth protecting," Cranamar said over vidcom.

"Does General Lagril Tazod of the Gaedian Legions agree?"

"Just one moment. Let me check," the station operator said. "He agrees, destroy the gate."

Nearing the Hypergate, Cranamar fired a laser blast at the Deceptor's engines and disabled it. He did another and destroyed it, leaving the freighter floating in space. Then, with the general's orders, they destroyed the Hypergate.

Exodus from Earth

1 The Underground City

Sitting at the multimedia desk console in the historic library section of an underground city, mission commander Kyle Preston of the SEED (Space Exploration and Extraterrestrial Discovery) Project, was scanning through the last century of post-nuclear history. He was appalled by the horrors that humanity had to endure during the past century. It was encouragement enough to find a place for future generations of human life to flourish. Kyle turned off the view screen and got up from the console and exited the long, velvet-like carpeted hall of towering data library CPUs. Kyle met Dr. Pavlowski in the long, cubic-like sterile white hallway.

"How are you feeling today, Commander Preston?" Eli said with a Ukrainian accent.

"Fine, fine … When are we due for launch?" Kyle inquired.

"As soon as the new Geostat satellite says we have clear skies," Eli said with confirmation. "We want the area of atmosphere above our launch site to be free of nuclear contaminants to ensure that we don't pollute other life-giving worlds with our own messes," Eli responded.

"Well, keep me updated on any further developments. See you later," Kyle said as he started to walk away.

The air outside the complex became unsuitable for human habitation and the refugees had to be moved elsewhere. They had to create genetically engineered humans for the underground city, because the scientists, who designed and built the structure, wanted it to be a sterile, white, clean environment. Besides, the place had to be for the mass driver Kyle helped the scientists and engineers design it. Most of the women were sterile and couldn't have children, so they had to preserve the future of the human race or they would die out and become extinct.

Kyle was a baby from a test-tube mother and was given to the Preston family, making Colonel Wayne Preston his great-grandfather. Kyle was twenty-five years old; he had dishwater-blond wavy hair and brown eyes. He was born inside the complex and had never seen the outside world. For a while, Kyle was a computer science specialist with a background in astronomy helping out with Project SEED to ensure that humankind had a future. It was their last chance and their only chance. Time was running out for the human race and their artificial atmosphere was limited. The subterranean complex project was undergoing construction during the infiltration crisis of North Korean troops into Russia in 2091. It was finished twenty years later in 2111 and Kyle was born in 2145. The present day was 2170 and five days before launch of the experimental Russian AV-forty shuttle transport. Scientists and engineers were testing and checking all the equipment very carefully to make sure that everything was in working order before launch, because they had only one chance at this.

Here's how the launch mechanism basically worked. The launch tube was dug at a sufficient depth underground, deep inside the Altal Mountains. Areas of energy storage and support were also built. To eliminate air resistance, the electromagnetic track, which was one hundred twenty-five kilometers long, was lined with capacitors, which were enclosed in an evacuated tube. The crew would have to endure ten G's for fifty seconds during launch. Launch capsules for satellites could get into orbit with thirty G's on the upper forty-five-kilometer track. The tunnel ran horizontally for most of its length and then gradually climbed when the spacecraft was accelerated to a velocity of five kilometers per second. When the spacecraft came out of the tube at an altitude of five to six thousand meters, it was already halfway into the atmosphere. The laser array propelled the craft by burning into ice made of liquid oxygen and hydrogen. The steam would propel the craft up out of the atmosphere by accelerating it to orbital velocity.

Kyle turned a corner a continued down another long corridor to a secure area and entered a code pass and a five-digit access code and the door slid open to his right. He entered a shorter hallway to an intersection of three doorways. He pressed a button on a door control and walked into a small briefing room with a cobalt fiberglass composite table and chairs. In front of him sat three people—an oriental young woman with her black hair in a ponytail, Dr. Eli Pavlowski, and a Hispanic man in his thirties. The woman wore a red, shiny jumpsuit with a patch of a Japanese flag on it. Dr. Pavlowski was balding on top and he was wearing a white lab coat, khaki pants, a white shirt with a green grid design of stripes, and he was wearing brown loafers. The Hispanic man wore a blue jumpsuit and it had a Spanish flag patch on it. To his right was another woman and she also had on a blue jumpsuit with an Irish flag on it. To his left was a young black man with thin black hair, wearing a red jumpsuit with a Zimbabwe flag patch on his right shoulder. Dr. Pavlowski addressed Kyle as he sat down.

"Mission Commander Kyle Preston, this is … Dr. Elaine O'Mara, psychologist with a background in anthropology." Kyle shook her hand as she sat down. As he was introduced, he shook everyone's hands. She had wild dark red hair and blue eyes.

"Kari Morimoto, technical engineer with a background in quantum physics." The doctor pointed to his right.

"Jose Gomez, geologist." The doctor pointed to his left.

"Dr. Kwasi Maica, biologist." The doctor pointed to his right. Kyle was holding what looked like a pen, but really was a remote-controlled pointer. He was standing in front of a wall-mounted video screen.

"Gentlemen, ladies! You were all selected for a very critical mission. As you already know, our planet is dying and you need to search out a new world habitable for human life," Dr. Pavlowski spoke. "I'm glad that the five of you have volunteered for this mission, because the five of you are our last hope to safeguard the future of humanity. Mission Commander Preston," Eli said as he turned the briefing over to Kyle.

"We have equipped the spacecraft with the latest in space technology. It will have a microwave radio telescope high-gain antenna array so that we can communicate over long distances and not be out of range. There will be oxygen replenisher tanks with algae growing hydroponically inside them. As you breathe, you feed the plants carbon dioxide and they feed you oxygen. There will be the latest in explorer probes and handy robots to help out during the trip and take samples of passing asteroids. We will have frozen sperm and eggs in liquid nitrogen for artificial fertilization for human colonization. There's a fluid reprocessing system to recycle bodily fluids. There will be food similar to the MREs, or meals ready to eat, used in the past century for this long trip for the five astronauts. We will be protected by reinforced metal shielding to protect the orbiter against micrometeorite bombardments. It will have photovoltaic cells to recharge the spacecraft's fuel cells and it will have a plasma propulsion drive. Solar energy is collected and converted into plasma."

An early twenty-first-century veteran space-shuttle astronaut with six flights under his belt, Chang-Diaz, described the Variable Specific Magneto plasma Rocket, or VASIMR, as a system using radio waves that heat rocket fuel—in this case, hydrogen to super-hot temperatures.

Diaz said that rockets tended to work much better the hotter the exhaust was and the plasma allowed them to go to temperatures millions of degrees rather than thousands of degrees in a conventional rocket engine.

Plasma, known as the fourth state of matter, was an electrically charged gas made up of atoms stripped of electrons. Plasma typically occurred in environments of high pressure and temperature, such as stars.

Thrust from the plasma engine could boost a spacecraft for a longer time and with better efficiency than conventional engines.

The heart of VASIMR was three magnetic cells that ionized, amplified the heating, and directed the flow of the plasma. The superconducting magnets worked a bit like a microwave oven by stimulating the hydrogen molecules, thus heating them.

Controlling and directing material as hot as a star had been a major challenge for researchers. No known solid could contain such super-hot gas, so superconducting magnets could generate a field that corraled the plasma. Development of such magnets had been the key to development of the engine.

In order to harness the plasma at those temperatures, the only way was to have a very strong magnetic field to hold it together. The only way to create those fields in a reasonable way in space was with superconductors. Another key feature of the plasma engine was its ability to throttle, which allowed it to increase or decrease in thrust when needed to enter or escape a planet's gravity. This was analogous to a car using a lower gear to climb a hill, then shifting to higher gear on the open highway.

Early tests near Earth used solar arrays. Deep-space tests would have most likely required nuclear power to provide the wattage needed to heat the plasma.

"To protect against atmospheric friction, the bottom of the orbiter is covered with a sandwich of special woven metallic mesh-like tiles of titanium/silicon carbide. Since we will not need them to maneuver in space, the wings are retractable and won't be damaged by micrometeorite bombardments. The landing gear will have skids instead of wheels to land on rough terrain. During the long trip into deep space, we'll be put in hyper-sleep chambers so that we are in a state of suspended animation. This will slow the aging process as well as our bodily functions. Any questions so far?" the mission commander said as he paused for inquiries.

"Five days from now, we'll be launched using a mechanism known as a mass driver. Basically, it's a gigantic catapult using magnetic levitation technology. The Geostat satellite will give the go-ahead to make sure we are free of any radioactive contaminants.

"Any further questions about the mission? Good, now Dr. Pavlowski will brief you on what we'll be doing on this mission. Doctor," Kyle said as he turned the briefing back over to Dr. Pavlowski.

"Dr. O'Mara, you'll be doing psychoanalysis on the crew if they require it as well as trying to understand the psyche of any intelligent life you discover, understand?"

"Understood, Doctor," she said with an Irish Gaelic accent.

"Kari, you'll be doing maintenance checks on all the equipment and provide technical assistance to any of the crew that needs it, okay?"

"Understood, Doctor," she said with gentle swiftness of a Japanese woman.

"Jose, you'll be operating the robotic sampling arm as well as outside gathering of rock samples from passing asteroids and giving analysis, understand?"

"Understood, Señor Eli," he said with a mild Spanish accent.

"Dr. Maica, it is your job to examine new forms of life and take samples if necessary, understood?"

"Understood, Doctor," he said with an African accent.

With understanding of what they were suppose to do, the group got up from their seats and shook hands with one another. They filed out of the room and walked and talked down the long, echoing hallway.

Dr. Eli Pavlowski was one of the original settlers of the underground city and helped develop much of the advanced technologies involved within the city. When he entered the city, he had to undergo decontamination as well as the refugees and early ancestors. He was born in the Ukraine in the year 2105 during the invasion of North Korean troops into what use to be Siberia. He left the Ukraine when he was nineteen and went to Georgia to study metaphysics and quantum mechanics. He also decided to get a degree in genetic engineering. He had a dream to send a deep spacecraft into space and find a new home for humanity. When he was thirty-two, he left Georgia and was called over to Kazakhstan to work on a top-secret project involving digging underground tunnels. Most of his life, he helped with the project and lived to see his dream come true.

Kyle walked down a long, narrow corridor to the bunking area and pressed a door-opening control, sliding it sideways to the right. Elaine was standing by her bunk, looking at a data tablet. Kari was kneeling on her bunk and looking over Elaine's shoulder. Dr. Maica was lying on his stomach looking at a data tablet as well. Jose was examining a small meteorite with a magnifier.

"Oh! Commander Preston, I didn't see you come in."

"What are you looking at, Dr. O'Mara?" he said with inquiry.

"It's a schematic of the ship. Pretty impressive, isn't it?" she said with astonishment.

"Quite a remarkable technological achievement," Kari agreed as she pointed to the fuselage of the craft.

"Excuse me, ladies, I'm going to check on Jose and Dr. Maica," Kyle said as he strolled over to Jose. He knelt down and asked, "Was that the same meteorite the crystalline cube came in?"

"I don't know. I'm not even sure it came in this rock!" Jose said with amazement.

"Is there any significance to this rock?" Kyle said as he pointed to the meteorite.

"Other than this crystalline texture on it, I would say no, not really," Jose analyzed.

"I'm going to go check on Dr. Maica. I'll see you later." Kyle got up and walked over to Kwasi's bunk.

"How's it comin' with those tree samples of ancient Earth?" Kyle asked with interest.

"I'm comparing the trees of two centuries ago that had pollutants with the ones that didn't a century before that," Dr. Maica said.

"What's the difference?" Kyle said with intrigue.

"Very little; the only effect it had was the amount of sunlight let in as a result of the high density of carbon dioxide released into the air," Dr. Maica answered.

"Thank you, Doctor, that was most intriguing," Kyle said as he bid his good-byes.

Dr. Elaine O'Mara was cloned in Scotland in 2137. She wanted to preserve her life, as well as her future, for the sake of humanity. In 2162, she pursued a career in parapsychology and studied the art of ESP as well as exploring other regions of the brain not yet understood by human knowledge. She was asked to be included on a special project somewhere near Russia.

Jose Gomez was born in Barcelona, Spain, in 2148, in a sealed nuclear fallout shelter encased in a sandwich of solid concrete, steel, and lead. Some of the fallout shelters like this one failed because they either didn't get sealed properly and allowed radioactive fallout to leak in or gave the people lead poisoning. Jose's mother died of breast cancer and his father was killed by an angry mob during a food riot. He was left with his only surviving aunt and his young sister, Maria. When his aunt died, he left Barcelona with Maria when he was sixteen in 2164. He passed through Sicily, Italy, and was so fascinated by volcanoes he went to examine Mount Etna on the eastern coast of Sicily. After that, he was so interested in rocks and minerals that he decided to become a geologist. He traversed through Austria, Slovakia, and the Ukraine until he met Dr. Pavlowski. The good doctor took Jose under his wing and taught him more about the scientific world.

Dr. Kwasi Maica was born in Zimbabwe in 2134. He left his homeland when he was fourteen to pursue a career in biology. He studied the remnants of life from a long-forgotten Earth. The Sahara Desert had spread to most of the continent over a century ago and fighting had expanded to the surrounding countries of Somalia as a result of a lawless government. He wanted to study the history of biology and someday discover life on other worlds and compare it to the kind of life that used to be on Earth. He was summoned to a top-secret project somewhere in Kazakhstan in 2170, present day.

Kyle sat in the pilot's seat of the AV-forty in front of the control panel.

"Mission Control, beginning systems check sequence on the AV-forty Deep spacecraft. Go or no go for launch?"

"Geostat satellite results of atmospheric check on airborne radioactive contaminants," Mission Control said to Commander Preston.

"Go!" Kyle replied.

"The Laser Array positioned and ready."

"Go!" Kyle said in response to the check.

"Are the magnetic-levitation capacitors charging up?"

"That would also be a go," Kyle said back as he flicked some overhead switches.

"Is life support on the hyper-sleep chambers in working order?"

"That would be an affirmative on the go."

"Is the robotic sampling arm operational?"

"We have a go on that."

"Is the propulsion fuel in place?"

"That would be a go."

"Is the radio wave stimulator charged and ready?"

"That would be an affirmative on that."

"Are the hydrogen gas tanks set and ready?"

"That's also a go."

"Are the superconductors charged up?"

"That would also be a go."

"Is the emergency nuclear generator charged up and ready?"

"We are a go for that as well."

"Are the retractable wings folded and secure?"

"That would be an affirmative go on that."

"Is the microwave radio telescope array functioning?"

"That is a go on that as well."

"The oxygen replenisher, is that ready?"

"We are a go on that."

"Is the hydroponics system in working order?"

"That would be a go on that as well."

"Are the frozen sperm and eggs stored away and secured?"

"A go on them as they sleep like a you-know-what."

"Is the fluid recycling system in working order?"

"That is a definite go on that."

"Is the food storage locked and secure?"

"That is another definite go."

"Are both fuel and photovoltaic cells charged and ready for the journey?"

"That is an affirmative go on that."

"Is the landing gear retracted and safely locked in?"

"I confirm a go for that."

"Finally, are the designated star system coordinates entered into the spacecraft's computer?"

"All systems are go." Kyle stood up, feeling proud of himself.

"Have a safe and pleasant journey."

"It is T minus ten minutes and counting."

2   The Launch

Kyle sat strapped into his seat wearing his usual orange flight spacesuit in front of the main control panel, flicking the overhead switches.

"It is T minus ten minutes and counting," the Russian said over the PA system.

"Well, let's have a look-see. The sky is as clear and blue as can be. We're just waiting for the go-ahead from mission control." Everyone on base called the guy over the PA system The Cowboy, because his southern accent reminded the Americans of good old-time America, before the war started.

Kyle remembered while the mass driver was under construction, when they finished the end part where the craft would leave the track. This was long before the laser array was built. They sent a capsule with the self-deploying Hypergate with coordinates to a designated star system. Astronomers said it was, possibly, somewhere at the edge of their universe. It was still in orbit as they waited for their vehicle to be deployed.

The scientists began walking across the gantry in their orange space-flight suits wearing their white helmets with their visors closed. They were also carrying their air conditioners, because the launch tube was sealed in a vacuum outside the ship to remove any air resistance that would interfere with the launch. The scientists entered the airlock and sealed it. They strapped themselves into their seats, lifted their visors, and disconnected their air conditioners.

"Mission control is giving you a go for launch. Hang on to your saddles, buckaroos, this is going to be a rough ride." There was laughter over the com. The gantry bridge lifted up and retracted.

"It is T minus one minute and counting," The Cowboy said to give a friendlier flavor to the atmosphere, instead of the strict, disciplined military attitude of the Russian.

"Beginning countdown sequence in fifty seconds." The crew looked at each other to see if everyone was okay and to basically give each other the look like, *Well, this is it, see you on the flipside.*

"The countdown begins now, ten, nine, eight, seven, six, five, four, three, two, one, zero."

At first, everyone braced themselves for an enormous concussion of force. All they got was a bone-jarring bump from the rear. Everyone exhaled when that was done, but it was just getting started. The next one was bigger. After that, it was huge and it kept going until they picked up enough speed to gradually catapult them high into the atmosphere. They finally got high enough for the laser array to take over, creating the steam to propel them into orbit.

"Happy trails, buckaroos," The Cowboy said, as the craft ascended.

3   Alien Contact

Once in orbit, the crew unfastened themselves and floated to their hyper-sleep chambers. Kyle programmed the artificially intelligent computer, coordinates to the designated star system, so the computer would wake them up. On that note, he climbed into his chamber, as the hatch closed. The coordinates in the computer automatically activated the Hypergate and the ship plunged into a tunnel of blue and white light created by elongated stars. Kyle and the scientists traveled while they were in a state of suspended animation for at least fifteen days after they left Pluto, the Kuiper Belt, and the Oort cloud, until it abruptly lurched forward and stopped.

The computer woke Kyle up. He checked the data. It turned out to be a passing comet. Kyle scratched his head for a moment and thought about how he was going to get their ship back on course. Then the idea hit him—use the microwave high-gain antenna to reestablish the link to the Hypergate. What he was seeing now was different random patterns of gas and dust in distant space. So, Kyle reprogrammed the computer for the ship to go back to its original jump point and start again. The ship disappeared and reappeared at the gate only to begin again. He finally climbed back into his chamber, where Kyle as well as the rest of the crew hibernated for at least eighteen years.

When Kyle and the rest of the crew finally came out of hyperspace, the whole crew was awakened. Then when everyone was done yawning and stretching, they all floated back to their seats and strapped in. The wings unfolded and they maneuvered via retrorockets through a larger solar system than what they were used to. The crew saw snowy worlds, worlds with electricity going between them, rocky worlds, and worlds that they'd never seen. They looked so alien to them compared to their own. They soared in and entered the atmosphere of the eighth planet of the solar system. They landed on a flat, grassy area next to some turquoise domes. They all attached their helmets to their spaceflight pressure suits and connected their air supply as well, because they weren't certain about the atmosphere.

They entered the main dome's doorway. Unsure about the air, Kyle took a chance; he removed his space helmet with his eyes and mouth closed. Then he exhaled. He finally inhaled, allowing him to relax and breathe.

"It's okay; you can take off your helmets now. The air is breathable," Kyle said as he coughed and struggled to catch his breath. The scientists took theirs off as well.

They were standing on a four step high white speckled bluish metal platform. The cubicle they were in seemed rather dark blue and dimly lit.

To their left was a curved wall. To their right, they saw three aliens, light green in skin color, with two long, pointy ears like a bat, two reddish-yellow eyes slanting inward, and two three-fingered, clawed hands. The aliens were shorter than average humans and very muscular. The aliens were wearing light blue uniforms decorated with a fiery-red-colored sash, golden-outlined shoulder pads, and an insignia pin with a golden circle overlapping three semicircles. Two of the aliens spoke amongst themselves in a jargon the humans could not understand. One of the aliens assumed to be the leader stepped forward and put one of its three-fingered, clawed hands on each of their foreheads. When they did that, the aliens were then able to speak English.

"How did you do that?" Kyle said as he stood up straight.

"We read your thoughts and got samples of your language so we could learn it." We know you have many questions and we are prepared," the alien responded before Kyle could ask another question. The alien waved its hand over something resembling a video screen and pictures appeared at random. The crew saw a picture of planet Earth, King Tutankhamen's burial mask, clear-cutting rainforests, cavalry shooting Native Americans on horseback, Geronimo, a traffic jam, the haze over Los Angeles, a red-eyed tree frog on a leaf, Neil Armstrong setting foot on the moon, a Pathfinder rover on Mars, the Enola Gay airplane, Albert Einstein, Martin Luther King marching with his fellow people, Adolph Hitler, the World Trade Center collapsing, the Los Angeles riots, a student waving a flag in front of a group of tanks in China, the Berlin wall coming down, a mushroom cloud.

Kyle backed away from the screen, awestruck, and turned around, facing the aliens, and asked, "How did you know?"

"We've been watching your species thrive and falter for thousands of years. We knew you had potential, but didn't know where to start. We did know that your world was in danger, because of rogue asteroids that you have no defense against and your star only has five billion years of fuel left. Help us make you known for your achievements and wonders. Besides, we need your help to protect and safeguard this side of the universe."

"We'd be honored to join in your quest," Kwasi said as he bowed down.

Another alien stepped forward, bent over, and said, "I think we'll have a bright and prosperous future together."

Kyle gently tapped the alien on the shoulder when he was done with Kwasi. The alien stood up and turned his head to face Kyle.

"Is the air outside these domes breathable?"

"It is for us. I'm not sure about you. You'd have to check," the alien answered.

"One more question, are you beings male or female?"

"We are both. We are known as Gaedians, after our home world, which was destroyed by our brother race, the Wizorans."

Kyle stepped outside while the others wandered about inside the dome. He did the same test that he did with the spacesuit. The air was breathable, Kyle thought as he felt a mild breeze on his face. He immediately told the rest of the crew inside. Later, Kari went over building and road schematics on her computer tablet with Dr. Shamaji.

One morning Elaine stood on a balcony holding on to a railing, overseeing the wildlife down below a steep hill. She was wearing a beige skirt with a pastel red T-shirt.

Jose came out of the dome to join her. "You're one of the first colonists to be artificially inseminated."

"That's great! A start to a whole new generation," she giggled as Jose hugged her gently.

One of the Gaedians came out onto the balcony and asked, "I was wondering if your team would like a tour of our solar system."

"That would be wonderful," Elaine replied excitedly with her Gaelic accent.

The aliens explained to the Terrans that they would prefer to be referred to as he or him, rather than she or her, because of their male characteristics such as their deep voices and enormous muscular strength. The Gaedian that greeted the two scientists had a sea-green pigment to his skin, like the ones that first greeted the astronauts. He had on a sky-blue lab coat and the same color pants. His brow ridges were more wrinkled, showing age. "My name is Dr. Ingro Shamaji. We'll be taking one of our ships. They are slightly faster than yours, because we have perfected the plasma propulsion technology."

Looking out the left porthole, the Terrans were awestruck at how such a system came to be. The Gaedians called this system Vorex.

The first planet was known as Yord. Yord was the first planet and was closest to the star. Its proximity to the extreme heat made this a barren and lifeless world. Its only uses were hydrogen and uranium mining.

The second planet was Nim. Nim was close to the star, and thus was very hot. It was covered with tundra and flat plains. There was some life on Nim, both animal and vegetable. There were few alpha habitations, and industries included weapons and armor (home of the Atron Company) and uranium mining. These industries occurred three centuries after the Terrans arrived.

The third planet was Xenthos. A neighbor to the imminently dead planet of Gaed, Xenthos had a dense mixture of gases in its atmosphere. It consisted of hydrogen, methane, and sulfur. The Gaedians once mined this moon's rocky and dusty surface for precious minerals like sulfur, nickel-iron, and zinc. On Xenthos, the core of it was over five hundred degrees Kelvin. Its surface composition was made of nickel-iron, zinc, and sulfur. The surface gravity was one point twenty-five compared to Earth's gravity, which was one. A day there was one hundred and eighty of Earth's days and a year was two hundred and seventy of Earth's days. It was also twelve times Earth's mass. Most of the surface was covered with Chivon dust and there were Argon gas vents just beneath it, keeping the surface cool. In extremely hot temperatures, the Gaedians wore a special insulated spacesuit that they had devised. The exterior was made of a thick coating of Chivon dust woven into the fabric, which was proven to be virtually heat-resistant.

The fourth planet was Saj Hari, a desert planet. Saj Hari was another hot world, but it managed to retain a thin but substantive atmosphere. The atmosphere was mainly nitrogen and oxygen. The planet itself was rocky with large mountain ranges and was 84.59 percent covered in desert. It was home to little animal and plant life. But many of the alpha races kept colonies. This planet was home of the Sedarian History Museum, where the Davonians were the caretakers of the facility as well as their colonies. Industries included tourism, silicon exports, highly radioactive Zeonium crystals, and other high-carbon minerals.

The fifth planet in the system was Baleto. This world was of varying climate and geography. It was a temperate world, and included large mountain ranges, plains, deep jungles, and vast oceans. It was highly inhabited by the Grioj amphibious alpha race and was also abundant in animal life and vegetation. The Griojs resembled tree frogs back on Earth, because they lived in tree huts. Its main industries were Zygate refining, textiles, and agricultural production. It was noted that Baleto exported much water to Saj Hari.

The sixth planet, Gaed, was one of the first planets discovered by the Terrans. It was rich in Gyrite ore, Magnellium, Dionium, and other useful minerals. Its rocky cliffs and canyons made it unsuitable for most plant life to grow. The only plant life growing there was a cave moss, which the inhabitants ate. Its atmosphere was thin, similar to Earth's upper atmosphere. The inhabitants had adapted themselves to such conditions.

The seventh planet, Patoa, or to humans, Terra-Gaea, was once a gaseous and frozen moon of the planet Gaed. At one time it had an atmosphere consisting of high concentrations of carbon dioxide and nitrogen. It was once inhabited by insect people who incorporated technology into their culture. Its surface composition was rich in minerals known as chromite and quartz. Patoa consisted of mostly frozen patches of ice over a rocky surface. It had oxygen frozen in patches of ice. Patoa's mass was .98 and its gravity was about the same. There were about five hundred days in a year's time. A day was about twenty-five hours, forty-six minutes and thirty-three seconds. Its axial tilt and rotation would be a little like Mars, only a little closer to the sun. Just by adjusting the planet's gravitational forces and using PSMs (planetary shift modules), both the Terrans and Gaedians were able to terraform or transform a dead and lifeless world into a livable and breathable planet, providing that the conditions were right. It was once thought that Patoa was hit by an ice comet millennia ago and got knocked out of its original orbit. The planetary engineers finally moved it back where it was. Now it was a sustainable biosphere teeming with living organisms ranging from the smallest of plants to the largest of animals, similar to Earth. Its geography included jungles, rainforests, large seas, and oceans. It was abundant in alpha race inhabitants and was the third most populated planet in the United Colonia. Industries included Dionium mining, and vehicle construction.

The eighth planet, Graelentag, this was the primary planet of the Colonia. It was the highest population (over eight billion) and was an industrial center. It had a variety of climates and geographical areas. Industries included weapons assembly, agriculture, and Ceronium and Magnellium mining.

The ninth planet, Us'anda, was the largest planet in the Septulon system. It was comprised completely of gas, such as hydrogen and nitrogen. Its only significance was many stations orbiting the planet as a tourist attraction.

The tenth planet, Vorden, was very far from its mother sun but still maintained a very fragile climate. Its surface was comprised of mountains and plains. The entire planet was covered in ammonia snow. Winds were constant and threatening. It carried little life, but alpha races had established many colonies and outposts here. It was the home of the Tactron Corporation. It was the maker of laser weaponry, robotics, and military computers. It also was abundant in Kazium and Tistat.

The eleventh and twelvth planets, Ionos Primus and Dominu … These twin worlds were almost exact copies of each other. Both were rocky and lifeless, lacking an atmosphere. They were a known source of magnetic disturbances and other unexplained phenomena. No industry was known on Primus but Dominu had small deposits of Micronium for daring prospectors to locate.

The thirteenth planet, Dolice, was another gaseous planet, quite smaller than the others. This planet, though, was home of few and strange life forms. It was a relatively unexplored world, and few ventured near it. It had no habitations or industry.

The fourteenth planet, Kitz'az, was a planet of great importance, even though it was rocky and bore no atmosphere. It was rich in Magnellium, Ceteranium, and Dionium. There were numerous colonies here and it was the hub of a great economic wheel and all other planets revolved around its material structure.

The fifteenth planet, Trehks'Icor, was a planet of high volcanic activity. Because of this, it maintained a warm climate despite its distance from the sun. It was inhabited by bands of alpha races, but there was no local life. Its economic outlet was the mining and refining of sulphuric chemical compounds.

The sixteenth planet, Webra, had been and still was a home for the pirates, smugglers, and cutthroats of the galaxy. The population consisted of mostly prisoners. It was a cold and flat world, with a thin layer of neon and no life. It had no industry and was supported by the UCP. The main feature of this planet was frequent electrical storms that activated the neon and gave the planet its warm blue glow. The planet Lyx was a tiny planet that had a very hot climate, and was covered in plains and jungle. It was only slightly inhabited, and then only by small creatures and vegetation. The races had only small settlements here, and its sole industry was uranium mining.

The seventeenth planet, Dimor, was the second most populated planet in the Colonia. Its climate was generally temperate, and its surface was plains and mountains, with some forests. It was rich in animal and plant life, and thus was heavily populated. Its industries included vehicle production, Zygate refining, and agricultural food production.

The eighteenth planet, Hosten's Deep, was named after its Gaedian discoverer. This world was 92.451 percent water. The temperature ranged from very warm at its moving equator to cold at the poles. It was the most abundant planet of the Colonia in plant and animal life, and was also inhabited by the races in floating and deep-sea cities. Its leading industry was tourism, which made up 78.4 percent of its economy. It also was a leading producer of algae and exotic seafood products.

The nineteenth planet, Kyrios, was the result of the efforts of millions of people over hundreds of years. It was created by capturing thousands of asteroids and molding them into one large body. After this, thousands of cities and stations were set up and interconnected to form a small superplanet, mostly artificial. There were huge chambers throughout the planet where millions of plants and animals lived and thrived in their race-made environment. Most industry was by automation, and was of the technological field. This occurred when the Gaedians encountered the Terrans, and with their engineering and ingenuity, this was made possible. From this time on, generations came and went, hoping for a bright future. The Terrans eventually got to know the Grioj people; with time they became more intelligent and less primitive.

The twentieth planet was a distant dead moon of Xanthu. It was a mining penal colony for captured prisoners of the Gaedians' brother race, the Wizorans. They were mining a very precious mineral for the Gaedians, Gyrite ore. A stronger metal could be made from it, stronger than Titanium, but lighter, Ecron steel.

Bright City Lights

Prologue

It is the year 2197, a century later after settlement on a Gaedian terra-formed moon with the help of alien technology. It is during times of fusion-powered and neon-decorated cities, we thought the city would be less busy than it was over a century ago. We are so naive to think that way. Cities will always be busy, as long as there are people around. The modern city has not changed much in the two hundred years that it has been in existence. Our old ways of living would be our undoing. Capitalism and social economics works people until they no longer have life in them. It doesn't give them any freedom and uses up the energy from their youth. When you have a way of life you are use to, it is hard to change it. Although this is the height of human architecture and alien technology, sometimes it can go too far. Now is the era of knowledge and understanding. This is a time when we know that our past is not the ideal way to live anymore and that we would have to unite our own cultures and change our old habits in order to maintain living tolerance amongst our alien friends. Since our encounter with the Gaedians, at last we are ready for a better tomorrow, or are we?

1 Fresh Start

Over a decade ago, a young Terran male's family was killed by the Wizorans when their cliffside home was destroyed by a Wizoran ship. An aging scientist named Ingro Shamaji took him in as his own and trained him as a scientist. Praden worked for Microcom, an electronics company, which was a front for a spy network of the Terran government, investigating alien phenomena. Employees would go in and come out of the Sungazer Government Services Building every day. No one had ever questioned the company's motives nor tried to figure them out. Praden was the only person who dared to think that way.

Years ago, Praden Garo was code-named Defcon, a mercenary who often assisted in Galactic Alliance conflicts. He was an enemy to the well-known bounty hunter Vexor. After a while, Defcon decided to go into something that paid more, like law enforcement. Ten years later, he was transferred to the Omni-Tech Alliance Intervention Organization as major defense officer.

It was during the nighttime hours that he went for a stroll. He exited his apartment and put up his collar on his trench coat since it cooled off outside. Watching crowds of pedestrians walk past and aeromobiles and hover cars float by, Praden often wondered what made a city a city. It had lots of people, vehicles to transport them around in. What made it feel as though it were alive were the lights. Without the lights, the city would feel empty. I guess that's what makes it a city. Most people don't think about it that way, they think of it as a part of life, because they're so used to it. Some people don't like the noise or just put up with it; maybe that's what makes it a city. That's why some people move to the country, where it's quiet, he thought.

At the dawn of a day, he was awakened by his vidcom.

"Praden Garo here," he answered as he pressed the pressure sensor for the receiver. The call came from the Microcom internal affairs office. They said it was urgent and that he should check out a strange disturbance down by the Pendrake Community Center. He signed off, sat up, and turned himself so that he was sitting on the side of the bed just so he could get awake. Squinting and rubbing his eyes, he stared around the room for a minute. He thought to himself, it was just another day, another job. Standard living quarters for government employees were furnished with a square round-edged table with smoothly rounded metallic legs and a firmly padded chair with smoothly rounded metallic legs as well. A desk with electronic working features to adjust for comfort and reduce body fatigue and an office chair with four legs on casters with a padded seat and backrest. Finally a standard sleeping unit with combination gel/foam mattress.

When he was fully awake, he then changed into his company-issue orange jumpsuit. Then he grabbed his orange cap with the Microcom insignia sewn on the front and placed it on his head. He fastened his Plk-5 laser side arm in the shoulder holster to his uniform and clipped his picture ID badge to his lapel. He slipped on his ankle boots and velcroed the sides shut. After he did that, he headed for the door and entered a three-digit code into the door control to lock it. The only way he could unlock it was if he ran his access card through the top slot of the door control. It was a surefire way to prevent break-ins. When that was done, the door slid open, he exited, and then it slid shut again. The electronic eye activated the door operating system after the code had been accessed.

He walked down the hallway from his living quarters to the central personnel lift. He pressed the call button and waited a few seconds for the doors to open. When they did, he entered and proceeded to the underground parking structure. Upon exiting, he walked over to his usual parking spot where his Vector Specter 970 series aeromobile awaited his presence. He entered a five-digit code into a small numeric keypad concealed in the door just below the handle in order to protect against car theft.

It seems like everything these days has to be push-button to be safe, he thought.

Vector aeromobiles were capable of flying by use of two dual-bladed turbo fans underneath the vehicle and were powered by an internal jet turbine that was virtually non-polluting. After completing the sequence, he reconcealed the keypad and almost immediately the door canopy opened. He hopped in and closed the scorch-proof hatch from the inside. He put on his shoulder harness and engaged the ignition switch down and to the left of the steering column. After releasing it, he heard a muffled sound of a jet turbine coming on from within the aeromobile. He pressed down on the acceleration pedal and smoothly steered the vehicle up a steep ramp and out of the parking structure. He then flicked a switch to allow the car to hover for a moment and pulled a lever that servodraulically raised the wheels to cut on drag. He piloted it away from the parking area and safely glided toward his destination. This vehicle basically operated on the same principle that the Harrier jet did.

As he flew over the paved roads, colorful motion blurs flashed by. He could almost visualize how complicated the humanoid forms of life were. Over time, they developed technologies to make life simpler and easier, that they had to move fast to keep up with the pace of life. Some things never changed in the course of humanoid living. They tried to invent ways to make life move a little smoother and now some of the methods developed were too complicated to operate, such that it took more time than needed. The real reason that most technological devices were too complicated to use was because there was too much science involved and time did not allow for thought. You would have to be a scientist of some kind to figure the machines out.

When Terrans traveled by land, they had two lanes on which to travel, speed lane one and two, slow or fast, rarely if ever used. Air travel and mass transit were the way to go. Almost as fast as the Autobahn in Germany, back on Earth. There was also a road that had magnets in it that allowed a car to hover. The lanes as mentioned before, not too many individuals took the slow route. As he drove down the open lanes. he could see that most structures were spread apart, exposing more vegetation and not close together in recent modern days, centuries ago. On Terra/Gaea, it was divided up into regions instead of provinces, states, or countries and there was one city per region. The way the planet was arranged allowed it to be less susceptible to overcrowding. Scientists, environmentalists, and ecologists had worked together to develop an atmospheric air cleaning system to keep the air breathable and free of any pollutants. The systems developed were called air filter stations and there were many stationed all over the planet. It worked by taking small air samples continuously out of the atmosphere and filtering out any particles of pollutants. Air travel had also gotten easier and safer over the past seventy-seven centuries. It was actually more efficient to travel this way and there were a variety of ways to do it. There were air buses, sky cabs, and Vector aeromobiles. Most air transports were jet powered. Air travel was a popular means of transportation amongst Terran inhabitants because it was faster.

2 The Rush

The report came in on his audio receiver. Garayen Yanx, a Sedarian/Elyzonian preacher, witnessed a loud electro-explosion and a voice spoke aloud in some sort of alien jargon and then an evil laugh outside the Pendrake Community Center. Glowing fluorescent green runes were left on the outside of the structure. Microcom investigators and law enforcement officials had already arrived on the scene.

When he first drove up, there was a Microcom minivan and two Prowler-1 police cruisers parked out in front of the community center. Zax Varren, his partner, and Zurasc enforcers questioned Garayen, one of his best friends. Garayen Yanx was one of the last Sedarians and grandson to one of the once enslaved ones. Garayen had a conflict between the reality of outside life and his people's true religious belief. He tried to tell him that most outside people didn't believe the same things that his people did because they had their own cultures.

Garayen said that he heard a loud voice speak out in some sort of alien jargon. It took a long time before he could understand this language similar to his. It sounded as if a message were being sent. He heard it in his sleep and he could understand what was being said. He heard the voice say, "Beware the spirit within, you are not welcome here!"

Police officials speculated that this strange disturbance came from the corrupt side of the Zurasc region. Years ago this area was left open to Terran development. Many building projects remained unfinished and unlived in because some of the Terrans were afraid to move in. They feared rumors that circulated around the small community about alien activity that occurred within that area for some time. Most settled in Terran colonies were afraid of new experiences, especially alien ones. Some of the rumors were true and some were not. Ignoring the rumors, some alien crime rings moved into the abandoned area.

This incident was classified as techno-cultural. Techno-culture was the incorporation of technological function into civil culture. Long before the Gaedian moon was ever terraformed, a techno-cultural civilization lived within the rocky caverns until a tremendous ice storm killed all the inhabitants and left the alien structures frozen in time. Some of the inhabitants were believed to be in suspended animation because of the storm. Investigators believed that either the spirits of the frozen beings or the actual beings themselves were awakening from their long hibernation.

He entered the community center along with Microcom investigators and Zurasc enforcers. One of the investigators approached the custodian of the facility and asked to borrow his code pass to enter the forum where community administrators and residents worked out their differences. As they walked down the dimly lit broad corridors, he noticed that the fluorescent tubular overhanging light fixtures were not functioning properly. The lights seemed to flicker on and off as they passed under them. He immediately brought his observation to the investigators' attention so that any vital clue such as this would not be left out.

The key investigator led them to where the disturbance was heard. Upon entering the forum, they noticed that all the chairs had been rearranged in unusual ways. Some were collected in the corner and some were even stacked in an untidy fashion. Most of the chairs were designed similar to the ones in his living unit but with different features. In the corner of the building it seemed as though part of the wall and the ceiling had somehow caved inward and cracked within the structure as a result of the explosion.

As they examined the room for clues, Praden noticed from the corner of his eye a shadowy figure peeking in the window from the outside. When he looked, the figure ran away from the window toward the front of the building and then he heard the same evil laugh heard by the witnesses, and so did the investigators and enforcers. He asked two of the investigators to follow him to the front entrance and find out who this mysterious character was. They scurried down the wide corridors where they finally came to the front entrance. Upon exiting the building, they heard a loud boom. They hid behind one of the doors for a moment and then they looked. Where his aeromobile was parked, there was an enormous fireball smoldering in what was left of it. He saw the shadowy figure again, running away from the scene; it paused when he shouted at it and then proceeded to escape. For a minute he had lost sight of it, then he looked again and an Ulstar 207 Quantum sped past. Knowing that it had traveled at an unreasonable speed, he assumed that it was the shadowy figure. Keeping an eye open for a means of transportation, a Prowler-1 police cruiser with its flashing lights on pulled up in front of the community center to find out what happened. He approached the vehicle and the law enforcer rolled down his tinted glass window. He explained to him that he saw a shadowy figure watching over us while we were investigating a strange disturbance inside the building and then his aeromobile exploded.

"I have reason to believe that it might have been the shadowy figure that caused it," he said.

"Could you possibly follow and track this mysterious character?" The enforcer advised him to get into the vehicle because he witnessed its actions. Obliging to his advice, he lifted the door handle upward and toward the front of the vehicle similar to a Lamborghini Countach back on Earth. He allowed him to seat himself, and he harnessed himself in for safety.

Cruising down the roadway, enforcer Sgt. Feneritt Malagen could trace the suspect heading for the Fensar region on his tracking unit. After having knowledge of an approximate location to intercept it, Enforcer Malagen accelerated with sirens blaring. Searching for the suspect in a suburban neighborhood, he spotted a red Ulstar 207 Quantum parked outside a white, low to the ground apartment complex. He signaled Officer Malagen to slowly cruise over to that location. That same moment, the shadowy figure ran out of the apartment, climbed into its vehicle, and sped away from the scene. They followed with lights flashing and sirens blaring down speed lane-2. The chase continued for five more minutes down the expressway, avoiding a collision with innocent civilians. Sgt. Malagen's Prowler-1 police cruiser and the red Ulstar 207 Quantum went airborne down a steep hill. They raced through an alley of an urban area and they swerved around a corner and the Quantum slammed into a disposal unit. The police cruiser swerved and stopped on the street corner. Using his car as a barricade, the enforcer got out and pumped his laser shotgun. He pulled out his Plk-5 laser side arm and clicked the arming switch. Holding the weapon two-handed in the air and against his shoulder, he climbed out of the vehicle. They slowly walked in a crouched position around their vehicle and over to the driver's side of the suspect's vehicle. Holding his position and keeping his weapon raised, he slowly opened the door.

Enforcer Malagen opened the other door and raised his 64k power pack Rlk-100 laser shotgun. When they did this, the shadowy figure offered no reaction to the intrusion. They saw a dark cloaked figure sitting motionless in the driver's seat. When Officer Malagen searched around the shadowy figure, he accidentally bumped the suspect's cloak and it collapsed onto the seat with no trace of its body. As stunned as Praden was, the sight gave him chills down his spine.

3   Melting Core

Years ago, before terraforming became a reality, the Gaedian planetary engineers had five metallic spheres installed, four spheres by the equator and one near the core. Inside these spheres were gyroscope-like devices that controlled gravitational fields to position the planet in a precise orbit with the sun. Keep in mind, this was a younger solar system. The Planetary Shift Modules were also designed to create heat while the planet was being moved to heat up the core.

One morning, Praden got a call from Dr. Ingro Shamaji on the vid-com, saying that he should come over to his place at Connor Apartments immediately. He took a quick shower, got dressed, and Enforcer Malagen was kind enough to give him a ride over there. He drove him to the front entrance and then took off. He entered the building and took the elevator up to the penthouse. He walked over to Ingro's apartment and used his copied code pass that Ingro gave him to open it. In Ingro's apartment there was a small desk with a flat-screened computer on his right as well as a sliding closet door. On his left, a white gel/foam bed similar to Praden's, to match the white decor. There was a small, round glass conference table next to the bed. In the center of the table was a media receptacle and lying next to it was a cube with a diamond-like crystal attached to it. He immediately plugged it in and a holographic image of Dr. Ingro Shamaji appeared. Ingro spoke:

"Praden, you must come down to the underground caverns immediately. I have just come across an amazing discovery."

He pulled it out, left the apartment, and entered the three-digit code to lock the door. He took a tram just off the magnetic freeway.

4 Intruders

Praden decided to take an unexpected detour and jump off the tram into a patch of vegetation with much success. He saw a cavern sloping downward, so he stepped gradually so as not to lose his footing. He met Ingro inside a huge dark gray cavern with stalagmites and stalactites and a deep crater where a ball of ice used to be, the core.

"What was it you wanted me to see?" said Praden.

"See those long shards of ice over there?" Ingro pointed to his left.

"Yeah. What are they?" Praden replied.

"Well, they certainly aren't stalagmites of ice." Ingro looked closer.

From what Praden could see, there were entities or something similar to a spirit. It seemed like these insect-like beings had ascended or had gone to a higher point of existence after being frozen in hibernation for eons. Praden noticed that there were other Patoan insect bodies lying about. They sort of looked like praying mantises, with an ant head and wings under their arms; their bodies were rust in color. He was startled by another Patoan thawing out but could barely breathe. He said a few words before he passed on.

"What is happening to us? Who are you and what are you doing here?" it said in its native tongue of clicks and snaps.

"My people, the Terrans, and several other species have made this planet habitable again. When we found your world, it had frozen over. We apologize for doing this. We didn't know that there was anyone living here but we needed a home." Ingro translated their dialect, similar to the Gaedians'.

"It is too late for us. We've been in hibernation for too long," the Patoan said.

"Besides, you're free; you can go anywhere you want. You've ascended to a higher plane without the need for bodies. I've seen it happen," Praden said with excitement. A light blue apparition came out of the Patoan and went into space as well as others. People were no longer afraid to live around their homes.

"Well, I guess I'm out of a job," Praden said.

"Not quite. Microcom may have some other assignments for you," Ingro replied.

www.ingramcontent.com/pod-product-compliance
Lightning Source LLC
Chambersburg PA
CBHW031314120626
46554CB00001BA/398